accidentally
FAMOUS

accidentally
FAMOUS

MARISSA CLARKE

Entangled Publishing, LLC
644 Shrewsbury Commons Ave., STE 181
Shrewsbury, PA 17361
Visit our website at www.entangledpublishing.com.

Amara is an imprint of Entangled Publishing, LLC.

Edited by Heather Howland
Cover art and design by Elizabeth Turner Stokes
Cover art by New Africa/Shutterstock,
kak2s/Shutterstock, Grandview Graphics/Shutterstock
Interior design by Toni Kerr

Print ISBN 978-1-64937-345-8
ebook ISBN 978-1-64937-346-5

Manufactured in the United States of America

First Edition February 2023

AMARA

ALSO BY MARISSA CLARKE

HIDEAWAY HARBOR

Accidentally Perfect
Accidentally Famous

ANDERSON BROTHERS SERIES

Sleeping With the Boss
Neighbors With Benefits
Chance of a Lifetime

ANIMAL ATTRACTION SERIES

Dear Jane
Three Day Fiancée
Love Out Loud

For Laine
I'm coming for you, babe!

CHAPTER ONE

The last time Cassidy James had seen Tristan McGuffy, he'd been wearing his medical school graduation robe, and she'd been wearing a mouth full of braces and her high school band uniform. At the time, she remembered thinking that nothing could have been worse.

Way wrong. *This* was worse.

Without even looking toward the door, she could *feel* his presence. Feel him staring at her, covered in dirt and dust as she leaned into the crawlspace under his dad's house to inspect a support beam. Closing her eyes, she pushed down a prickly wave of disappointment.

For two months, she'd known he'd planned to return to Blink to visit his dad. And for two months, she'd imagined this moment…well, not *this* moment, but rather what this moment *should* have been. In her fantasies, her childhood—now adult—crush would walk in, stop in astonishment, and marvel at how grown up and put-together little Cassidy James had become.

At least she'd gotten the first two parts right: he'd walked in and stopped in astonishment.

Slowly, she straightened to a kneeling position, and since her hands were so filthy, she resorted to blowing some escaped strands of hair out of her face. Of course, they fell right back across her eyes. Oh yeah. So grown up. So perfectly put-together.

No doubt he hadn't said anything because he was struck silent with lust. *Not.*

She pushed the hair out of her eyes using the back of her forearm and forced herself to twist and face him, wood flooring plank in one hand and prybar in the other.

Sure enough. Her dream man, Tristan McGuffy—*Dr.* Tristan McGuffy—stood in the doorway with a small suitcase in hand.

A suitcase? Two months ago, when his dad, Roger McGuffy, had said that Tristan was going to drive in from Portland, Cassidy had assumed it would be a day visit, like the few times he'd stopped by during the years back before his mom had died.

He didn't enter but instead scanned the room, which gave her a moment to compose herself. Her memories didn't do him justice, which surprised her, considering those memories kept her up at night.

For a moment, she was transported back to her favorite memory of Tristan McGuffy. She'd been sixteen and had just finished helping her dad install a new water heater at the Starfish Diner, which, back then, had been the only restaurant in their tiny town of Blink, Maine.

While her dad gave the tank a final leak-and-pressure test back in the kitchen, the owner, Sally, had treated Cassidy to a root beer float at the counter, one stool over from Tristan.

He had driven home from med school for a day visit and was waiting for his parents to join him. He had ordered a cheeseburger and a strawberry milkshake with extra whipped cream. She remembered that because it was her favorite meal at the diner, too. In fact, since ninth grade, she'd cataloged what she and Tristan had in common, which pretty much boiled down to three main things: both grew up in a teensy town with a population hovering around two hundred, they both had a love of reading as evidenced by his always having a book on hand, and they both had an appreciation of Sally's cheeseburgers—though this similarity was probably shared by anyone who had ever tasted one of Sally's cheeseburgers.

Her sixteen-year-old self had been thrilled at being seated only one stool over from Tristan. He was a lot older than she was, but in her mind, that was no obstacle. By the time he finished medical school and she graduated from high school the year after that, she'd be grown up enough to catch his eye. Her dad had told her that the older a person got, the less age mattered. In fact, her parents had been over a decade apart in age.

"So, Cassy," Tristan had said. "You're a freshman now, right?"

"Junior," she'd corrected, wanting to be sure he knew she was older.

He'd swiveled on his stool to study her for a moment, and she remembered her heart racing like her hamster, Rosco, on his exercise wheel.

"I bet you're going to be a knockout when you grow up," he'd said.

A knockout.

Sally'd backed through the swinging kitchen doors carrying a box that, judging from the way she was leaning back to counterbalance it, was heavy. Tristan had dropped his burger to his plate to run around the counter to relieve her of it.

"Where to?" he'd asked.

"Always such a helpful boy," Sally had crooned, pointing to an open space under the service window. "I'll unpack it later."

Helpful, handsome, and a soon-to-be doctor. Cassidy was still basking in Tristan's knockout comment when her dad stuck his head out through the kitchen door. "All done. Let's go, Cassy, baby."

Baby. Ugh. Reluctantly, she'd slid off the stool and placed her napkin on the counter.

"So, I remember your nickname at church used to be Sassy Cassy. Do they still call you that around here?" Tristan had asked, slipping back onto his stool at the counter.

Her little brother, Luke, had come up with that nickname when he was in kindergarten, and she'd still not forgiven him for it all these years later. She really should let that go. Her brother was in college now, for goodness' sake.

"Not if they want to live another day," she'd answered.

Tristan had laughed, and she remembered feeling proud and sophisticated that she'd amused him.

"Cassy, let's go!" her dad had hollered from the kitchen.

Giving Tristan one last longing glance, she'd skirted the counter and headed toward the kitchen doors.

"Hey, Sassy Cassy," Tristan had called.

Holding her breath, she'd turned to face him, heart spinning on that exercise wheel, too excited to even be angry about the nickname.

"See you soon," he'd said with a wink.

In Cassidy's sixteen-year-old mind, that was only a few inches off of asking her out on a date. "See ya," she'd said before dashing through the swinging kitchen doors.

Only two more years, she remembered thinking. In two years, she'd be all grown up. In her mind, eighteen had been the magic number—only it hadn't been magical at all. Tristan's mother had died the year she'd turned eighteen, and he'd stopped coming to Blink altogether.

Cassidy pulled herself back to the present and studied the current Dr. Tristan McGuffy as he entered the house and pulled the door closed behind him. Maybe it was her grown-up perspective, but he was more handsome than she remembered. And taller. And a little bit intimidating. His blond hair was impeccably styled and groomed, like he'd come straight from the barber. He had a business-casual vibe going with khaki slacks and a crisp, white dress shirt like you'd wear with a suit—the perfect pairing with her paint-splattered, dust-covered clothes, her usual state since she took over her dad's construction business three years ago.

She swallowed hard. The reunion wasn't supposed to happen this way. She was supposed to be clean and made-up and dressed like the knockout he'd told her she'd be. Instead, she was... She glanced down at her sawdust- and grime-covered overalls over her torn Wonder Woman T-shirt and stifled a groan. She was a mess.

"I was told the house was being renovated. Sorry to interrupt you," Tristan said with a nod, striding past her toward the staircase.

Open-jawed, she stared after him as he climbed the stairs without even saying hello. She sagged back onto her heels as her heart seemed to drop below her ribs.

Had he not recognized her?

All these years of anticipation, buildup, and smokin' hot fantasies, and the guy didn't even remember who she was. She couldn't believe it. She blinked several times. In her most vivid daydreams, she'd pictured him in a black tux and her in a white, beaded gown and veil, like perfect wedding-cake toppers.

She stared down at the pitted support beam she'd exposed. Sometimes in her business, damage could be repaired with epoxy, or additional fasteners, or bracing, but sometimes a damaged thing simply wasn't salvageable. And in the span of less than a minute, this whole day, along with her life-long crush on Tristan McGuffy, had fallen into the latter category—unsalvageable.

She gave a defeated sigh. Teen fantasies were just that—fantasies. This was real life, and this house was her real job. She had to pick her heart back up and get back to work. Any mourning for the past she'd always dreamed of would have to be done later, preferably when she was tucked into her own bed.

Forcing herself to focus, she tossed the floor

plank onto the pile behind her and set the prybar next to her knee. The exposed support beam had a two-and-a-half-foot section that was riddled a few inches deep with holes and wafer-thin husks of wallowed-out wood. The Powderpost Beetles had evidently thrown a party under the old Victorian house. At least someone was having fun around here.

From underneath the house, two green eyes stared up at her through the hole in the floor. "Meeerrrooow!" The sound was raspy but got the point across.

"Hey, Lolo. Wanna take the shortcut?" Cassidy patted the floor next to her. The ancient cat crouched but didn't leap. Instead, she stared and made a hissing sound like a compressor hose quick connect.

"Okay, I get it. Help's on the way." Cassidy climbed down into the hole and lifted the cat into the room, then climbed out herself. "You could have come up the porch steps and through the front door, you know."

"Mrrrrrew."

Cassidy smoothed the dusty, ruffled gray-and-white fur on Lolo's back. When the front door opened, the cat slunk out of the room, probably to her usual hidey-hole under the staircase. Lolo was not into people these days.

She could relate.

Ordinarily, Cassidy was positive and satisfied, but for some reason, lately, it felt like her life was off-balance — as if something was missing. After her dad died, she missed him, of course, and then her little brother went away to college, and she missed him, too, but this was different. It made her uncomfortable like an itchy tag on a shirt.

"Hey!" Her best friend Amanda's voice came from where Tristan had stood only minutes earlier.

"Hey yourself," Cassidy said, trying to sound neutral, which was probably futile, since Amanda could read her moods as quickly as the trashy tabloids she consumed like candy. Amanda was the only person in the world who knew about Cassidy's decade-long infatuation with Tristan. Nobody else was in on the secret, *especially* Tristan.

"Ready to shoot today's video?" Amanda was wearing a bright-red floral top with a scoop neck and flowing bell sleeves that fluttered when she brandished her phone like a magic wand. As always, she wore large, coordinating earrings—roses, this time, that hung on wires well below her close-cropped, curly black hair. Amanda's tastes ran on the flamboyant, vintage eclectic side, and she pulled it off like a boss.

"Yep. Ready to film." Cassidy had been chronicling her work on the house and posting it to YouTube to share with the handful of remodelers she'd befriended at a seminar on restoring old houses she'd attended two months ago in Bangor. All five people in her group were in various stages of restoration on their projects and shared tips with each other weekly. Her house, which she'd affectionately named Dolores, was in the best shape of any of the others in her group. Of course, it wasn't *her* house. It was Roger McGuffy's house, as in the father of the man who, in all his golden-haired glory, was somewhere on the floor above her. She stared at the ceiling, then back to the hole in the floor.

"You okay, Cass?" Amanda asked.

"Yes, fine."

Amanda stared at her for several moments, no doubt seeing right through her, like she always did. "Whose car is out front?" she asked as she wiped the camera lens of her phone on one of her flowing sleeves.

"Tristan's," she mumbled.

"Really?"

Yeah, really.

"Roger said he was coming in to check out the clinic, not the house." She lowered her voice, her eyes twinkling. "Any chance he's here to check *you* out, too?"

Cassidy fought back a groan, grateful the man was upstairs and out of earshot. "Definitely not."

Amanda scanned the entry hall and both rooms flanking it. "Is he here?"

Cassidy shifted to sit with her legs dangling into the hole she'd cut through the subfloor. "Yeah. He had a bag, so I guess he's going to spend the night."

"*Here*?" Amanda, sleeves flapping, gestured wildly to the partially demolished entry hall and living areas.

"The bedrooms are still intact. I'm only working on structural issues and the first floor," Cassidy said, reaching out to pull the tins of epoxy and activator closer to her, along with a cup to mix them in.

Amanda's face lit up. "Did he tell you how long he's going to stay? Old man McGuffy would give an arm or a leg to keep him here." She winked. "And I imagine you would offer up some choice body parts as well."

"No, he didn't say anything to me at all other than an apology for interrupting."

Cassidy immediately regretted the words as her insightful friend studied her long enough that she had to resist the urge to squirm.

Finally, Amanda said, "That's odd."

It was odd, all right. Cassidy had dreamed about Tristan for years, and he hadn't even recognized her. She felt...forgettable.

"What are you going to do?" Amanda asked. "Can I help? I mean, this is perfect, right?"

Perfectly awful. "Please don't do anything," Cassidy said. "Let me see how it goes, okay?" Knowing Amanda, she'd try to do some painfully unsubtle matchmaking and create a huge mess out of an already awkward situation.

"Suit yourself. I'm sure we could find a creative way to jar his memory." Amanda held her phone up. Its rhinestone case glittered in the sunlight slanting in from the tall sash windows in the dining room. "In the meantime, let's get filming."

Cassidy considered going to the bathroom to wash her hands and brush her hair, but why bother? Her videos hadn't found a following at all. The only people who watched were her buddies from the seminar, and they looked equally grubby in their own videos. Besides, she was about to reach into the dirty underbelly of the structure again anyway.

An image of the handsome man upstairs flooded her brain, and she shook her head. He'd already seen her like this. No point in trying to right the wrong first impression.

Cassidy focused a work light on the beam spanning the gaping hole in the floorboards and motioned Amanda over. "Hey, restoration friends," she said after Amanda nodded to indicate they were rolling. "I crawled under the house and only spotted a suspicious area on the top of one support beam, so my demolition was minimal. Since I'll be refinishing the floors as part of this project, I removed a few of the pitted planks and a small area of subfloor to access the area from above, since that was where the damage was concentrated. As you know, houses of this age were constructed of old-growth wood, so I'll make every effort to retain as much of the original material as possible. In this case, the area of Powderpost Beetle damage is small. I'll use an epoxy made for this purpose to fill the voids and strengthen the area rather than replace the beam."

Cassidy's thoughts momentarily flitted back to Tristan and how easily he'd ignored her as he'd strode past without a glance. What she needed was an epoxy that could fix broken fantasies—or maybe something to fix *her* so that her fantasies could become reality. No. That was totally the wrong attitude. What she needed was to let those fantasies go and begin living her life—the real one she'd carved out and created all by herself.

Now, if she could just get her heart on board

with the idea…

"That was great. You get better every time," Amanda said after they finished the shoot. She was doing something on her phone. Probably uploading the video, since they filmed it in one shot and it didn't need an edit. Her eyes narrowed. "That's strange."

Cassidy wiped her hands on the tops of her denim-clad thighs. "What?"

"Your subscription numbers." She didn't take her eyes off her phone screen.

"All whopping five subscriptions from my restoration friends?" Cassidy said with a grin. She'd only had one view that wasn't tied to her group, and that one didn't subscribe, unsurprisingly. No one else in her group had been successful at growing an audience for their channels, either. "Better turn off the subscriber notifications so they don't blow up your phone."

Amanda's brow furrowed as she studied her screen. "Huh…" She continued scrolling, still looking puzzled. "Well, you don't have five anymore." She turned the screen to the analytics page for Cassidy's YouTube channel. "You have over five thousand."

CHAPTER TWO

Jack Winston sat back in the soft, leather sofa and stared at the sprawling L.A. skyline outside the bank of windows lining the wall of his penthouse apartment—and tried to ignore his assistant's fidgeting. Dee had worked for him for over a month now, so he knew this wasn't her normal behavior. She'd gone from hand-wringing to foot tapping as she pretended to study his weekly schedule and incoming emails. He took a sip of coffee and studied her.

Evidently feeling his eyes on her, she looked up. "Would you like more coffee?"

He saluted her with his cup. "No, thank you. I'm good."

But *she* clearly wasn't. Maybe her boyfriend had dumped her. Did she have a boyfriend? They never talked about anything personal even though she spent eight hours a day either with him or somewhere nearby. His manager kept her busy with this and that, but he didn't know much about her other than she was in her twenties and had been hired straight out of undergrad.

He studied her as she tapped a pencil on the desk, eyes unfocused as she stared at the computer monitor. "You okay?"

She met his eyes briefly, and for a moment, he thought she was going to say something. But then she looked away, evidently finding the enormous fireplace at the end of the room fascinating. He'd always found the fireplace puzzling. Who in L.A. needed a fireplace? He sighed. It was all for show, just like everything and everyone in this town.

A familiar, confident, staccato snapping of heels sounded from the hallway behind him, and when he glanced back at Dee, she looked relieved.

Oh, yeah, something was definitely wrong. Nobody *ever* felt relief at the approach of Marion Hill. Terror, maybe. Dread, absolutely, but never relief. He focused on maintaining his relaxed pose on the sofa as he braced for his manager's entrance. Being an actor paid off in moments like this. If Marion smelled weakness, she was like a shark with blood in the water, leaving nothing but carnage behind. It's why she'd been hired to handle the business side of his career, a brilliant move on his part.

"Why aren't you dressed for your photo shoot, Mr. Winston?" Marion's harsh, nasal voice said from somewhere behind him.

Jack glanced down at his bathrobe, lounge pants, and slippers. "I wasn't aware there was a photo shoot."

He could practically feel Marion's glare burning holes in the back of his skull. *She works for you*, he reminded himself.

"*Hollywood Weekly* is doing a feature on you to coincide with the announcement of *Mad Planet 4*," she said.

He flopped his head onto the back of the sofa and groaned. He should never have agreed to a fourth movie. The storyline was exhausted, and so was he. "Tell them to use the outtakes from their shoots for *Mad Planet 1, 2,* or *3*."

It was unnerving that Marion was still hovering somewhere behind him, but he resisted the urge to turn around.

"They need current shots. You look different now."

Well, that was true. He looked healthier now. He *was* healthier now, physically, emotionally, and mentally, and he planned to keep it that way. If he was honest with himself, this harpy of a manager was in huge part responsible. "Where's the shoot?"

"At their studio, of course."

He glanced over at the desk where Dee still fidgeted with nervous energy. Her dark skin paled, and her panicked eyes darted to his. "I...um. I must have forgotten to tell you about that, Mr. Winston."

Huh. As an actor, it was his business to study human behavior, and he'd never seen her like this. Dee was nothing if not extremely organized. He opened his mouth to say something reassuring, but Marion had already sensed blood in the water.

"You're fired, Miss LaPorte," Marion said in that terrifying, authoritative voice of hers.

The hairs prickled on the back of Jack's neck as he fought the urge to tell Marion to back off. Instead, he remained still in his relaxed position and calmly lied, "Oh, yeah. I remember you telling me about this photo shoot, Dee. I totally forgot. My bad. Please give them a call and ask if they can shoot here instead."

That should work. They loved to do features in

celebrities' homes, and he couldn't imagine Marion contradicting him over this.

As if shot from a cannon, Dee launched out of her chair and ran from the room, her sneakers squeaking on the bamboo flooring all the way down the hall.

"Stop covering for her. She's underqualified and inexperienced," Marion said, striding to sit at the desk Dee had vacated. "She needs to be replaced."

She'd just graduated with honors from Berkeley. She was overqualified for a job like this, but arguing with Marion never ended well. Best to stick to a less combative, personal approach. "I like her."

"Liking someone gets you nowhere. I thought you had learned that lesson."

Yeah, he sure had. He'd hired and surrounded himself with people he'd thought were friends for a decade, and it had almost destroyed his career and his life. It's why he'd coaxed Marion out of retirement. The self-proclaimed battle-ax had cleaned house, so to speak, and saved his ass. If not for Marion Hill, he'd probably be back stocking grocery store shelves. Still, he couldn't let her fire Dee for one mistake. God knew he'd made plenty of them and had been given chance after chance after chance.

"I want to give her another shot," he said finally.

He'd never seen Marion roll her eyes before. It was incongruous with her meticulously styled and dyed two-tone brown hair and her stiff suit jacket.

Jack recrossed his legs and studied Marion as she tapped her manicured nails over the keyboard. The woman was a Hollywood legend, and based on her career timeline, she had to be in her early eighties. She was either blessed with eternal youth or had some work done by a doc with real talent because she looked decades younger. She wore glasses with stylish red frames that matched her blouse and possessed the most prominent resting-bitch-face he'd ever seen.

She turned her gaze on him, and he resisted the urge to flinch like a naughty child. Yeah, she was *that* good. "Your agent is having the revised screenplay for *Four* sent by courier. It should be here any minute. Oh, and they're sending another script with it. It's a new series from HBO that, according to the producer, screams your name."

It could scream all it wanted and so could she. He wasn't doing a TV series right now. What he really wanted was some downtime. While he appreciated the improvements to his life and his bank accounts Marion had produced, he was feeling the stress of her ambitions. His mind drifted back to Dee. Maybe that's what was wrong with her, too—Marion's ceaseless pressure.

"I'm going to go see my sister and her kids in Malibu," he said.

"You have a lot going on right now. I don't advise that, Mr. Winston."

Of course she didn't. The more money he made, the more she made. He admired her drive and was grateful she'd taken him on, but he really needed a break from her, from L.A., from *Mad Planet*, and

most of all, from the constant pressure squeezing
him from all aspects of his personal life—if one
even could call it that. He didn't go out anymore.
He didn't date. He may never date again, at least
not seriously. It never ended well. In fact, it ended
horribly every single time. He got that from his
mom, he supposed. At least his sister had been
spared the curse.

"I won't be gone long. I'll take the revised
screenplay with me and learn some lines. I'll review any other scripts when I get back." He stood
while she opened and closed her mouth silently
like a fish. He fought back a smile. It was reassuring that he could render the dragon speechless.
"I'll go change—unless you think the Hugh
Hefner look works for *Hollywood Weekly*, in
which case, I'll stay in my bathrobe."

She snapped her mouth shut and shook her
head.

"Set the photographer up anywhere you think
would be best," he called over his shoulder as he
strode down the hall.

As he neared the stairs, he heard muffled crying
from the kitchen. He paused with his foot on the
bottom step and tilted his head. The cook and
housekeepers wouldn't arrive for at least another
hour. It had to be Dee. Entering the kitchen, he
found his assistant at the white quartz island with
her head down on her folded arms, sobbing.

"Hey," he said. "Marion's cooled off. Don't
worry about it, Dee. It was no big deal. Did you
get the photographer to agree to come here instead?"

Not lifting her head, she sniffed and said, "Uh huh. On her way." Then she sniffed again.

He had the urge to pat her shoulder but stuffed his hands in his robe pockets instead. He learned long ago to not get close to anyone unless it was on set and in the script, a family member, or he was serious enough to read about it. Platonic friends didn't exist on the pages of the tabloids. "See? Everything's fine."

Like a startled deer, she lifted her head in a quick motion and stared at him with tears running down her cheeks. "No. It's *not* fine. I messed up, Mr. Winston. Really messed up."

"But...it's all over now?" He made a helpless gesture in the general direction of the front door, as if indicating where the photographer would come in. In truth, he was finding it hard to stand still when this poor girl was in such distress.

"Not that." She glanced at the door as if she expected Marion to come crashing in like Godzilla. "It's something else."

Jack leaned a shoulder on the doorframe and crossed his arms, dreading whatever she would say, because it could result in Marion letting her go. "What happened?"

Again, Dee glanced at the door. "Remember how after you talked to your sister on the phone this morning, you asked me to tag her on Instagram with a picture of you from *Mad Planet 3* saying, 'I'm coming for you, babe'?"

"Yeah." That's what his character, Blake Crusher, said in all three *Mad Planet* films way too many times and no doubt would say over and over in the fourth movie. He and his sister had a running joke about it.

Dee took a deep breath. "Well, I—"

The unmistakable strikes of Marion's shoes ricocheted down the hall like a jackhammer as she strode toward them. "Get dressed, Mr. Winston. Do something useful, Miss LaPorte," she ordered from the hallway behind him.

Dee jumped to her feet, and Jack pushed away from the doorframe like they were a couple of naughty toddlers raiding the cookie jar. "We'll talk about it later," he whispered to Dee over his shoulder before mounting the stairs.

Jack felt a little bit better knowing what had rattled Dee was just a silly Instagram post for his sister. How bad could it be?

CHAPTER THREE

"This is terrible." Cassidy stared at Amanda's screen. The idea of thousands of people watching her while she remodeled a house was unnerving. She swallowed and took a deep breath. "Why would so many people subscribe to my channel all of a sudden?"

"Because you're adorable and swing a mean hammer?" Amanda said. "Besides, I thought you wanted to bring attention to your business so Luke has something to do with his life after college. This seems like a good thing."

Her little brother was graduating with a degree in business management in the spring, and the plan was always that he'd come home and join the family business. "This kind of attention wasn't what I had in mind." Cassidy blew her bangs out of her face, then flipped her head to finish the job, but the irritating things fell right back into her eyes. She needed a haircut, but she had way too much going on to take time out for something like that. "Why are these people subscribing? I mean, my last video was about wood-joining techniques in the early nineteen hundreds. Probably my most boring topic yet. Seriously. It has to be a YouTube analytics error or something."

"You've gained a few dozen more subscribers since we've been standing here talking about it," Amanda said, scrolling. "If it keeps up at this rate, you'll break ten thousand by tonight."

What the actual heck? Frowning, Cassidy climbed out of the hole in the floor and brushed herself off with her hands. Amanda stepped back out of the way of the sawdust and dirt storm.

"Maybe it's some kind of bot attack," Cassidy said. "Or an online troll army or something."

"Why would anyone target an obscure, niche channel about repairing a Victorian home? I'm sticking with you're cute and swing a mean hammer." Amanda shoved her phone into her red, rose-shaped handbag. "You coming to my deck for dinner? Lillian and Caleb will be there."

The interaction—or rather lack of interaction—with Tristan, along with the YouTube glitch, had put Cassidy in a foul mood. She wasn't up to dealing with the inevitable PDA and joy that Caleb and Lillian oozed from every pore since their engagement. She was thrilled for them, but she was still stinging from her fantasy bubble being deflated in such a demeaning way.

Before Cassidy could decline, Amanda held out her hand like a traffic cop, momentarily distracted by her own neon orange nail polish. "Hold on. Before you say no, think about it." She grinned. "You *have* to come. Lillian is an online wizard. She'll be able to tell you what's going on with your channel subscriptions for sure."

Amanda wasn't wrong. Lillian was queen of the online lifestyle empire, *Living Sharpe.* Her business also had a TV show, magazine, and several cookware lines. Lillian would definitely know how to fix Cassidy's subscriptions—and goodness knew that fixing *something* in her life was in order about now.

Loud scraping and banging came from the floor above. From the corner of her eye, Cassidy spotted a terrified Lolo sprinting from her spot under the stairs to disappear somewhere in the direction of the kitchen.

"Is the doc redecorating?" Amanda asked.

Something big was clearly being moved from the sound of it. "I've no idea."

Amanda grinned. "Let's go see." She grabbed Cassidy's hand and yanked her in the direction of the stairs.

"No. Wait. It's none of our business."

Amanda managed an impressive, theatrical wink while still steamrolling toward the stairs. "*Everything* is my business. Besides, you should take advantage of every interaction." She stopped at the foot of the stairs. "You've been waiting for this for years, am I right?"

Yes, she was right, but now that the time was here, Cassidy wasn't so sure how she felt. It was easy when there were no emotional stakes—when it was nothing but a dream. She nodded and followed Amanda up the stairs.

When they reached the top landing, they found Tristan lugging a mattress through a doorway and into the hall. Even wrestling an ancient, floppy mattress, he looked put-together and perfect—just like in her fantasies.

"Hi. I'm Amanda. Want some help?"

Cassidy remained frozen in place beside her friend.

"I'm Tristan McGuffy," he said with a brilliant, heart-melting smile she remembered so well. "Good to meet you, Amanda." He met Cassidy's eyes. "And you are?"

And you are? Her face grew hot. That certainly wasn't a line from any of her million dreams about the guy. He honestly had no clue who she was. Well, maybe that was a good thing considering the cheesy band uniform and braces she'd been sporting the last time he'd seen her.

"I'm Cassidy James."

His eyebrows rose, and he stared at her for an uncomfortably long time. "No way. Little Sassy Cassy?"

Great, just great. Amanda would have a field day with that one.

His smile widened. "Wow. Time really flies, doesn't it?"

Not really. Not for her, anyway. She felt like it had been a million years since she'd last seen him, but then, time in Blink seemed to run on an entirely different schedule from the rest of the world. Seven years felt like centuries.

"I'd love some help," he said. "Thanks for asking, Amanda. I'm trading this old mattress my parents used for the newer one in my old room."

With Amanda and Cassidy on one end and Tristan on the other, they managed to maneuver the floppy old mattress down the hallway and into his childhood room. Cassidy had intentionally not wandered into these bedrooms out of respect for the family's privacy. She'd been hired by Tristan's father to restore the exterior and first floor, and if that went well, he'd said he'd expand the project. She'd assumed he was prepping the house to move back in.

Roger and his wife had moved into the cottage behind this house when she got sick several years ago. After her death, he remained, saying he preferred living in the smaller cottage. He'd said that this house was too big for him to keep up with, but Cassidy was pretty sure it was because everything in this large house reminded him of his wife. With his son living in Portland, Mr. McGuffy was probably lonely.

They leaned the old mattress against a bookcase on the left wall and helped him tip up and slide the newer one off the bed.

"Mom bought this new mattress before I came home to celebrate my med school graduation, and I think I've slept on it three times total," he said. "I'd rather sleep in the master, so I'm trading mattresses." As he looked around the room, his cheerful expression fell. "This feels…wrong." He blinked rapidly a few times, took in a deep breath, then shrugged. "But it made Mom happy to decorate it like this when I went off to college."

Cassidy studied the room. It was a shrine to his high school years. School pennants. Loads of trophies and award plaques. The walls were covered in framed certificates and photos of groups he had been a part of.

"If I'm stuck in this town for a while, I'd rather not be stuck in my high school glory days." He grinned, and when Cassidy glanced at Amanda, it was obvious that his grin had totally worked. Her friend's eyes were glazed, and she wore the wistful expression of the charmed.

Cassidy could relate.

Wait. He'd said he'd be stuck here *a while*. She took a deep breath, refusing to get her hopes up. "How long will you be in Blink?"

He grabbed the back edge of the mattress as she and Amanda clutched the front.

"Not long, I hope." With a huff, he pushed, setting the mattress in motion with much less effort than it took to move the older floppy one. They slid this newer mattress down the hallway and into the master bedroom.

"Wow." The word came out of Cassidy's mouth as if from somewhere else. Her reaction to the beautiful room was involuntary. The tall ceiling still bore the original plaster medallion from the late 1800s above the light, and all the ornate moldings were still intact, including those around the gorgeous fireplace highlighted by the original hand-painted green tiles.

They slid the mattress into place, and Cassidy walked to a corner and stared up at the plasterwork. "Wow," she repeated.

Tristan squared up the mattress on the four-poster bed. "This old house is pretty impressive if you didn't grow up in it, I guess." He gave a dismissive shrug, then smiled. "Thanks for helping me move the mattress." He straightened, feet apart, arms folded over his chest like a pirate captain or something. A completely masculine look that made Cassidy want to sigh.

"Anytime," Amanda said. "We're meeting at the

harbor with some friends for dinner. Wanna join?"

Cassidy found herself holding her breath.

"No, but thanks for the invite. I need to have a talk with my dad. Rain check?"

"Absolutely," Amanda said with a grin. "Ready, Cass?"

Cassidy pulled her gaze away from the handsome Dr. McGuffy and with a nod gave the gorgeous details of the room one last perusal. Her online buddies would freak out about the condition of this place—her stomach flipped over—all five thousand–plus of them. Definitely a computer glitch. Hopefully, Lillian could help her put a stop to whatever was causing the falsely inflated statistics.

"Sassy Cassy," Amanda teased in a sing-song voice.

Yeah, and Cassidy needed a way to put a stop to *that*, too.

CHAPTER FOUR

"Thank you," Jack said as the crew packed up their equipment and wardrobe racks. Fortunately, the shoot hadn't involved wearing his heavy outfit from *Mad Planet*. The studio had provided stills of him in the ridiculous armor for them to use, so instead, they posed him casually in designer clothes in front of the huge, modern fireplace and long bank of windows overlooking L.A.

Not wanting to hang around for awkward small talk with strangers, he headed straight upstairs to pack to go see his sister, leaving Dee to oversee their departure.

Marion knocked on the doorframe and stood outside his open bedroom door. "Again, Mr. Winston, I'd like to emphasize this is a bad time for you to leave."

She said this every time he left the house. He certainly wasn't a prisoner, and she'd never try to keep him against his will, but his will was weak compared to hers. *Everyone's* will was weak compared to hers. And even though her advice was sound, it had become confining.

He took a deep breath and pulled a blue T-shirt out of his dresser drawer and placed it in his duffel. No need to ask why it was a bad time. Marion would lay it all out in excruciating detail, no doubt. She was nothing if not thorough.

"HBO needs a quick answer and—"

"Tell them no," he said, cutting her off.

"No?"

He turned to face her. "No. I don't want to do a series right now."

She took a deep breath through her nose with a give-me-patience expression that reminded him of his high school acting teacher when he purposely went off book during a performance. "Mr. Winston, you hired me to help you. I left a lovely resort in the French Riviera to come back to L.A. and clean up the mess you and your *friends* had made of your career."

And you're paid well for it. He tossed some socks into the duffel. "And I'm grateful."

"Our agreement was that if I came back to Hollywood, you would honor my opinions and follow my directives," she said, brown eyes narrowed, lips drawn thin.

"And I have." He strode to the bathroom to grab his travel kit. He returned to find her still in the doorway, tapping her foot, eyebrow arched.

"Until now," she said. "You've been fine with my directives going on two years. What's changed?"

He threw the leather travel kit into the bag. "I can't do it, Marion."

Her expression didn't change, but her foot stopped tapping. She'd probably heard it all in her very long career, including these exact words. Maybe hundreds of times. Maybe thousands.

"I need a break. I'm uneasy and restless, and I don't want to feel this way. I need to go see my sister and her kids for a short while. That's all." He craved normalcy for a moment. He wanted to just be Uncle Jackie and nothing else.

Her lips tightened even more.

"It helps me," he said. "The one-on-one connection with people who love me helps keep me grounded."

Her eyes never left his. "Are you clean?"

For a moment, he was offended, then he remembered something his mom had always said: "People judge a man by the company he keeps." Marion had every right to ask him that based on what she'd dealt with when she arrived two years ago. The people he'd allowed into his life had been a mess, and the more time that went by without them, the more he realized they'd never been his friends in the first place. He held up a hand like in a scout pledge. "I'm completely clean. You know that."

She gave a brisk nod, then shifted her gaze to the window. "Many of my clients over the years have fallen prey to…vices." For a moment, she stared past him, as if deep in a memory. After a breath, she met his eyes again. "You hired me to manage your career. It's my job to make sure you're okay when you say you feel off."

That seemed fair. "Thanks for your concern."

"How long will you be gone?"

"I'll be back by dinner tomorrow."

Her shoulders relaxed. It would be his first night away outside of filming since she'd agreed to work with him. It was part of their agreement. No drugs, no parties, no disappearing—none of which were an issue for him. He was to be a homebody with a stellar work ethic. Something he'd lost touch with before she came onboard.

"I'm truly grateful for what you've done for me," he said again with absolute sincerity.

"It has been a satisfactory arrangement so far, Mr. Winston. I'm hopeful it will continue as such."

That was as close to a compliment as he'd ever heard come out of her mouth. He gestured for her to enter the room.

She strode across the room and stared out the window on the far wall before turning to face him, expression serious. Her expression was always serious, though. "We need to discuss some things. The *Hollywood Tattler* ran a story about a woman named Desiree Smith who claims you were drunk on a date and left her at the restaurant with an unpaid $800 dinner bill."

He sat on the bed, facing her. "Funny, because I haven't had a drink or taken a woman to dinner in ages, and you know it." Marion Hill practically lived in his pocket. She arrived at the crack of dawn every single day and knew where he was at all times, thanks to her constant communication with his staff. She was the consummate den mother.

She cleared her throat. "A woman named Sable Burke told *The Inquisitor* this week that you are the best date ever. The *best* in every sense of the word."

"I am," he said, grinning when Marion's eyebrow cocked up in amusement. "But I've never met, much less dated, a Sable Burke. Why are you telling me what's in the tabloids? They're always running fake stories." This entire city was fueled by fake stories. It's the one thing he disliked the most about his career. If he was out in the social scene like he used to be when his friends lived with him, the press latched onto everything he did and blew it all out of proportion. If he maintained his privacy and laid low, like he did now, they made things up about him. It was a lose-lose.

"You hired me to manage your career, to be the primary contact between your agent, PR firm, attorneys, accountants, and every other troublesome side of things you had neglected so long."

He studied her shiny black stilettos. The woman made him feel like a scolded child.

She continued, evidently satisfied he was properly remorseful. "A part of managing your career, and a large part of my function, is maintaining the proper image. I'm satisfied that you left the clubbing and socially self-destructive behavior behind when you left your so-called friends behind. Now it's time to create the image that best facilitates your success. All entities working with you, including your agent and PR firm, are in agreement on this."

The hairs on Jack's neck prickled. This couldn't be a good thing. His dread expanded down his spine when she picked up her phone and said, "Miss LaPorte, please bring the document in the printer to Mr. Winston's room."

"Can this wait until I get back from my sister's house?"

"No."

She stared out the window while he finished

packing until Dee entered the room. She was out of breath, no doubt from running up the stairs.

"Please hand it to Mr. Winston," Marion ordered.

He took the paper and stared down at it. It was a list of names, some he knew, and some he didn't. Those he recognized were in the industry. "What's this?"

"A menu," she said. "We need more control over what the tabloids and media put out about you. It will strengthen your image if you're seen with a regular partner, even if it's only for a short period of time—a couple of weeks would do, but longer would be better, of course, if you and whomever you choose can pull it off. These are your options from which to select."

His breath quickened as he studied the names. "I don't even know some of these people."

"It doesn't matter. It's only for show. Fabricated romances are as old as the movie industry itself."

"Fabricated romances…" His voice trailed off.

"Pick someone. All of the names on that list are open to a public romantic relationship with you."

He lowered the paper and stared at her in disbelief. "They know about this?"

"Of course they do."

He looked down at the list of women and a few men typed neatly down the left side of the page. Dee shifted uncomfortably in the doorway, pulling his attention from the list.

"Thank you, Miss LaPorte," Marion said with a dismissive wave of her hand. Once Dee left, she continued. "You need to control the narrative, Mr.

Winston. You and whomever you select will benefit from the free publicity. No more Sable Burkes
muddying the waters. This puts you in charge of
your image. An image which I have worked hard
to improve. Now, you need to do your part by creating a relationship that will interest the public
and put you in the spotlight in a positive way." She
stood. "You should also have a hobby that will interest your fans."

He took a deep breath and pushed down his
irritation. "Like what?"

She lifted one shoulder. "Like art or tennis or
music or cars. Something relatable for your fans.
Something personal and positive."

When he simply stared at her, she added, "It
doesn't have to be something you're good at,
though it would help if you were. You need to be
seen doing something regular people do."

Regular people. That was where his self-image
collided with his life. He thought of himself as just
a regular guy. The movie star thing seemed foreign
and uncomfortable. Like a coat that was too tight,
even after all these years.

Marion waved her hand in a dismissive circle.
"No rush. Let me know who you choose from that
list tomorrow when you return, and I'll contact the
agent of whomever you select."

Jack didn't move until the sound of her shoes
clicking on wood faded to silence. Then he sat on
the edge of his bed. What she said made sense, but
he was repulsed by it. Letting out a huff of breath,
he shook his head. He had loads of actor friends
who were in relationships. How many of them

were fake?

He stared at the fireplace at the far end of his bedroom. Again, it struck him how silly it was in this climate where on the few days it was cold enough for a fire, central heat made it redundant. He thought back on winter nights as a kid living in Kansas when they couldn't pay the bills, so he and his sister and mother had huddled together under a blanket pretending the cold radiator was a warm, crackling fireplace.

He stood and zipped his duffel bag, ran a hand through his hair, and let out what sounded like laughter but felt hollow in his chest. "Look at us now," he said. His sister was married to a hotshot plastic surgeon in Malibu, and he was living in an L.A. penthouse with fireplaces that were only for show while considering a relationship that was only for show. What a world.

"Mr. Winston?" Dee's voice said from the doorway.

"Come on in," he answered, standing.

She took a few tentative steps into his room, looked over her shoulder, then held out a paper.

"Did Marion come up with another list of potential fake partners for me?" he asked with a smirk. "Or maybe it's a list of false hobbies."

He'd expected her expression to lighten, but it didn't. In fact, her lower lip trembled and the paper in her hand fluttered.

He crossed to her, took it, and scanned the words. *Oh, hell no.* "You can't resign," he said. "I won't accept this letter."

She took a deep breath. "You'll accept it when I

tell you what I did."

He doubted it. He made a motion with his hand, indicating for her to continue.

"When I put up the post you asked for on Instagram with your picture from *Mad Planet 3* with that caption, I thought I'd tagged your sister, but I accidentally left the underscore out of the username and tagged the wrong person."

He let out a breath in relief. "That's it? That's what all this is about?"

She wrapped her arms around herself. "It kind of blew up. I took it down when I realized I'd tagged the wrong person, but it had been twenty minutes by then, and it was too late. There were lots of screenshots circulating on social media and in chat rooms, and your fans did what they do…"

He didn't handle his own social media. His publicity firm handled all his sites, but Dee kept an eye on his sister's and closest friends' profiles and occasionally posted at his request—almost always personal jokes. The publicists loved it when he had Dee post because it made the sites more "authentic," which was a joke regarding anything about this career. "Exactly what do my fans do?"

"They dig deep. They cyberstalk."

They stalked for real, too, which was why Marion pushed him so hard to hire a team of bodyguards. So far, that hadn't been necessary except for bigger events or promotional tours when movies came out. He and Marion had compromised, and only one bodyguard was a full-time employee—Flex, a thirty-something-year-old former police officer. He'd decided early on that he preferred security work to being an officer on the beat.

Flex's security job was easy. For the most part, Jack hung out at home, and it was a super-secure building with his own floor, a keyed, accompanied elevator, and a security guard 24/7 in the lobby. A beautiful, safe cage.

"So they cyberstalked the person you accidentally tagged?" he asked.

She studied her feet. "Yes. And the tabloids found her based off that."

He closed his eyes. "Who is she?"

"A woman named Cassidy James. She appears to play the cymbals and do construction work in a small town in Maine. A normal person." Dee let out a frustrated huff. "Well, normal until I screwed her life up. Now, she's being hassled from everywhere, I assume."

No doubt the paparazzi were falling all over themselves to get a piece of this. The reclusive superstar of *Mad Planet* had tagged a woman in a post saying, "I'm coming for you, babe."

Since he'd dropped out of social life, the tabloids had been starving for information on secretive Jack Winston. Now they had something, or rather some*one*, to sink their teeth into…some normal, everyday woman from a small town—he shook his head—who played the cymbals and did construction work? Suddenly, he found himself interested in her himself.

"I'll hang on to this, but I'm not accepting your resignation right now," he said, folding her letter and stuffing it into the side pocket of his duffel bag. "I'm going to spend some time with my sister and her husband and their kids in Malibu. I'll be back tomorrow night. Send me the contact info for the cymbal player and I'll reach out."

Dee's mouth dropped open. "Mr. Winston. No. That's... You can't do that."

"Why not?"

She threw her arms up in exasperation. "Because you're Jack Winston!"

He grinned at her. "Thanks for clearing that up. I'd forgotten."

Finally, a glimmer of amusement crossed her face.

"Okay, I'll stay out of it. Contact her and apologize for the mistake on my behalf and offer her airfare, lodging, and tickets to the premiere of *Mad Planet 4* or something." He picked up his duffel and slung it over his shoulder. "I'll call the PR folks to clear it up. The paparazzi will tire of her in no time when they find out it was simply a mis-tag on social media."

She nodded.

He stopped before he made it to the door. "Dee, don't tell Marion anything about this. I'll be a good client and make a big show of dating somebody from the list she gave me and the fans and paparazzi will forget all about this woman from Maine." He shrugged and smiled. "Who knows? Maybe this was a stroke of good luck for this Cassidy person. Maybe it will improve her construction business or something." He thought about his early days of fame. "Maybe she likes attention and it's the best thing that's ever happened to her."

CHAPTER FIVE

"It has to stop!" With a groan, Cassidy declined the incoming call on her phone, the dozenth or so in as many minutes. All came from unfamiliar numbers, the last three in rapid succession from the same California number.

She turned off her ringer and picked up her sandwich. She'd asked one of the first callers how they'd gotten her number, and they said it was by searching her name and location, and boom, up comes her website and relevant info: *Miss Fix-It Renovations, Blink, Maine, Owner/proprietor, Cassidy James*, complete with phone number, which happened to be her cell. "Small businesses must have an online presence," she'd been instructed at the last builders' conference she'd attended. "Be sure to make yourself easy to find and accessible," they'd said. She groaned.

"I know you're frustrated, Cass," Lillian remarked from across the picnic table, "but maybe your sudden notoriety can be turned into a good thing."

The four of them had gathered on the deck in front of Amanda's business, Miller Mercantile. Lillian and her fiancé, Caleb, sat across from Amanda and Cassidy at the bright turquoise picnic table. The evening sun reflected off the ripples in the harbor, causing the water's surface to shimmer like glitter. Along the boardwalk ringing the harbor, Caleb's dogs chased any seagull with the audacity to attempt a landing on the pilings.

It was business as usual for everyone except Cassidy.

She declined another unknown caller, sighed, and set her turkey sandwich down on her plate. "How? How can I turn it into a good thing?" Cassidy moaned. "My phone hasn't stopped all day."

Lillian stared out over the harbor and shrugged. "I don't exactly know *how* it could be a good thing. Maybe it will amp up your remodeling business?"

With Blink's growth spurt, Cassidy had hoped to use the videos to generate new business. The odd messages on her phone from strangers all over the country asking for interviews didn't seem to be related to her construction business at all. She took a bite of sandwich and chased it with a chug of Sprite.

"Why is this happening all of a sudden?" Amanda asked.

Lillian glanced up from her phone. "I'm checking the comments on YouTube, and more than one has mentioned an affair between you and Jack Winston."

Cassidy's face grew warm. "A couple of the text messages mentioned that, too. Clearly they're confusing me with someone else."

"Jack Winston?" Amanda bounced on the bench, and Cassidy grabbed the edge of the table in case her friend's exuberance toppled the whole thing over. "Jack Winston? *The* Jack Winston as in

Blake Crusher from *Mad Planet*?"

It made no sense whatsoever. None. Why would anyone think she was with Jack Winston? Her face went from warm to hot. Amanda had dragged Cassidy to every one of the *Mad Planet* movies even though superhero action-adventure was not her thing. Pop culture wasn't her thing, either, but even *she* knew who Jack Winston was. His handsome face was often on the cover of Amanda's tabloids along with his Hollywood exploits. Cassidy would be lying if she said the man wasn't eye-catching as he stared back at her from the covers of magazines at the grocery checkout in Machias.

"Oh, here we go," Lillian said, turning the screen to face them. "The source of the rumor was Instagram."

Amanda leaned closer to the phone and read a comment that said, *"Hey, found you from insta congrats on bagging the big one."* The odd comment was followed by a string of alternating winky and flame emojis.

What on earth did that even mean? Cassidy swallowed her bite of sandwich, glad when it went down the right way. She hadn't logged in to her Instagram account since high school. The jump in subscribers to her YouTube channel was uncomfortable, but the thought of thousands of strangers viewing photos on her long-abandoned account was mortifying. Heaven only knew what was there. She shuddered and glanced down at her own phone screen full of new missed call notifications and texts from randos wanting interviews or statements.

"What's your name on Instagram?" Lillian asked.

Cassidy shrugged. "I don't remember."

Lillian's eyebrows rose. "Seriously?"

She wiped her fingers on a napkin. "I haven't posted or visited that site in years. Not since high school."

Lillian popped a chip in her mouth. "Try logging in. Do you have the same email address you had back then?"

"I think so." Cassidy picked up her phone. After doing a lost password reset, she successfully accessed the page and groaned as it all came back to her. "The name is @BNforever." She cringed, remembering how cool she'd felt when she had picked the name. *Band nerd forever*. With a grimace, she scrolled the photos from her long-abandoned account, feeling anything but cool.

"Oh my God. Look how cute you were in your little marching band uniform!" Amanda said. "And those braces!"

Caleb studied Lillian's phone as she scrolled. "I remember you in those days." He looked up from the screen and winked at her across the table. "You've come a long way since then."

Cassidy could feel the blush raging up her neck and over her face, and for a moment, her thoughts ran to Tristan and how she'd hoped he'd be the one to say something like that.

"You didn't make any posts about Jack Winston." Amanda's brow furrowed. "Wonder what triggered the flood of people over on YouTube. I doubt a video of you in a blue bathrobe holding up a hairbrush like a microphone, singing 'Let It Go' from *Frozen* would've done it."

Cassidy groaned, dropped her phone on the table, and covered her hot face. People seeing her restoration videos was fine. Watching a terrible Elsa impersonation was absolutely not.

"Bingo!" Lillian said a few moments later.

When Cassidy opened her eyes, she realized Lillian had picked up her phone from the table where she'd laid it.

"It's in your notifications. You were tagged by Jack Winston this morning. His fans found you from that post on his profile page. The original post is down now, but there are loads of notifications tagging you that contain screenshots of the post from his account." She turned the phone toward Cassidy and Amanda.

Amanda gasped. "Oh my God! You were tagged by Jack Winston! Holy crap, he's hot." She fanned her face and heaved a melodramatic sigh.

Cassidy read the caption under the photo of the actor wearing a huge, futuristic armored suit. "Hey, @BNforever! I'm coming for you, babe." Even in the cumbersome gear with the large helmet, the guy was gorgeous. Not in a pretty way. In a pure male way with dark hair and even darker eyes.

Cassidy shifted on the bench. "Why would he tag *me*?"

"Because you're cute and swing a mean hammer?" Amanda said. "Um, maybe because you look adorable in your band uniform holding those cymbals." She snickered. "They're almost as big as you are!"

Caleb laughed. "That's it. The guy has a cymbal fetish."

"Or a thing for braces and freckles," Amanda added.

"It's not funny," Cassidy grumbled. Though she knew it truly was. High school Cassidy was hilarious and unashamed...and 100 percent cringy.

"Your *Frozen* karaoke has close to two thousand likes and a zillion views," Amanda said between giggles.

Okay, so not *that* funny. "I have to make this stop."

Lillian handed her phone back. "It's definitely the tag by Jack Winston's account that caused the flood of followers. And I'm not surprised the post was deleted. Very few celebrities of his status handle their own social media accounts. If I were guessing, I'd say it was an accidental tag made by someone on his publicity team. He probably doesn't even know about it."

Well, that certainly made more sense than a movie star tagging *her*.

"If you don't want the attention, deactivate your account. It's that simple," Lillian said.

"Girl, I'd ride this as long as it lasts," Amanda said. "Jack Winston! You grab that fifteen minutes of fame and run with it all the way to the finish line."

To Cassidy, fame held no appeal. She liked her low-key life and planned to keep it that way.

She stared down at the photo of Jack Winston smiling up at her from her phone, and she couldn't help but smile back. Weird. Maybe that's what people meant by "star power."

Maybe Lillian was right and she could turn this into a good thing. All she had to do was delete her Instagram account and carry on as usual with a much bigger YouTube audience. If she was lucky, maybe a couple of jobs would come out of it. Relieved, she raised her Sprite can in a toast. "To my return to peace and quiet."

They all raised their drinks, and Amanda said, "To peace and quiet!"

Cans lifted for the toast, Caleb and Lillian froze, mouths open in shock. Next to her, Amanda twisted around and gasped.

A prickly wave of dread moved from the base of Cassidy's spine up over the top of her head. "What is it?" she whispered, too uptight to even look.

"I don't think you're going to get your peace and quiet anytime soon," Lillian said.

"Cassidy James!" a male voice from behind her on the harbor walkway called. "How long have you been seeing Jack Winston?"

"Is the affair serious?" a woman's voice asked.

"How did you and Mr. Winston meet?" a third voice shouted.

Cassidy was pretty sure what she'd see when she finally managed to turn around, but nothing could have prepared her for the reality of it.

Paparazzi. Lots of them.

Clicks of cameras filled the air when she finally

twisted in her seat. They were on the boardwalk, just outside the patio railing, some with cameras, some with microphones, and all looking straight at her. She glanced down at her paint-spattered overalls and winced. Well, at least she wasn't in a high school band uniform with a mouth full of braces.

"My car is parked on the other side of my store. I can walk Cass through the store, get her to my car, and drive her home if you guys will distract them," Amanda said in her best drill sergeant voice.

Cassidy's body flooded with itchy anxiety. She didn't like being in the cabin alone to begin with since her dad died, but she really didn't like the idea of being there if these people were going to be following her around, shouting questions and snapping pictures. Even if Amanda could sneak her out, the paparazzi would find her there. Her business address was listed online as a PO box in Machias, but all it would take was a quick check of the tax records to know where she lived.

Lillian must have been thinking the same thing, because she glanced at the cluster of photographers and said, "I'd rather you not go home right now, Cass."

"That's a wise choice," Caleb said. "Let's get her inside the store."

"You can stay with me tonight," Amanda said. "We'll figure it out from there."

"When will you be seeing Mr. Winston next?" one of the people called as the four of them hustled toward the door of Amanda's store.

"This deck is private property," Caleb shouted

over his shoulder. Evidently, those were magic words because they stayed put on the boardwalk.

"I need to go back to Roger's house to work," Cassidy said, pulling the curtain aside an inch or so to peek out the window. A few of the paparazzi had remained just outside the deck, but most had moved on. Probably to case the front of the building and who knew what else.

"I wouldn't advise going back to work," Lillian said. "Since Jack Winston took the post down, they might move on soon, depending on how his team spins it. No need to subject yourself to this."

"You work too much anyway," Amanda said, rummaging around under the counter. "You know the guest bedroom is always yours."

She used to stay with Amanda frequently after her dad's funeral. Recently, though, Cassidy had forced herself to spend time at her family cabin. She'd cleared out all the clutter that her dad had accumulated, and refurnished the place in a clean, comfortable style that would be perfect for her little brother when he returned next summer from college to help her run the business.

She let the curtain slip back into place. She hadn't really considered what she'd do after her brother moved back to Blink. The cabin was small, and no doubt they could tolerate living together like they had as kids, but that hadn't been her plan. In fact, she didn't have a plan.

She thought of Tristan and kicked herself mentally. She'd never imagined anything past the reunion where he extolled her maturity and the image of them in wedding garb. Maybe she'd just assumed they'd ride off into the sunset together and live happily ever after in Happilyeverafterville. How ridiculous.

"I'll take you up on the offer of your guest bedroom," Cassidy said.

"Binge watching is in order." Amanda turned over the "open" signs on the front and back doors. "Ooo. I know! Let's watch all three *Mad Planet* movies!"

The last thing she wanted was to watch movies starring the man who had caused all this trouble. Cassidy delivered the quelling look usually reserved for her little brother, Luke, that shut him right up. It worked on her friend, too, evidently.

"Okay, no Jack Winston," Amanda said. "How about comedy?" She walked back to the counter and fiddled with the computer. "We'll watch TV, eat popcorn, and laugh until we can't stand it."

After Caleb and Lillian left, Cassidy followed Amanda up the stairs while her friend chattered about what series they should watch and how cool it was Jack Winston had tagged her.

As she glanced through the window at the second story landing, Cassidy saw a couple of photographers in the front parking lot. *Yeah, cool*, she thought with a grimace, backing out of their view.

She was a prisoner because of this. She glared at the window and crossed her arms over her chest. Here she was in hiding because of some stuck-up movie star who didn't even know what was happening to her because of his careless mistake—or the mistake of someone who worked for him. She didn't need to be wasting time watching an entire season of some silly sitcom. She needed to be working on Roger's house. With a huff, she climbed the rest of the stairs. This was ridiculous.

As she watched Amanda scroll through the show menu, she slumped down onto the sectional and glowered, letting her anger heat up to boiling. If she ever got the chance, she had a choice word or two for Mr. Jack Winston. But first things first. She pulled out her phone and deactivated her Instagram account.

CHAPTER SIX

On the TV screen, cool, collected Captain Blake Crusher skillfully piloted his damaged ship through an impossible crash landing in a wheat field. He left a blazing trail of destruction behind him, accompanied by some gratuitous explosions, of course. A beautiful young woman hanging clothes on the line outside her meager, rustic farmhouse located conveniently in the middle of nowhere stared in breathless wonder as he calmly pushed up the glass windscreen dome and, miraculously uninjured, climbed out of the smoking, destroyed ship. Dramatic music swelled as their eyes met and held, making it clear to the viewers that the life of that woman was about to change forever, and so was Captain Blake Crusher's.

With a sigh, Jack picked up the remote and muted the volume on the television, careful not to disturb the sleeping kids on either side of him on the sofa. They were growing up so fast. Sidney was seven now, and her brother, Mason, was five.

Jack's sister, Bryn, stuck her head into the living room from the hallway. "You want me to put them to bed?"

He smiled. "I'll do it."

She stared at him for a moment. "I'm glad you came by. So's Nate."

And so was he. He brushed some hair out of Mason's face. The boy turned over, draping an arm across Jack's lap, knocking a book about dinosaurs to the floor. "You did great, sis."

Curled in a ball with her head on the arm of the sofa, Sidney cracked her eyes open, smiled at him, and drifted off to sleep again.

"You've done pretty well yourself, Mr. Movie Star." She moved into the room and sat on the ottoman in front of the sofa. "This is your first time to visit in a while. Everything okay?"

Bryn knew him too well. No. She knew him well enough to care, which he appreciated. "Yeah. I'm good."

She tilted her head and studied him. "Don't get me wrong; I love it when we talk on the phone or FaceTime or touch base on social media, but tagging each other with silly jokes on Instagram isn't the same as teasing you in person, little brother."

She was right. He glanced down at the kids next to him and how much they'd grown in the several months since he'd last spent time with them, and his throat tightened. He'd do better and make sure he scheduled more frequent visits. "I've been busy with pre-production on the next *Mad Planet* film. My manager is keeping me in line, so smooth sailing, I suppose."

Mason rolled over and settled again.

"I worry about you, you know," she said.

He gave what he knew from years of practice to be a convincing smile. "I'm good. I promise." And for the most part, that was true. Marion had his career back on track, and after spending time with his niece and nephew, he felt much more at ease. He was glad his sister's family lived so close to

L.A. so he could drop in like this without a lot of fuss or a big security detail like he would have to endure if they lived somewhere distant. As much as he was not a fan of Hollywood life, he'd stay for this reason alone—plus it was convenient business-wise. According to Marion, living in L.A. was essential at this point in his career so he could keep his finger on the pulse of the industry.

Bryn tilted her head. "You seeing anyone?"

Leave it to his prying big sister to dig in instead of give up. She asked this every time they talked. People in good relationships always wish the same for friends and relatives. Only in his case, it was a lost cause. "No."

"You should."

With a sigh, he leaned back into the sofa. He knew Bryn only wanted him to find happiness and love like she and Nate had. Jack's chest pinched painfully. He rarely regretted his career choice, but when he did, it was usually the result of loneliness. He was surrounded by people all the time, but like his mom, he never seemed to be able to make deep connections that lasted. Unlike his mom, though, when Jack's relationships ended, the news was splattered like blood all over the front pages of the tabloids, making his failure even more pronounced.

"We've talked about this," he said. "My lifestyle is not conducive to dating. It's a disaster for me to even attempt a relationship." Everyone wanted something from him. He'd learned that the hard way one too many times. In fact, the more he'd thought about it, the more Marion's fake relationship scheme made sense.

"The right person just hasn't come along yet." She reached over to touch him but dropped her hand instead, maybe because she didn't want to wake her son draped across Jack's lap. "Don't let past mistakes, including Mom's and Dad's, hold you down, Jack. Time's too precious."

Bryn was several years older, but she didn't have any memories of their father, either. He'd left when their mother was pregnant with Jack. He'd never met the man. As for his mom, she'd tried to find a father for them on a regular basis. None of them stuck around.

Bryn was right. The older he got, the more he realized how precious time was.

For a while, they sat in silence. In the flickering light of the TV screen, Bryn stared at Jack in that big sister way he loved. The one that said, *I'll love you the same way no matter how bad you screw up or how successful you become. I love you for you and nothing else.*

She stood. "Okay, then. See you in the morning." She kissed him on the cheek and disappeared.

For a long time, Jack sat in silence as Crusher lived out his exciting life on the muted TV screen and his niece and nephew slept peacefully on either side of him. He'd sent his bodyguard to the guest house long ago.

Across the room, a clock ticked, and the bubblers on a huge saltwater fish tank hummed behind him. After a few moments, he found himself breathing in a slow rhythm, the clock's steady beats acting as a metronome. Spending time with family had been the perfect balm for his edginess. He felt his old self after some fierce rounds of hide-and-seek with the kids, dinner, and some TV time — even if the kids had insisted on watching *Mad Planet*. He smiled. They had watched it so many times, they could recite the dialogue. This time, though, they'd fallen asleep before Crusher had even set off on his mission to save the universe. He let out a sigh and closed his eyes. He doubted even Marion could wind him up right now.

His phone buzzed in his pocket, and he struggled to retrieve it without disturbing the sleeping children.

It was a text from Dee: *I can't reach Cassidy James. Will try again tomorrow. Hope you're having fun with family.*

Jack replied: *Having a great time. Thanks. Don't worry about Cassidy James. We'll sort it out. Get some sleep.*

Dee replied with a thumbs-up emoji, but he was certain that didn't reflect how she felt at all. She'd been way more shaken up by this than he'd expected. To him, her worry seemed completely out of proportion to the problem.

Before he and Flex had left his penthouse to drive to Malibu, he'd spent a few minutes scrolling Instagram. The post on his account that had caused all the trouble was gone, as expected, so he scrolled through recent notifications and found several that tagged his account with posts containing screenshots of Dee's post to @BNforever before it was taken down.

The mix-up was easy to understand. His sister's username was @BN_forever. She had opened her account around the time she and Nate had gotten engaged. Bryn and Nate forever certainly suited. They were as in love a decade later as they were when they first met.

When he'd checked out his private messages, Jack found several attempts to contact @BNforever from his account. That'd be Dee, reaching out on his behalf. He clicked on the other name, and Cassidy James's profile had popped up. There was only a brief bio. "I make noise and build stuff."

He'd liked her immediately.

In scrolling through her photos, Jack had learned that Cassidy had played cymbals in her high school marching band, at one time had a pet hamster named Rosco, loved lemonade, had a little brother, and adored her father. She also couldn't hold a tune. He winced at her pitiful karaoke rendition of "Let It Go" in a hideous blond wig. Sadly, her Instagram posts ended once she left high school, years ago. No telling what she was like now, though he couldn't imagine she had changed much. At least he hoped she hadn't. She was funny with a quirky sense of humor.

Nowhere on her Instagram page had Cassidy revealed her name, so it must have taken some real sleuthing on the part of his fans to find her on YouTube...or maybe not. It was clear she was from Blink, Maine, and built stuff with her dad. Perhaps it had been simple to find her based off that. If there was one thing he knew for sure, it was that fans and paparazzi could find anyone or anything.

Fortunately, he didn't have to search at all because Dee had sent him the link to her YouTube channel.

To his left on the sofa, Sidney shifted, then settled back to sleep.

Careful not to wake the kids, he put his earbuds in and clicked play on the first video, grinning at the petite, messy-haired, paint-splattered woman giving a tour of the outside of a white Victorian home and explaining some repairs she planned to make, waving her arms wildly. In the video, she walked the perimeter with someone else clearly filming her. The footage was wobbly and too far away for her to be filming herself.

There was something about that house tour that made his chest ache. It was an old longing— one he'd pushed aside when he moved to California. He found himself leaning forward, riveted to what she said. No. It wasn't what she said, it was the way she said it. Her admiration and respect for the old house flowed from her, which compounded the ache he already felt.

After the video ended, he watched another, then another, and his focus switched from the house to the woman. He found himself studying her like he would if he were preparing for a role. The way she picked at her left thumbnail with her right hand when she was deep in thought. The way her voice pitched higher when she got fired up about something. She rocked up on her toes when she was happy. When she tried to remember something, she squinted. And most frequent of all, she messed with the fringe of bangs that hung over her eyes. They clearly bothered her, but no matter how many times she pushed or blew them back, they went right back into her face. She was cute. Absolutely approachable and honestly...enchanting.

"Uncle Jack?" With a start, he looked up from his phone. The movie had ended, and both kids were awake. He took out his earbuds, turned off the TV, and smiled at them.

"Wanna play another game of hide-and-seek?" Mason asked, stifling a yawn. "I'll be 'it' first this time."

He rubbed the boy's head. "It's a little late for that. Maybe in the morning. I told your mom I'd see you two to bed when the movie ended." He glanced down at the time on his phone screen. The movie had been over for almost an hour. He'd been so absorbed in Cassidy James, it had felt like ten minutes.

After reading out loud about a giant prehistoric shark from Mason's dinosaur book, he tucked his niece and nephew into their beds and went to what the kids called "Uncle Jackie's room." Bryn and Nate's Malibu house was on a hillside, over-looking the ocean. Peaceful, even at night with the moon reflecting on the water below.

He brushed his teeth and with Marion's list in hand slid into bed. He crossed out half the names of willing participants immediately because he knew them well enough to know that even with all his training and experience, he wasn't a good

enough actor to pull off a believable fake romance
with them.

Then he did an internet deep dive on the first
three on her list that he didn't already know. In his
mind, one was just as good or bad as the next. All
in the industry. All beautiful. And most troubling,
all willing to enter an agreement to fake date him.
He folded the paper and pitched it onto the night-
stand. Maybe he'd be in a more receptive mood for
this charade in the morning.

Sleep would help, but sleep didn't come.
Instead, he kept thinking of Cassidy James from
Instagram and YouTube playing the cymbals,
showing off her hamster, singing bad karaoke, and
talking animatedly about an old house that reminded him of the one on his street growing
up—the one he'd promised himself he'd live in
someday when he became rich and famous.

At seven, he'd dreamed his mom and sister
would live with him in that old house, and his
bedroom would be way up in the top of the round
tower at the corner of the building. His mother
had told him an elderly woman lived in the house,
but he'd never seen her, which allowed his imagination to run wild. Maybe he'd never seen her
because she was a ghost. Maybe she was a prisoner. The old house had always piqued his curiosity.
He and his sister walked by that property every
day on their way to school and made up stories
about who lived there and what the inside looked
like. Bryn insisted it was like a fairy castle draped
in pink fabric, and Jack was certain it was all fancy
with dark, carved wood, like a house from one of

those British PBS dramas his mom liked so much, only with spiderwebs and bats hanging from the ceiling.

Sadly, they would never know. He'd visited his hometown briefly on a whim years ago and had discovered the historic old house that had fired so many childhood fantasies had been torn down.

After tossing and turning for a while, he gave in, picked up his phone, and googled, "construction company in Blink, Maine." A website called *Miss Fix-It* came up as the first hit. It was definitely her site, complete with name and phone number. He entered the number but didn't hit the call button. It was late—after midnight, even later in her time zone. She'd certainly be asleep, like he should be. Besides, what would he say? Sorry wasn't enough. No doubt the paparazzi and his fans were making her life hell. In a little town like she lived in, it was probably a nightmare for everyone there, not just her. He owed the whole town an apology. Frustrated, he fluffed his pillow and rolled over, dropping the phone on the pillow next to him. After ten minutes of restlessness, he groaned, threw back the covers, and got out of bed.

Outside the window, clouds covered the moon, making the water below inky—the darkness so different from the light-filled view of frenetic L.A. from his own balcony. He glanced back at the phone. What was it about Cassidy James that intrigued him so much? Maybe it was her unabashed enthusiasm and love of life, which was something he craved. She was genuine, the opposite of Hollywood—a normal person living a normal life.

Well, if he knew the paparazzi, her life wasn't so normal now, and that was his fault. He had to make this right somehow, whatever it took. But how?

Looking at the little app icons scattered across his phone screen over a picture of him, Sidney, and Mason on his balcony in L.A., he clicked on Instagram, then entered @BNforever. An error message popped up.

Maybe it was a bad connection or something. He had a good wifi signal and five bars, so maybe it was an app glitch. He closed the app and re-opened it, then entered Cassidy's username again and received the same error message, "User not found."

Something in his chest tightened, and he lowered himself on the edge of the bed, feeling hollow like he'd lost a friend. He shook his head. He didn't even know the woman. Well, he sort of did. He knew more about her than he did about most people. He knew, for example, it made her furious when people painted over stained trim in historic houses, and she didn't like the texture of those American cheese slices individually wrapped in plastic, and even though she lived in Maine, she couldn't stand the taste of lobster. She was left-handed, liked math, and loved spiders. He shuddered. Spiders?

Staring at his phone screen, he swallowed hard. Cassidy James had deleted her account. Now what?

Through the enormous window, the moon slid out from behind the clouds and the room brightened, sharpening the edges of the shadows. He would have to tell Marion about this. As awful as that would be, she would know what to do. He'd just have to make sure Dee didn't take the blame. At least that part would be easy, even if nothing else was.

CHAPTER SEVEN

After what felt like an eternity, Cassidy had finally convinced Amanda to end the binge watch of *The Office* and retreated to the guest room, exhausted. She was glad to not be alone in her family cottage, though. Even now, a couple of the tabloid vultures cased Amanda's place hoping Cassidy would appear. She wondered how long her life would be disrupted and how long she would harbor a deep resentment for Mr. Jack Winston, who, if Lillian was right, didn't have a clue what trouble he'd caused, directly or indirectly. Ignorance is bliss, as they say. Must be nice.

Phone in hand, she pulled down the duvet and slid into bed, leaning back against the mound of pillows that were the hallmark of decor in Amanda's home. Chairs, sofa, beds, even the corners of every room were filled with brightly colored, multi-textured pillows. None of them matched, but all of them seemed to fit together.

She stared at her phone screen and took a deep breath. The messages from randos were still coming in via text, but at least nobody would be watching her sing "Let It Go" on Instagram anymore—if you could call it singing.

The subscriber numbers on her YouTube channel were still going up, too, which she had decided to consider a good thing. She was determined something positive was going to come out of this, but right now, it was hard to get past her frustration with a movie star who probably didn't care a bit about how he'd disrupted her life.

She dropped her phone on the bed next to her and leaned back into the nest of pillows, jaw clenched. She shouldn't have to endure this online nonsense, and she shouldn't be forced to hide out in her friend's guest room, either. Maybe Lillian was right and whoever had mis-tagged her on Jack Winston's account would have his publicity firm clear up the mistake and the photographers would go away.

Then her life could go back to normal. Predictable, reliable, normal.

Tristan's voice ran through her head: *And you are?* Yeah. Predictable, reliable, normal, boring, and evidently invisible. She pounded the top two pillows and flopped back again.

Her phone screen lit up, casting a blue hue up to the ceiling as a text notification came in. No doubt another tabloid wanting an interview. If this was how it went for a normal person, she couldn't imagine how it was for a superstar like Jack Winston. Paparazzi must follow him around as thick as the flies at Mr. Gibson's pig pen.

Unable to resist her curiosity, she picked up her phone, ignored the six new text notifications, and googled "Jack Winston actor."

He was beautiful. No. That wasn't the right word. He was…stunning. She clicked on the first image which was of him in a tux on a red carpet with some tall, skinny, perfect woman wearing a sparkly gold gown. The woman was looking at him adoringly while he smiled directly at the camera, which made Cassidy feel he was smiling right at her. The jerk.

A light knock came on the door. "It's me," Amanda said.

"Come on in." Cassidy placed her phone on the bed next to her.

Amanda was wearing a deep lavender kimono-type robe and the kind of slippers with puffs on top Cassidy had only seen in old-fashioned movies or Barbie dolls when she was little. Amanda kicked off the slippers and sat on the edge of the bed, one leg folded under her. "How are you holding up?" she asked.

"I'm fine," Cassidy lied. It had been quite a day, for sure.

Amanda stared down at Cassidy's phone, lying face-up on top of the duvet. "He's hot, huh?"

The picture of Jack Winston and the perfect woman was still up on her screen. "Yeah. He's a handsome man," Cassidy conceded.

"So is your doctor."

Her doctor. How many years had Cassidy thought of Tristan McGuffy that way? "He's a handsome man, too."

Amanda shifted uneasily. "I think it's a good thing he didn't recognize you at first back at the house."

"How so?"

"Well, he hadn't seen you in a long time, right?"

"Years."

"It's a testament to how much you've changed."

Or, more likely, evidence of how little he'd

thought of her over the years. "It's silly, really. The whole crush thing." Amanda gave her a look Cassidy was sure was pity, which suited, she supposed. "When you grow up in a town of two hundred people, the pool of prospective boyfriends is microscopic—or, in this case, limited to one guy who goes off to college, and then med school, and then moves away without ever noticing you at all. My crush on Tristan was probably fueled by some kind of self-protective instinct or something—a way to fill my time and not worry about dating, or a lack thereof that comes from living in a place like Blink."

Amanda picked at an embroidered crane on her kimono. For all her meddling and bluster, her friend was a good listener when it mattered, like now. When Cassidy's father's Alzheimer's had become advanced, Amanda was Cassidy's rock, always ready with an ear or shoulder to cry on. After his funeral, they'd spent hours talking, just like this.

"My crush on Tristan gave me hope, you know? I mean, think about it, Amanda. You moved away with your mom and then went to college. You met lots of people before you came back to run your grandparents' store—had lots of fun experiences you can't get here." Cassidy leaned back into the pillows. "I've never left for more than a week at a time. Imagining a future with Tristan, no matter how unrealistic, gave me a goal or a purpose or something." Saying it out loud, even to Amanda, made her feel ridiculous.

"Purpose? You took care of your dad,"

Amanda said. "You worked and stayed here so your brother could go to college."

She shrugged. "True, but even if given a choice, I probably wouldn't have left anyway." She loved her life here. Until recently, she hadn't felt a twinge of regret or even considered potential missed opportunities.

Amanda stood, pulled back the covers, and slipped between the sheets on her side of the bed—just like she'd done so many times after Cassidy's dad's funeral. "So what are you going to do about Tristan?"

Cassidy sighed. "I don't know. It's not like there's anything to do, really. There was nothing there to begin with. The whole thing is something I'd created in my head years ago to appease my teen hormones."

"And your *adult* hormones," Amanda added. "I hope you put that vivid imagination of yours to good use."

"You bet I did."

Their laughter filled the room and wrapped around Cassidy like a warm, comforting blanket.

"So?" Amanda turned on her side to face her. "What now?"

"So I go on like I always do. My crush on Tristan got me through lots of tough times, but I think I'm ready to let it go finally."

"But what if while he's here, you two—"

Cassidy cut her off. "Nothing will ever happen between us." Besides, even if he finally noticed her, she knew he had a big medical practice in Portland, and there was no chance he'd move back here, which was non-negotiable for her. Blink was and would always be her home.

"So what about one of the new guys who moved here with the Living Sharpe team?"

"Which guys are those?" Cassidy teased. "The married ones, the gay ones, or the ones younger than my little brother?"

Amanda huffed. "There are some eligible guys here now."

"I know. You've set me up with all three of them."

"And?"

"And they're silly."

Amanda arched an eyebrow. "And you are so serious?"

"I act like I'm out of middle school at least."

"Hmmm. I get it. You like older men—probably because of your infatuation with Dr. McGuffy."

"He's not *that* much older than I am."

Amanda reached between them and picked up Cassidy's phone, turning the screen toward her. "Jack Winston is about Tristan's age." She waggled her eyebrows. "And flamin' hot."

"And a further departure from reality, even. Don't be absurd. Besides, his ego is too big to fit in Blink."

Amanda's brow furrowed. "It's not like you to be so judgy."

Her friend was right. Cassidy usually tried to keep an open mind and find the best in people. Sadly, this situation had brought out the worst in her. "The guy has really screwed up my day." She took her phone back and closed the browser, then opened her YouTube app. The subscriber count was now over eleven thousand.

Amanda said, "So, if you're abandoning all hope of a thing with Tristan, what are your plans?"

And that, Cassidy supposed, was the real issue. Her decade-long crush on Tristan McGuffy had allowed her to float along without any real plans, other than waiting. Waiting for him to return, waiting for her dad to pass, waiting for her brother to graduate from college. Waiting wasn't much of a plan. "I don't know."

"Are you going to live with Luke when he gets back?"

"I'm not sure. Bethany graduates in two years and plans to come back and work as a layout designer for *Living Sharpe Magazine*. I assume if they're still together, I'd be in the way." Like really in the way. Bethany was Caleb's daughter. She'd been dating Luke for several years now, and things were getting pretty serious between them.

Amanda pursed her lips. "Okay, so, I'm going to ask you what my mom asked me every time I was at a crossroads."

Was she at a crossroads? Her day had sucked, yeah. Her decade-long crush had come to an end, and a bunch of goons with cameras were hunting her because of some stuck-up movie star's mistake, but was it a crossroads, really?

Amanda smoothed the sheet. "Mom would ask, 'When you see yourself in the future, what do you see yourself doing, where do you see yourself doing it, and who are you doing it with?'"

Cassidy's shoulders relaxed. That was easy. "I

want to do exactly what I'm doing, right where I'm doing it, all by myself."

Amanda threw the covers off and sat up. "Oh, no. That's a cop out. You're telling me you want to be single in Blink, working on that big old house, and sharing a tiny cottage with your little brother and his girlfriend?"

Well, no. Once or twice, she'd imagined living in the big white Victorian with Tristan but hadn't put much more thought to it than that, probably because she knew deep down that was nothing but starry-eyed fantasy.

Cassidy crossed her arms over her chest and stared at the abstract painting on the opposite wall that looked like someone had chugged a six-pack, put on a blindfold, and thrown some paint at a canvas. "I love Blink, I love my brother, and I love that big old house."

A minute or so of silence ticked by while neither of them spoke, which Cassidy knew was a real feat for Amanda. Cassidy also knew her friend was right. Her answer had been a cop-out, but these were the kind of questions she'd avoided and skirted after her father had become ill. Maybe this really *was* a crossroads.

"Okay. I'll be more specific." Cassidy sat forward and stacked some pillows against the headboard before scooting back to sit upright. "I want to remodel homes, especially historic homes. My brother is the only family I have left, and I want to help him out in any way I can when he returns to build up Dad's business again." She closed her eyes, took a deep breath, and dug deep. What did she want? *Really* want? "I want to live in…no, I want to *own* Roger McGuffy's Queen Anne Victorian house, and I want a partner. Someone who shares my love of this town and is real. Not some fantasy I cooked up. Not some fake, out-of-reach fantasy. I want real this time, if that makes sense. I'm done with dreams."

"That makes total sense," her friend said, sliding on her slippers and cinching the belt on her robe. She stopped just inside the doorway. "You know, Cass, sometimes it's okay to let yourself dream. Sometimes dreams come true."

Cassidy fought the urge to throw one of the ornate pillows at Amanda as she shut the door. She'd been dreaming of Tristan for years and had done such a good job at it, she'd fallen in love with a fantasy. No more of that. No more dreams.

Tomorrow was a new day. Hopefully, one that was predictable, normal, and boring.

CHAPTER EIGHT

On his penthouse balcony, Jack pushed his sunglasses up on his nose and squinted through the late afternoon sun at L.A. sprawling below. The caffeine from the two cups of coffee he'd chugged when he got back home from his sister's an hour or so ago had finally kicked in. He used to be able to stay out at clubs and parties with his friends until all hours, day after day. Now, one late night wiped him out.

He smiled. That would amuse Marion, no doubt. Watching videos of Cassidy James restore an old house had been a lot more fun than clubbing with his friends had ever been.

He smiled over the patio table at Dee, who evidently found her laptop fascinating. "You still worried about that Instagram mix-up?" he asked.

"I can't get in touch with that Cassidy woman," Dee said, sounding frustrated. "Sending her DMs was a bust, and she doesn't answer a phone number tied to her business. I've left multiple voicemails and texts."

Before he could reply, the sliding door whooshed behind him.

"I thought you were going to pick someone from my list," Marion said, placing a tabloid beside his water glass.

"Hi, Marion," he drawled in his most charming voice. "Great to see you, too. Yes, my visit with

Bryn and the kids was great. How are *you* today?"
He ignored the tabloid and twisted in his chair to
face her. She didn't look as angry as she sounded,
thank goodness. He glanced over at Dee, who was
frozen in place, like she'd been zapped by one of
the Medusa lasers from *Mad Planet*—the ones that
turned the victim into stone. Her eyes were locked
on the tabloid to the left of his plate.

"The Movie Star and the Construction
Worker," the headline read over a terrible doc-
tored photo that looked like he was with Cassidy
in one of her home restoration videos. He was in a
T-shirt and jeans, and she was in her overalls with
a circular saw in hand. Her bangs almost covered
her eyes, and she was staring straight at the camera, clearly a still from one of her renovation
videos. His was an old candid photo taken from a
distance when he was out walking somewhere,
looking away. It was obvious it was two photos
smashed together with different lighting and an
obvious seam, but no doubt it would draw readers
in.

Dammit.

Poor Cassidy. The paparazzi hounded Jack re-
lentlessly, but he'd intentionally sought fame. Now
that they'd latched on to her, it would be hard to
shake them, but if anyone could do it, it was
Marion Hill.

Marion pitched another magazine on the table.
This headline read, "Jack Winston's Secret Affair
Exposed." There was a picture of a clearly
freaked-out Cassidy with huge eyes and her mouth
drawn tight at a blue picnic table with some other

people. The paparazzi vultures were obviously hunting her based on the startled look on her face.

"Who is she?" Marion asked.

Dee shifted in her seat. "Um, she's—"

"She's a historic home restoration specialist in a small seaside town called Blink, Maine," Jack answered before Dee could finish. "She's a super-cool person. I watched some of her YouTube videos and liked her content." That much was true, at least. "I tagged her on social media, which had the unintended side effect of sending up the Bat Signal for the paparazzi."

Marion's eyes narrowed as she studied him. Narrowed eyes on Marion Hill was never a good thing.

"I'm..." He fought the urge to glance at Dee, worried she'd confess. "I'm going to make it right." Somehow.

"And what, exactly, do you plan to do to make it right?" Marion asked, placing yet another tabloid rag in front of him, this one with a grainy picture of Cassidy awkwardly stepping over the bench of the same blue table, probably in an attempt to escape from the cameras. The headline read, "Jack Winston's Secret Girlfriend."

"I really don't know. I was hoping you would have some suggestions," he said. "I thought maybe it would be enough if the PR team put out there that I tagged the wrong person and I don't even know the woman."

Marion arched a skeptical eyebrow and stared down her nose at him—a move she'd perfected before he was born, no doubt. Great. Way to make him feel like a grade-school kid. And then she turned her attention to the tabloids on the table, drumming her fingers on the one closest to her.

Marion looked up and met his eyes. "Have you made a selection from the list of potential romantic partners I gave you?"

"You mean fake romantic partners? No, I—"

"Good," Marion said, one side of her mouth pulling up in a smile that reminded him of the Grinch. "Don't. This is better."

Jack felt like the bottom of his stomach had dropped out. Marion's Grinch smile was always trouble. "What's better?"

She picked up the closest tabloid and studied the picture. "She's pretty—in a rustic way." She pitched the paper back on the table. "Miss LaPorte, please get someone from Mr. Winston's team at the PR firm on the phone."

Dee scurried from the balcony, fingers flying over her phone as she went.

"You say this woman is a historic home restoration specialist?"

He nodded. From the next room, he could hear Dee's soft voice as she spoke with someone on the phone.

"Are you handy, Mr. Winston?"

Dread wrapped around his chest and squeezed. What was Marion up to? "Sometimes."

Her eyebrow arched.

"A call from PR will be coming for you now, Ms. Hill," Dee said from the patio door to the balcony.

Marion, smile still in place, slipped her phone

from her handbag and took the call. "Edward!" she said as if delighted. "You saw the papers then?" After a couple of moments in which Edward Jones, Jack's main representative at the PR firm, spoke, she said, "No, no. Don't silence it. We want to go with this. It's perfect." Again, she listened, then said, "Yes, I believe it will work. Kansas boy turned movie star rolls up his sleeves to save a historic house with his small-town girlfriend he met online through her DIY videos. Very relatable. His fans will love it. Every girl-next-door from the most obscure of places will believe that she, too, could win the heart of a movie star."

Jack's gut lurched. Surely, she wasn't serious.

Marion laughed. It was a light, practiced, tinkling kind of laugh. "We'll leave first thing in the morning. No. Don't alert anyone yet. I'll come by in an hour or so to iron out the details. See you then, *mwah*."

Marion Hill had made a kissy noise. Jack shook his head in horrified disbelief, not only at Marion's anomalous behavior—*mwah?*—but at the prospect that she intended to involve Cassidy in a fake romance scheme with his PR firm. His jaw clenched. He glanced past Marion to Dee, still hovering in the doorway. She looked as shocked as he felt.

This was a ridiculous plan. He willed his heart to slow and took a deep breath. If there was anything he'd learned over the last two years, it was that once Marion Hill set her sights on something, it was as good as done. And she had evidently determined that Cassidy James would be his next fake girlfriend, and resistance was futile.

Dee had returned to the table and flattened her napkin in her lap, eyes on Marion, who was typing furiously on her phone, no doubt rallying the troops to invade Blink.

Jack gave a resigned sigh, a little bit of positivity loosening the tightness in his chest at the prospect of actually meeting Cassidy. After studying her online content, he had to admit that he wanted to meet this cymbal-playing, family-loving, small-town woman with her paint-splattered overalls and non-pretentious demeanor. She was everything Hollywood was not, and it appealed. He'd been restless recently, and a trip to the East Coast could be a great distraction—not that he had a choice.

Marion looked up at him, nodded as if finalizing some aspect of her diabolical scheme in her mind, then went back to typing.

The dragon knew what she was doing, but from his viewpoint, there was a major flaw. How would it make this mess right for Cassidy? His turning up in Blink would not make the paparazzi go away. In fact, it would bring a new squadron of them in to attack her.

When he glanced over at Marion, she was staring at him with an arched eyebrow and an expectant half smile. "It appears we're going on a field trip," she said. "I'll arrange the appropriate publicity to offset the tabloids. I'll also see that additional security is hired. Flex is not enough."

Jack leaned forward in his chair. "We need to go in quietly, Marion, with as little fanfare as possible. It's evidently a really tiny town with only a few hundred residents."

Marion shook her head, but he cut her off before she could get a word out.

"I know small towns. I grew up in one. A big entourage will not go over well."

"The fanfare started when you tagged the wrong person and called her 'baby,'" Marion said, gesturing to the tabloids on the table.

Obviously, Marion had never seen a *Mad Planet* movie.

"Babe," he corrected.

She turned her attention to Dee, who had folded and refolded her napkin so many times, it had become a little square of linen origami. "Miss LaPorte, arrange airfare, ground transportation, and accommodations for you, Mr. Flex, and Mr. Winston for tomorrow morning. It will be easier for me if Mr. Winston does not travel with the reporters. Instructing them will be easier if he's not around to distract them."

Dee nodded.

"I'll take care of my own travel and that of the security detail and selected press. I'll need some time to get everything arranged for the campaign," Marion added.

Panic bubbled in Jack's chest. *Campaign?* Oh, hell no. "It's not warfare, Marion. And it's not politics, either."

Marion lifted her pointed chin, which gave the impression she was looking down her nose at him despite how much taller he was. "That's where you are wrong, Mr. Winston. Success in this business is nothing but war and politics. It's why you hired me." She stiffened her already square shoulders and lifted her chin even higher. "You asked me to help you set this woman's life back to rights, and I will, but I'm going to do it *my* way." Jack fought the urge to squirm as she eyed him down her straight nose. "I've waged many a Hollywood campaign, Mr. Winston, and I always win." She paused for dramatic effect, then repeated, "Always."

Before disappearing back inside the penthouse, she turned and said, "I will see you tomorrow in Blink, Maine. We can't risk word of your arrival leaking to the paparazzi, so under no circumstance let Miss James or anyone else know of this trip. If you arrive before me, do not seek her out. No contact unless I am present."

Jack heaved a sigh after the door slid shut behind Marion.

Dee took a deep breath and let it out with a whistle, then picked up one of the tabloids. "I'm not sure this is a good idea," she said.

Neither was Jack, but once the Battleship Marion had selected her course, there was no turning back.

CHAPTER NINE

The bells on the door of the Starfish Diner smacked the glass above Cassidy's head as she slammed the door shut. With a grunt, she turned the thumb lock and spun to lean back against the door. Breathing hard, she glanced around the diner. Fortunately, there was almost nobody here on Thursday nights, and the ones who were, she knew.

"Good heavens, Cassy! You running from a bear?" Sally called from behind the counter. Sally had operated the diner since Cassidy was a little girl and played the role of second mom to the town, especially Cassidy, who had lost her mother as a child.

"Worse," Cassidy said. "I could have scared a bear off by now, but I can't shake these guys. They followed me from Amanda's to Mr. McGuffy's house and then tracked me here." Getting work done was going to be a challenge with the vultures waiting behind every bush for a photo op. She'd tacked paint drop cloths over all the first-floor windows of the house, so at least she had privacy while inside.

Behind her, someone knocked on the door. She didn't turn around because she knew they'd pop off a bunch of shots on their huge cameras.

"Step away, honey," Sally said, striding to the door. With a harrumph, she yanked the pull-down shade on the door, then closed the blinds at the

booth in the corner. "Shut the blinds at your table," she said to the only occupied table. Amanda
reached up and lowered the blinds in the face of a
photographer peering in.

There were only six windows and the door, and
in no time, the camera-wielding goons were effectively cut off. "We're closed," Sally called through
the door. "Go away."

Yeah, good luck with that, Cassidy thought,
swallowing hard. The guys were dug in like super-
glue on skin. Completely immovable.

Cassidy joined the group at their booth at the
corner of the room—her makeshift family of sorts.
Roger McGuffy held his usual spot with his back
to the wall so he could see everyone who came in.
Amanda and her on-again, off-again boyfriend,
Niles, sat across from Roger. Both twisted in the
booth to study her.

"See? This is what I was telling you. Cassidy's a
celebrity now," Amanda said.

Niles scanned Cassidy head to toe before turning back around in the booth. Niles Sharpe was
the handsome star of the highly successful lifestyle
empire, *Living Sharpe*, and was the undisputed
celebrity in Blink since the entire enterprise had
relocated here two years ago, breathing new life
into her tiny, dwindling town. Knowing Niles, attention on anyone else rubbed him the wrong way.

Roger patted the booth next to him. "Have a
seat, young lady."

As Cassidy slid into the booth, Roger's phone
dinged. He glanced at it, winked at Cassidy, and
called out, "Hey, Sally. I invited my son to join us.

He's at the door wanting in."

After a worried glance at the door, Sally strode to it and peeked out the side of the shade. After a deep breath, she unlocked the door, and jerking it open, commanded, "Only Dr. McGuffy. We're closed to everyone else."

A harried-looking Tristan slipped inside, and Sally locked the door behind him, bell clanging at the top as she peeked around the edge of the shade. "Most of them are returning to their cars now," Sally said. "Only a few are still hovering near the building." She ran her hands down the front of her apron.

Tristan approached the table. "What is going on around here? There are so many reporters in that parking lot, it looks like the president is visiting or something." He smoothed his blond hair back. "They asked me if I knew you, Cassidy."

A brief glance at Niles confirmed Cassidy's assumption. Yep, he was envious of attention on anyone else. His eyes narrowed on her.

"It's not my fault, Niles," she said.

Before she could explain further, Roger put his hand over hers and said, "I think all of us should avoid answering any questions at all from these people. I also think we should give Cassidy some peace and not talk about it unless she wants to." He gestured to the next table over. "Pull up a chair, son."

Tristan nodded a greeting at Cassidy as he slid a chair over, placing it at the end of the booth.

"Hi, Amanda," Tristan said. He extended his hand to Niles. "And you are?"

"Niles Sharpe." He shook Tristan's hand, clearly disappointed that he hadn't recognized him.

"Okay, Cassidy and Tristan, what'll you two have?" Sally asked, notepad in hand.

Something about being paired, even for a food order, with Tristan sparked that old, familiar longing. Nope. No more of that. "A cheeseburger and fries for me, Sally," she said. "And a Dr Pepper, too."

"Just water, please, Sally," Tristan said. "I had a protein shake before I came."

Cassidy had eaten here hundreds, if not thousands, of times in her life. For a while, the Starfish Diner had been the only place to hang out in Blink. Thanks to Lillian's business moving and filming here, and Roger re-opening his family mill, the population had grown, and so had business development. But even with two new restaurants on the harbor, Cassidy's friends always tried to meet up at the diner at least every other day. It felt like home.

Sally delivered the Dr Pepper and Tristan's water. "Glad you're here, Tristan," she said. "Missed seeing you all these years."

Cassidy remembered sitting in this exact booth with her dad and little brother, watching Tristan and his high school friends laugh and kid around with each other at the counter. As a young girl, it seemed like the entire town of Blink revolved around Tristan McGuffy. Growing up, he *was* Blink to Cassidy.

She studied him while he fiddled with his phone, looking sleek and perfect. An odd, hollow feeling filled her chest. Tristan seemed totally out of place here now—maybe because she wasn't used to seeing him in this setting. Well, in truth, she wasn't used to seeing him at all, but she'd imagined him a billion times, just never in the diner. Usually, her daydreams about Dr. Tristan McGuffy had been blurry at the edges with a nondescript background as he studied her with adoring eyes and flashed his brilliant smile as he told her she'd grown up to be a knockout.

There was nothing adoring about his expression right now, though. His eyebrows drew together in concern as he turned to her. "Why are those reporters out there asking questions about you?"

"I'd rather not talk about it," she said, grateful Sally arrived just in time to prevent more questioning.

"Here ya go," Sally said, placing the cheeseburger in front of her. "Extra cheese and pickles, like always."

"Heart attack on a plate," Tristan said as he went back to his phone.

Cassidy assumed from his light tone of voice that he'd been kidding, but his words made her skin prickle. Yeah, he was a doctor and all, and granted, a cheeseburger was not the healthiest meal, but it was delicious, and honestly, what she ate was none of his freaking business.

While Niles and Roger discussed the new soundstage being finished out at the Living Sharpe complex, Cassidy found herself wondering if someone as lofty as Jack Winston ate cheeseburgers or only dined on steak and caviar.

Amanda reached over and took a fry from Cassidy's plate. "I'm having my usual Friday night gathering tomorrow night on my deck. Would love it if you joined us, Tristan."

Like the Tristan from Cassidy's memories, he relaxed into the chair and gave a charming smile. "I'd like that, thanks, but I'm not sure I'll still be in town."

Roger stiffened, but his expression didn't change.

"What's the party theme?" Niles asked.

Amanda shrugged. "No theme this time."

"I'll get the word out to the Living Sharpe team," Niles said, reaching across to also swipe one of Cassidy's fries. When she looked pointedly at the smattering of fries left on his own plate, he shrugged and said, "Yours are hot."

Cassidy's phone dinged, but she ignored the notification like she had the dozens of others so far today, leaving it facedown on the table.

"I'm meeting with two more potential employees at the clinic this evening when they get off their shifts at Machias Hospital," Tristan said. "Dad, I'd like to talk to you when I get finished with that." He was still studying his phone screen. "I have openings in my schedule after eight p.m. What works for you?"

"Son, I'm available all day, every day. Just tell me when and where."

Tristan glanced up from his phone. "That's new."

"How's that?" Roger asked.

"You've never been available, much less let

anyone tell you when and where to do anything," Tristan said before returning his eyes to his phone.

Holy smokes, that was unexpected. Cassidy couldn't imagine what had happened between these two to cause that kind of interaction.

Cassidy's phone dinged again, and she turned it over and glanced at her screen. She'd gotten messages yesterday and today from the same California number. It was someone calling herself Dee who claimed to be Jack Winston's assistant and had offered her tickets, airfare, and hotel for a movie premiere, but Cassidy hadn't replied, assuming it was a scam. Whoever they were, they were certainly persistent.

She flipped her phone facedown on the table, intentionally keeping her expression relaxed.

"What's wrong?" Amanda asked, voice urgent.

"Nothing." A weird churning swirled in her stomach. What if it really was his assistant?

Amanda reached across the table and grabbed her phone.

Cassidy stared at the fries on her plate, avoiding a glance across the table at her friend as she read the texts from this Dee person.

"Holy crap!" Amanda finally said. "Jack Winston's assistant says he wants to send you tickets to the premiere of *Mad Planet 4*?"

And airfare and hotel for two. It really felt like a hoax or a scam.

When Cassidy glanced over at Tristan, he was studying her. "Are we talking about Jack Winston who plays Blake Crusher in the *Mad Planet* movies?"

"We certainly are," Amanda said.

Tristan was still studying Cassidy. "Why would Jack Winston's assistant be contacting *you*?"

Granted, that was her first thought, too, but it sounded awful coming from someone else—especially a guy she'd always dreamed would come home and be totally into her. At first, his dismissive words and tone hurt, but only for a moment. Then the hurt turned to anger.

"Why not?" she snapped back, grateful she hadn't revealed the embarrassing truth that the only reason this was happening was because she'd been accidentally tagged on her obsolete Instagram account.

Thankfully, Tristan's phone rang, and he excused himself, moving to a stool at the counter to take the call.

When Niles and Roger were once again deep in conversation about the Living Sharpe sound stage construction, Amanda slid into the booth next to Cassidy and whispered, "I told you dreams sometimes come true. Oooh. Wouldn't it be cool if you went to the premiere and got to meet him?"

"Oh, sure. I could ride out in my carriage made from a pumpkin with mice as footmen."

Amanda tapped the side of her nose with her finger. "I remember hearing about that happening somewhere."

Cassidy rolled her eyes. "Trust me, the texts are a hoax or a scam. My phone is full of weird messages."

"Well, if it's legit, you're taking me with you, right?"

"Only if there's room for two in my fairytale pumpkin carriage."

Amanda laughed. "There needs to be room for three. Jack Winston would join us, of course." In a terrible imitation of the man, she said, "I'm coming for you, babe."

Cassidy groaned. It was a ridiculous line in her opinion. Certainly not worthy of being a hallmark of the *Mad Planet* movies. Maybe it was in the delivery, like Arnold Schwarzenegger's "I'll be back."

"It's a scam," Cassidy repeated. "Besides, that man's ego would never fit in a pumpkin."

CHAPTER TEN

Jack grinned as he parked the rental car in front of the tall, white Victorian he recognized from Cassidy's YouTube videos. It had been simple to find because it was visible from the road leading to Hideaway Harbor, the main feature in Blink.

A quick glance over at his bodyguard sitting in the backseat told him that the man found this trip far less entertaining than he did.

"We should wait like Miss Hill told us to," Flex grumbled for the dozenth time since Jack had headed up the hill toward the house.

Like all the times before, Jack ignored him.

"We need more security," Flex said, eyeing the half dozen or so photographers gathered on the opposite side of the street from the house. Behind them was a steep drop-off. The small harbor glimmered below, ringed by a wooden walkway and some quaint-looking buildings—like something out of a movie set. Flex twisted in the car seat to look behind them. "Way too many variables for me to cover alone."

Dee sighed from the passenger seat, no doubt still thinking this was her fault. She'd said it several times since they'd left his penthouse back in California for the airport.

"What dangers do you think lurk in a place like this?" Jack asked, feeling the end of his patience rope nearing. Between Dee's nervous guilt and

Flex's intensity, he found himself fighting to keep his spirits up. He was determined to meet Cassidy before Marion and her entourage of security, reporters, and who knew who else descended like starving locusts to devour the rest of whatever joy remained.

"Bad things can happen anywhere, anytime," Flex grumbled. "Even in a place as remote as this. I hardly got a chance to research it, and no one had the time to scout it out in person. Again, I suggest we follow Ms. Hill's instructions and wait to contact Miss James until she arrives with backup security."

Jack conjured his best I'm-in-charge voice. He'd heard Marion use it so many times, he'd perfected it. "You work for me, Flex, not Marion. I intend to meet Miss James as soon as possible—preferably before Marion gets her claws into her." He hit the unlock button. "Everybody out!"

Dee opened her door immediately and stepped into the sunshine.

With a frustrated huff, Flex got out and opened Jack's door, looking around as if they were at a crowded event and not a tiny coastal village at the ends of the earth.

Evidently, the paparazzi had not gotten word that he'd be arriving, because the look of surprise on their faces when Jack got out of the driver's seat of the car was obvious, even from this distance. And it was hilarious. They practically fell over their own feet, gearing up for battle. Cameras out, they swarmed toward them. Flex placed his bulk between Jack and the reporters, giving them his best "back off" glare. Jack smiled. He'd used his bodyguard's glare as inspiration for the facial expression he used when Blake Crusher stared down hostile alien creatures.

As effective as his bodyguard's glare was, the paparazzi didn't even slow down. Flex placed his familiar hand on Jack's shoulder as he guided him toward the huge wraparound porch of the house as the group in pursuit shouted questions.

"Private property," a tall man with short brown hair called from the porch to the reporters. "Stay across the street like we discussed."

"The street isn't private," a woman with a huge telephoto lens shouted back.

The man on the porch looked surprised as he scanned Jack, Dee, and Flex, then gestured for them to come up the stairs.

"If I'm not mistaken, you're Jack Winston," he said, holding out his hand when they reached the top step. "I'm Caleb Wright."

Behind, from the street, camera shutters snapped.

Jack took his hand. "Of Wright Boat Works we saw on the way in?"

The guy smiled, and Jack liked him right away. Open and friendly.

"The same," Caleb said.

"How long have you been seeing Cassidy James?" a man shouted from the street.

"Where did you two meet?" a woman yelled.

Flex blocked the stairs from the paparazzi who remained at the curb while Jack took Dee's hand and pulled her closer. "Caleb, this is my assistant,

Dee LaPorte, and this is Flex, who works security for me."

Dee exchanged a shy handshake, but Flex never took his eyes off the paparazzi. He made a grunt of greeting, though, which was a step in the right direction, Jack supposed.

"Wow. I knew about the Instagram mix-up but certainly didn't expect you to show up here in person," Caleb said.

Jack's stomach churned. "It was a last-minute decision." Possibly a terrible one.

"Will you be taking Cassidy James back to Hollywood with you?" a photographer called.

"I don't like this," Flex grumbled over his shoulder. "We need to notify local law enforcement that we're here."

"Blink doesn't have a police department, but I'll call the county sheriff's office to send someone to make sure these folks stay off private property," Caleb said. "They've been pretty good so far, but now that you're here, they might get carried away."

"Good," Flex said. "We'll have more people here soon, I hope."

"How long will you be in Blink?" a guy shouted from the street. "Is your affair with Cassidy James serious?"

"You might want to come on in," Caleb said, opening the door. With a glance back at the paparazzi, Dee strode inside immediately.

Jack took a deep breath. Ordinarily, he greeted new situations with calm confidence. But as he stood just outside the doorway of the house he'd seen in the videos, there was nothing calm about him. He felt the twisting, churning knots in his stomach he always got before an important audition, and it had nothing to do with the reporters shouting questions from the street. He'd imagined what he'd say to Cassidy James over and over on the plane on the way here, and now, he was finally going to meet this stranger he'd watched on YouTube, who somehow felt like a long-time friend.

He took a deep breath, then with Flex's hand on his shoulder—a technique his bodyguard used so they wouldn't get separated in crowds—they entered the house.

It was just as he'd imagined the Victorian in his childhood neighborhood would look—minus the cobwebs and bats, of course—with tall ceilings and elaborate, carved woodwork. It smelled like fresh-cut wood and paint, and the strange, distinctive scent of old house overlayed with something feminine. Honeysuckle, maybe?

There was a gaping hole in the floor to the left of the staircase he recognized from Cassidy's latest video about repairing a support beam. A grizzled-looking cat stuck its gray-and-white head out from under the staircase but tucked back out of sight almost immediately. On Jack's left was a huge, empty room lined with bookshelves, and on the right, voices drifted in from the other side of a half-closed pocket door. He took a step forward to get a look into the room.

And there she was. On her knees in front of a large, tiled fireplace with a wood mantel, brushing a clear liquid onto the white paint she'd complained about in an earlier video. Her back was to him, but he'd know her anywhere. Shorter than average with sandy brown hair pulled into a ponytail and wearing a bright green T-shirt and paint-splattered overalls...well, they weren't only splattered, they looked like she used them to wipe paint off her hands. In fact, there was a yellow handprint strategically placed over her right back pocket.

"Cass!" the woman standing over Cassidy filming with a phone said. She poked Cassidy on the shoulder hard. "Girl, round up your pumpkins and footmen and mice and call your freaking fairy godmother."

Still kneeling in front of the fireplace with her paintbrush in hand, Cassidy James looked over her shoulder and their eyes met. It was a weird moment. Like the one in the first *Mad Planet* movie where Captain Blake Crusher encounters the woman hanging clothes on the line—only there was no dramatic, swelling music or sweeping close-ups. Just a frozen moment where they stared at each other, comparing what they knew about each other against expectations. Well, at least that's what *he* was doing. And she far exceeded expectations.

And then, her surprised expression shifted. Her eyebrows pulled together, and her clear, gray eyes narrowed. He had obviously not exceeded *her* expectations—at least not her positive expectations.

At this point, he wished there *had* been dramatic swelling music to soften the silence that seemed to stretch on forever. The woman appeared to despise him, and honestly, he didn't blame her.

"I'm Amanda Miller, Cassidy's very, very best friend," the woman who had been filming with her phone said in a breathy voice that was overly loud. The fan voice. He would know it anywhere. With a stiff gait, probably from nerves in combination with some super-shiny yellow platform boots, she crossed the room to shake his hand. Her dark, curly hair was cropped short, and she had on some huge, gold, star earrings that swung back and forth against her neck.

He shook her hand. "Jack Winston."

Staring with wide eyes, she said, "I know," in that same loud, breathy voice.

He dropped Amanda's hand and glanced at the other people in the room. In addition to the guy named Caleb who'd met them on the porch, there were Cassidy and Amanda, an older man who looked to be in his eighties, and a guy with blond hair.

Jack reached his hand toward the old man. "I'm Jack."

"Roger McGuffy."

"Roger! I understand from Cassidy's videos you own this beautiful house."

"For a little while longer, anyway." The man grinned, then shot a look at Cassidy, whose eyes widened with surprise at this news. "This is my son, Tristan." He gestured to the blond guy.

"Hey, Tristan." Jack extended his hand.

The man gave him a brief, firm handshake, then shot a curious glance at Cassidy as if he'd never seen her before.

"How long are you here?" the older man, Roger, asked.

Jack met eyes with Cassidy, who was studying him with a wrinkled-nose expression like she was standing too near a stinky trash can. He looked down at himself to find his clothes were still clean and tidy. Yep, she was 100 percent angry. He should have followed his gut and defied Marion's orders and let her know he was coming. "I don't know how long we're staying yet. The rest of my group arrives later today. It all depends on what Cassidy has planned."

Again, the blond guy shot a puzzled look at Cassidy.

"Where ya stayin'?" Roger asked. "Not any hotels here yet. We're working on one, though." The old man's chest puffed out like he was proud of that.

"Ms. Hill says she is bringing our own accommodations," Dee answered, voice tight. She was clearly uncomfortable. Dee was a rule follower, and Jack had broken the rules. He'd been told to wait to contact Cassidy James until Marion was present. Well, the rule made no sense. At least from Jack's perspective, it didn't. He needed to talk to Cassidy alone before Marion came in guns blazing and frightened her or made things even worse.

"Bringing accommodations?" Roger repeated.

"That's what she said," Dee answered, giving Jack a look.

"Ms. Hill is very resourceful," Jack said, in the

understatement of the year. Maybe she'd arranged
for RVs or travel buses, though with the entourage
she had planned to bring, she'd need a fleet of
them if that was her plan.

"It's great to meet all of you, and I look forward to seeing Blink," Jack said. Marion would
arrive any minute. He approached where Cassidy
was still kneeling in front of the fireplace, paintbrush in her hand. "Is it possible for me to have a
private word with you?"

"We were all just leaving," Caleb said. "Come
on, Amanda." Caleb took her elbow. "Let's get
back to our jobs at the harbor."

"But…" Amanda looked longingly over her
shoulder as Caleb all but dragged her to the door.
"There's a party on my patio tonight. Invite him,
Cass."

"I'm off to conduct my last interview," Tristan
said, following Amanda and Caleb out. "Good to
meet you, Jack." After another puzzled look at
Cassidy, the man nodded at Dee and Flex and shut
the door.

Roger was the only person remaining. "I'll go
make another pot of coffee," he said with a wide
smile before disappearing through a doorway at
the back of the dining room adjoining this big
empty space he assumed was the parlor Cassidy
talked about in her videos.

Jack held out a hand to Cassidy, still kneeling
by the fireplace mantel. Her brow furrowed as she
stared from his hand to his face. For a moment, he
was afraid she'd refuse him outright. Then she
wrapped her brush in a baggie next to the

paint-stripper bottle. After wiping her hands down the front of her thighs, she placed her hand in his and allowed him to help her to her feet. Her hand was small and a little bit rough. No pampered, silky skin or long, manicured nails. No artifice in this woman at all.

A strange sensation bloomed in his chest like it had several times on the way here. It was the buzzy anticipation of beginning a new adventure like when he had moved to L.A. or when they began the first shoot on a new project. Though the buzzing faded as he stared at Cassidy's guarded, distrustful expression.

"I should have let you know I was coming," he said.

Hand still in his, she looked down at her work clothes, then she lifted her head and blew her bangs out of her face. "You're right. You should have."

Outside, something caused the paparazzi to begin shouting, and the sound of footfalls came from the wooden porch. Flex strode to the front window, pulled aside a makeshift drop cloth curtain, and peered outside. His shoulders stiffened, and Jack knew exactly why. With a resigned sigh, he looked down into Cassidy's gray eyes and said, "I'm really sorry about this."

As the footfalls on the porch got louder, he could make out a voice he would recognize anywhere. And at that moment, Jack wished, not for the first time, that he were someone other than Jack Winston, star of *Mad Planet*.

CHAPTER ELEVEN

Jack Winston was exactly what Cassidy had expected. Confident, oozing charm, and exuding that star-power vibe she'd noticed from his photos online. And, as expected, he was smoking hot. Like, the wow kind of hot pictures didn't adequately capture—so hot, the paint she was stripping might just melt off the mantel if he got close enough.

He was dressed all casual-perfect in worn jeans and a T-shirt, which suited him better than the fancy tuxes she'd seen online in his red-carpet photos.

But even with all that in his favor, he was an irritating, unwelcome problem. And his admission that he should have given her a heads-up that he was going to turn up in all his superstar glory? Simply not enough.

Outside, the paparazzi made some commotion, like they'd done on and off since this whole thing began. It was louder this time, probably because Mr. Movie Magic was here now. *Oh, goodie.*

She studied him. His dark eyes were warm, like melted chocolate—warm like his hand she was still holding. *Oh, crap!* She sucked in a breath. She was holding Jack Winston's hand. She jerked her fingers from his.

"She's here, boss," the bodyguard said.

Jack's assistant's shoulders rose and her whole body appeared to tense as the bodyguard guy strode to the front door, expression grim.

Who on earth was outside?

"I wish we'd had a chance to talk before she arrived. She's not nearly as bad as she comes across on first impression. I promise," Jack whispered. "Lots of bark. Very little bite...usually."

Cassidy faced the door, half expecting there to be an army of zombies or maybe someone in a hockey mask brandishing a chainsaw on the other side based on Jack and his team's tension, but when the bodyguard opened the door, a slim older woman in a pretty, pale-blue pantsuit with stylish red glasses was standing on the threshold. There were some people behind her, also dressed in business clothes. Cassidy let out a relieved breath. These people couldn't be nearly as bad as the paparazzi who had hounded her since yesterday.

The bodyguard stepped aside, and the woman strode in without a greeting. Five people followed her in, the last two of whom were men who stationed themselves on opposite ends of the entry hall—obviously more bodyguards for Mister Hollywood. Through the open door, Cassidy noticed other security guards taking up posts on the front porch. This whole thing was surreal.

After giving the state of the house a cursory once-over, the woman turned her focus on Cassidy, who, fighting not to fidget, decided she had been wrong: this woman was worse than the paparazzi—she was certainly scarier.

Cassidy felt frozen in place as Marion's eyes scanned her thoroughly from head to toe and then back up again as if cataloging every single paint splatter and physical flaw. It was all Cassidy could do to not squirm under the woman's intense and obviously disdainful scrutiny.

No way. She was stronger than this. Cassidy lifted her chin and met Marion's eyes directly.

The woman arched a perfect eyebrow as if surprised, then smiled.

Jack took a step forward. "Marion, this is—"

"I know who she is," the woman interrupted. Then her smile returned. "It's a pleasure to meet you, Miss James."

The words were a warm greeting, but Cassidy's body registered them as a threat, causing the hairs on the back of her neck to tingle.

"Is there a place where we could all sit down and talk?" Marion asked.

Cassidy took in the well-dressed strangers who had come in with Marion. There was a man in a gray suit and two women with briefcases. What on earth was going on here? Mice as footmen and a pumpkin carriage were no more farfetched than this scenario for sure.

Cassidy led the group through the parlor into the dining room. It was the only room on the first floor with furniture because of the renovation. The table was too massive to move easily, so she had left the room intact since her work in here would be minimal. In fact, she only planned to repair pulleys and replace the sash cords in the windows of this room.

Flex and the other bodyguards must have remained at their posts near the front of the house because the only people in the room aside from

Cassidy were Jack, Dee, Marion, and the three business-looking people.

Marion took the seat at the far end of the table, but the others remained standing.

"I know your life has been disrupted by the attention you have been receiving, Miss James, and we are here to rectify that and leave your life better than before," Marion said. "We would like to make you an offer that anyone in your position would jump at."

Her position?

Jack, who was standing near the carved mahogany sideboard, shifted uneasily as the others took seats at the table with the exception of his assistant, Dee, who remained standing near the entrance to the room.

Marion held up a finger. "But..."

That one word out of the woman's mouth caused a jolt of fear to shoot up Cassidy's spine. Somehow, Cassidy got the feeling that making her life better was the last thing on Marion Hill's mind.

"...before I make introductions or we discuss our offer," Marion continued, "I must insist you sign a nondisclosure agreement, Miss James."

Cassidy had heard of nondisclosure agreements but had no clue about their specifics or why on earth would she need to sign one. She could hear her own heart hammering. This was way out of her league.

She shot a look at Jack, and her teeth clenched. This whole thing was his fault, and all he could do was look at her with a sincere expression. No doubt, a well-rehearsed act. She didn't like Jack Winston or this woman with her predatory stare.

"I'm not unreasonable," Marion said. "I want you to feel comfortable. If you wish to consult someone, that would be fine. If that person signs an NDA as well, you can have them present when we discuss our proposal."

The thought of taking on something this foreign by herself was terrifying. Amanda would be her first choice, but she was no savvier about things like this than Cassidy. And ignorant though she was, Cassidy knew signing this thing was swearing to keep something secret—a real weak point for Amanda. Lillian probably had experience with this kind of thing, but she was shooting an episode of *Living Sharpe* right now. Roger would know what to do. He'd run businesses and she trusted him. He was also a master secret keeper who thrived on schemes.

No doubt he'd cranked his hearing aids up and had been eavesdropping from the next room—a favorite trick of his—because he peeked his head into the dining room at that moment. "I have a fresh pot of coffee on if anyone is interested."

Jack stepped forward. "Roger McGuffy, this is my manager, Marion Hill."

Roger approached the table and extended his hand to Marion. "Ms. Hill." She took his hand. "Welcome to my home," he said with a smile.

"I need your help, Mr. McGuffy," Cassidy blurted out, hoping to head off any more small talk. "Can you sit in on this meeting, please?"

Yep. He'd been listening. He didn't ask any

questions or even try to look surprised. "My pleasure, Cassy."

Roger took the seat next to Cassidy, and they were introduced to Jack's publicity team leader, a lawyer from Jack's agency, and a legal assistant. Within five minutes, they'd reviewed and read through the NDA, which was mercifully brief and straightforward. In fact, when she got to the last page, she felt relieved, until she reached the "Penalty of Breach" section and her breath caught.

"Hold on," Cassidy said, squinting down at the document. "If I disclose anything about my interactions with Jack Winston or any of his associates, representatives, or employees, or share any information I learn about his career, his private life, or…basically anything having to do with him at all, I have to pay…" She pointed at the number on the page. "You've gotta be kidding me. I don't even have that much money."

Marion smiled, one corner of her mouth rising higher than the other one. "Then I would advise you to not violate the NDA, Miss James."

Cassidy glanced at Roger, whose face was neutral. He was leaving the decision up to her. Then she glared at Jack, the cause of all this mess, and he gave her a reassuring nod. She held his steady gaze for a moment, and her heart rate slowed enough to gather her thoughts.

She took a deep breath. "So, if I sign this NDA, you'll tell me what you're offering that will make my life so much better. The magical thing that any person in my position would jump on?"

Marion folded her arms in front of her on the

table. "Yes."

She turned toward Roger, who smiled and said, "Well, they've got *my* attention, Cassy girl. I'd be willing to keep my trap shut to find out what they have in mind, but I don't have any skin in the game...well, unless I blab." He winked. "Do what you're comfortable with."

For a moment, she wanted to get up and walk away, but then she remembered the horde of camera-wielding goons outside and relaxed back in her seat. Jack's sincere expression was now tinged with a hint of hope.

"You can make the paparazzi go away?" she asked.

Marion nodded. "Without a doubt."

The sooner this nightmare was over, the better. She picked up the pen the lawyer had given her and turned to the last page of the contract, signing with a flourish.

How bad could it be? Any plan that would rid her of Jack Winston and all the awful things that came with him, from rabid fans texting her to cameramen literally hiding in trees, was a good plan as far as she was concerned.

CHAPTER TWELVE

Jack relaxed against the dining room wall and gave Cassidy what he hoped was a confident, encouraging smile when she set the pen down after signing the NDA. Good thing he'd taken all those acting classes because this whole thing was a disaster, and he was anything but confident.

She held his gaze for a moment, then brushed her bangs out of her eyes and folded her hands in her lap, waiting for Marion to commence the big reveal. Jack closed his eyes and took a deep breath. This was going to be awful; he could sense it. No way was Cassidy going to go for this ridiculous scheme—though he should know better by now than to underestimate his manager when her mind was set on something.

Marion was intimidating on a good day, even to him. She'd be overwhelming to someone like Cassidy. Not that Cassidy was weak, as she'd shown by her behavior so far, but Jack doubted she was accustomed to swimming with sharks like Marion Hill. In fact, Marion had been at it so long, she was more like one of those enormous prehistoric sharks his nephew talked about constantly—the ones with teeth the size of a man's hand. He imagined the page from the book he'd read to Mason dozens of times depicting the prehistoric predator. What were those things called?

Megalodons. That was the name he was looking

for. Marion Hill was a Megalodon.

The whole meeting, Jack had found himself focusing more on Cassidy than the legal mumbo jumbo his lawyer had spouted when describing the terms of the NDA. He'd not allowed himself to get his hopes up that the funny, kind woman he'd come to know on YouTube was actually the woman he would meet in Blink. He'd assumed she'd be much different in person. He of all people knew someone's onscreen and online personas differed vastly from how they behaved face-to-face. Over and over, he'd been disappointed or surprised by fellow actors when meeting for the first time. There was no disappointment with Cassidy. She was real all the way through.

And so was her shock when Marion laid out the plan in one abrupt sentence. "The agreement is for you to enter into a public romantic relationship with Jack for the duration of two weeks, after which time you will break up with him, again, publicly, and end your association altogether."

Roger leaned back in his chair, the wrinkle lines bracketing his mouth becoming more pronounced with his amusement.

Cassidy was not amused. She looked horrified. "You can't possibly mean…" She shot a startled look at Jack. "You mean we make it look like we're dating?" Cassidy stood. "Why? How could that possibly make any of this better?" She gestured to Jack. "I would never date someone like him." She shook her head. "The answer is no."

Jack wasn't surprised. It was clear from the moment he set foot in the place the woman wasn't a fan, and for good reason. Heck, he wasn't a Jack Winston fan himself at that moment.

Marion *was* surprised, however. As if she couldn't wrap her head around anyone not wanting to be seen with him. She stared at Cassidy with pursed lips and wide eyes as if she was waiting for a punchline to a joke. The joke was on her, though. Cassidy James was serious.

Despite her obvious dislike of him, Jack found himself admiring Cassidy more by the minute. She'd defied the Megalodon, and that took guts.

"Suit yourself," Marion said, standing. She retrieved the NDAs Roger and Cassidy had signed and handed them across the table to the lawyer, who placed them in her briefcase. "You are bound by the NDA regardless. You may not disclose to anyone anything discussed or witnessed here today."

"No worries there. Who'd believe it anyway?" Cassidy lifted her chin. "If you'll excuse me, I need to finish stripping the paint on Dolores's mantel."

"Dolores?" Roger repeated with a smile. "You named this house after a grumpy, arthritic old cat?"

Cassidy stopped in the dining room archway. "Lolo is a special old lady, just like Dolores."

Roger got a faraway look in his eyes as he stared into the middle distance. "Yes, she is. And loyal, too. That cat didn't leave my sweet Mabel's side until she took her last breath." Shaking himself out of the memory, the old man stood. "Nice to meet all of you." He extended his hand to Marion again. "A real pleasure, Ms. Hill."

Marion wore an expression Jack hadn't seen before. Empathy, maybe? She stood and took his hand. "Same, Mr. McGuffy. Thank you."

"Roger," he said, patting the top of her hand clasped in his.

"Roger," she repeated.

The old man released her hand and shuffled back into the kitchen.

Marion took a deep breath and straightened her shoulders. "Miss LaPorte, make return arrangements for the three of you. I'll take care of my end."

Dee pulled out her phone and immediately got to work.

And that was that, Jack supposed, as he watched everyone pack up their papers, pens, and electronics. Only it wasn't. Not for him, anyway. They couldn't just pull up the tent stakes and fold camp, leaving this mess behind. "This won't do," he said. "I caused this."

Marion snapped her leather folio shut and braced her palms on the table. "I beg your pardon?"

Jack glanced through the archway into the room where Cassidy was covering up the paint stripper–coated mantel with what looked to be saran wrap. "I can't just leave her with this mess."

"Miss James was offered the opportunity to remedy her situation. She declined to accept." Marion glanced at her watch. "I need to get the legal team to the Bangor airport. Do you have a solution or simply a complaint?"

Ouch. The Megalodon was in fine form. "I hope

to have a solution. Give me ten minutes alone with her."

Marion arched a brow, then glanced down at her watch. "Five minutes."

Ten, five, it probably didn't matter anyway. He was going to give it his best shot, though. As if entering a stage from the wings, he rolled his shoulders back, straightened his spine, took a deep breath, and practiced his lines in his head as he headed onstage. Showtime.

CHAPTER THIRTEEN

Cassidy ripped off another piece of cling wrap from the roll and smoothed it over the sticky, paint stripper–coated mantel, imagining how much better the fireplace would be once the paint was removed and the gorgeous wood was exposed again. Just like she'd be better once this stuck-up actor and his self-important manager were gone, along with their lawyer, and notary, and PR person, and the army of security they'd brought to protect their precious movie star from the big, bad residents of Blink, Maine.

"Good riddance," she muttered under her breath.

They were still talking and packing up when she glanced over at the dining room archway.

Shaking her head in disbelief, she pulled off another length of wrap. She still couldn't believe that their great-and-mighty proposal—the one that would change her life and make it better— was a fake relationship with Jack Winston. She huffed and blew the bangs out of her eyes. *That* was the offer that anyone in her position would jump at? Seriously?

She looked over again to find Jack's expression dark as he said something to Marion, like he was mad, too.

With hard strokes, she flattened the final piece of plastic over the wood. Good. She hoped all of them were as angry as she was. She didn't ask for this.

She sat back on her heels and took in her handiwork. In a few hours, she'd check and see if the paint was loosening up. Until then, she'd take a sledgehammer to the dilapidated shed between Dolores and Roger's little house.

She couldn't imagine choosing the guest house over Dolores, but maybe there were too many memories here for Roger. She sighed and glanced around the room, breath catching when she saw Jack striding purposefully toward her. The look on his face wasn't the confident, easygoing one he'd come in with. He looked stormy. She'd probably wounded his overly inflated superstar ego.

He stopped abruptly ten or so feet away, and instead of the indignant rant she'd expected, he huffed out a breath and ran a hand through his thick, dark hair.

"Cassidy, I'm sorry," he said. "I feel terrible about all of this." He gestured behind him to his team in the dining room. "This is not what I'd intended."

What was she supposed to say to that? The guy sounded sincere. Maybe he was. He certainly *should* be. She folded her arms across her ribs and waited.

He glanced back at the dining room, then said, "Is there somewhere we can go and talk in private?"

She gestured toward the front door. "No. Thanks to you, there are clowns with cameras and microphones everywhere."

He closed his eyes for a moment. "I'm sorry."

Dang. She could almost believe he meant it. It wouldn't hurt to hear him out, she supposed. "The library is out of their line of vision, at least."

They passed the bodyguards at the door in the foyer. When they entered the library, Cassidy slid the enormous pocket doors closed, proud of how easily and silently they rolled into place since she'd reworked the hardware. She felt a prickle of pride when she turned to find Jack running a hand over the carved wood wainscoting near the tower window seat.

"This is as private as it gets around here," she said.

Jack did a three-sixty, taking in the room. "The house is beautiful."

"At least there's one thing we agree on," she said, not sure why everything about this man made her irritated and snappy. Amanda was right. This wasn't like her. She took a breath through her nose. This guy had made her life a nightmare. She had every right to be snappy.

"Cassidy, I…" He lowered onto the circular window seat of the tower as if he were defeated. "What can I do to make this right?"

To her, the answer was obvious. "Leave and take your people and those photographers with you."

He shook his head. "The paparazzi won't simply leave because I do. Especially now that I've been here."

She placed her hands on her hips. "That would have been a good observation for you to have made *before* you arrived."

Elbows on knees, he leaned over and covered his face with his hands. After a moment, he lifted his head. "Marion only gave me five minutes."

"You'd better get to talking, then." She sat on the seat opposite him. This little conversation nook was her favorite feature in this room, and this was the first time she'd ever used it. Too bad it was with Jack. Even with the light from the windows muted by the drop cloths tacked up, Cassidy noted there were little gold flecks in his irises, like stars in a night sky.

She shook her head. *Stop it.* This man was a problem, not some painting to admire. *Stars in a night sky...sheesh.*

"I came here with every intention of making things better for you," he said. "I had no idea Marion was going to hit you with an NDA or throw her agenda out there so harshly."

"Her agenda?" Cassidy stood. The nook felt too small suddenly, and she had too much energy zinging through her muscles to sit. "What's *your* agenda, Jack? Truly, what do you want from me?" Her work boots sounded overly loud on the wooden floors in the vast, empty room as she put some distance between them.

"I don't want anything from you. I want something *for* you. I want to make it right. To put things back in an acceptable way for you." He stood but only took a couple of steps in her direction before her glare froze him. "The Instagram mis-tag has caused you a lot of trouble. I know my showing up here unannounced was rude and threw you off, but

I also know, now that I'm here, we can find a way to make this work to our benefit. Just you and me. No publicity reps, no lawyers, no Marion the Megalodon."

"The what?"

He made a dismissive motion with his hand. "Megalodon. It's a big, nasty, prehistoric shark. A brutal predator. Giant sharp teeth. Eyes that roll back in its head when it feeds. A total terror. Fits her perfectly."

Cassidy's lips twitched as she fought a smile.

A light knock sounded on the doors to the library. "Mr. Winston?" a light voice called.

"Come in, Dee," Jack answered.

The door slid open, and the petite woman slipped in. Dee was about Cassidy's age, maybe younger, her tight curls pulled back in a bun. "Ms. Hill wanted me to tell you she's about to leave."

He held up a finger to Dee, indicating for her to wait a moment, then turned back to Cassidy. "Are you willing to give me a try at fixing this? If we work together, I know we'll come up with something."

Part of her wanted to toss this man out of this house and out of her life this very minute, right along with the rest of his entourage. Another part of her, though, the less angry, more familiar part, was willing to hear him out and maybe come up with an agreeable plan to put an end to this madness.

She nodded.

A look of genuine relief crossed his handsome face. He turned to Dee. "Please wish Ms. Hill safe travels and tell her that we will be remaining in Blink."

As Dee slid the doors shut, Jack paced the room. "Okay, so, the way this whole thing was presented to you was wrong," he said, turning to stride to the bookcase at the far end. "Marion held out the fake-dating ruse like it was a big favor to you or something."

Cassidy leaned against one of the built-in mahogany bookcases. "An opportunity that someone in *my position* would jump at? That simply being seen with the wildly successful, exceptionally talented superstar, Jack Winston, would fix all my problems and make my life better? You mean *that* favor?"

He stopped and raked his fingers through his hair. "Yes, when in fact the opposite is true. Being seen together would benefit *me*. A lot."

Well, that made no sense whatsoever. "How?"

"For all her flaws and harshness, Marion Hill is one of the best managers in the business. She knows how to promote success, and she's convinced I need to have a public girlfriend for myriad reasons I won't bore you with."

At that moment, Cassidy didn't find herself bored even a little bit.

"I was supposed to form an alliance with another celebrity," he continued, "but when the press latched on to you because of my mistake, Marion decided to make the most of the situation."

She crossed her arms over her ribs. She knew this whole thing seemed off before she even signed the NDA. "So it wasn't about making it better for me at all, was it?"

"I can't speak for Marion, but I came here to make things right. And I will, I promise." The look on his face was so open and sincere, she found herself wanting to believe him. Maybe he really hadn't known Marion the Megalodon was going to bring lawyers and contracts. Or maybe he was just that good at acting.

She picked at a fleck that had left a bump under the primer coat on the wall plaster next to the bookshelf. "You know, this entire problem could have been solved yesterday by having your people make it crystal clear in a public way that the Instagram tag was in error, and you didn't know me." She gestured to the drop cloth–covered window. "And then all those creeps with cameras would go hunt the girlfriend you had really intended to tag."

"I'd intended to tag my sister. Her profile name is similar to yours. I was going to visit her family. I used that photo and text because we have an inside joke about the awful line from the movie."

Well, that was a surprise. It almost made him real. "It's a ridiculous line."

"I completely agree. I have no idea why it took off. Memes everywhere online. Now, the writers use it throughout every *Mad Planet* script like salt on potato chips."

A weird silence stretched between them from where they stared at each other from opposite ends of the library. A truce of some kind, Cassidy supposed.

Finally, he spoke. "Can you imagine any way

that this situation or your association with me could benefit you personally?"

She took in a deep breath and dropped her arms to her side. "My YouTube channel stats are through the roof since this happened." She tucked her hands into the pockets of her overalls. "A boost in future business for when my little brother takes over next summer would be the only positive thing I could see coming out of our association. Other than that, I can't see any benefit to knowing you at all."

He winced, and she felt a momentary pang of guilt. It had been a tacky thing to say. He recovered quickly and said, "Good. I have a proposal for you then, Cassidy James."

"I'm listening."

CHAPTER FOURTEEN

Jack strode to the front window of the library, pulled aside a paint-covered drop cloth that had been tacked up, and peeked out at the growing pack of reporters across the street from the house. Clearly word had gotten out that he was in Blink, since there were many more than when he'd arrived. He should have requested Marion leave some of the security.

When he looked over his shoulder at Cassidy, she was studying the view through the window with wide eyes. The paparazzi must be terrifying to her.

"I think I know how to fix it and make it up to you at the same time." He dropped the cloth in place over the window.

She flipped her bangs out of her face.

For some reason his mouth had gone dry, and a swirling pocket of dread made his gut churn. He could tell from her closed-off stance and skeptical expression she still didn't trust him. "How long-range are the projects you're trying to attract?"

She shrugged. "Luke will be here full-time next summer, so the projects couldn't begin until then, but he could line things up and start scheduling now. The big projects he hopes to take on are years in the planning and involve lots of sub-contractors."

"This is perfect, then. I have a pretty big platform—"

She snorted.

"Okay. I have an enormous platform, and if we hang out together and make some videos, it could boost your clientele. It would certainly improve your views and subscriptions."

"No doubt," she muttered. A rapidly tapping foot joined her closed-off body language. She raked her bangs out of her face and stared at him, clearly uncomfortable. "What do you mean by 'hang out together'?"

This was the tricky part. He had to word this carefully or he was back at zero. "Exactly that. We would make the videos and then, for the benefit of the paparazzi…and me, we would act like we're more than friends in front of the cameras."

When her jaw tightened, he added, "It will only be when we're out. You can go back to hating me in private." He held out his hand. "Deal?"

"I don't hate you," she said, not taking his hand. "I don't know you well enough for that."

She was softening, at least. Not necessarily toward him, but toward the plan.

He walked across the room and stopped several feet away from her. "Come on, Cassidy. A couple of weeks. A few videos. Some hand holding and loving looks deep into each other's eyes." He could tell she was about to laugh. "We both end up in a better place." He extended his hand again, unsettled by how important it had become to him that she accept. "Deal?"

She eyed his hand as if he were holding a fat, hairy spider. Wait. She liked spiders. A snake, then.

For several seconds, the room remained quiet

except for Cassidy's shallow breaths.

"Fine," she said, extending her hand. "We have a deal."

"Excellent," Jack said, relief flooding his body as he shook her hand. "Thank you."

"Don't thank me yet," she said. "There's still plenty of ways for this to go wrong."

No doubt about that. "Dee!" Jack called, striding toward the doors. When he slid them open, Roger, Dee, and Flex, huddled just outside the doors, jumped back like they'd been electrocuted.

"Were you eavesdropping?" Jack asked.

"Absolutely!" Roger said with a grin. At least Dee and Flex had the good manners to look ashamed.

"Right. Then you know we're going forward with the plan," Jack announced. "We'll need a place to stay, Dee."

"I've found a hotel in a town north of here," she answered.

"Nonsense," Roger said. "You can stay here. You too, Cassy. No sense in you fighting the cameras when I have six bedrooms here."

Cassidy was standing almost next to Jack in the doorway. Close enough for him to confirm that she was the source of the honeysuckle notes in the house.

"That's really generous of you, Roger. Thanks," Jack said.

Dee cleared her throat. "Ms. Hill texted and said she can't get back before tomorrow."

Jack stepped out into the foyer. "Thank God."

"I think she's angry, Mr. Winston," Dee said.

"I hope so." From an opening under the stairs, the grizzled gray-and-white cat stared at him, no doubt Lolo, the namesake for the house.

A loud knock on the door caused the cat to duck back out of sight.

Cassidy's friend, Amanda, came in, all smiles. "I am here to take you to the Living Sharpe studios, Cassidy," she announced. "Caleb is out there with the motor running. And since you're still here, Mr. Winston—"

"Jack," he corrected.

"*Jack*," she said with a grin. "Since you're still here, I want to personally invite you to my party on the patio tonight, since I'm sure Cassidy forgot."

"In her defense," Jack said, "she's been pretty busy."

"Hold up," Cassidy said, raising both hands up in front of her. "I have work to do. Why am I going to the Living Sharpe studio?"

"To get ready for the party, of course." Amanda linked her arm through Cassidy's. "Because we have a theme now that Mr. Winston...I mean, *Jack* is here."

Cassidy closed her eyes and groaned as her friend led her toward the door. "What's the theme?"

Amanda escorted her friend through the door, causing the paparazzi to begin shouting, then turned back and said over her shoulder, winking at Jack, "Helloooooo, Hollywood!"

CHAPTER FIFTEEN

Standing between Amanda and Lillian, Cassidy scanned the partygoers on the deck behind Amanda's store, Miller Mercantile.

"Stop pulling on your dress, Cass," Amanda hissed under her breath, waving at a gaggle of older ladies from the church assembled by the railing of the deck who were wearing enough sequins and feathers to supply all of Vegas. Everyone in Blink loved Amanda's parties, and if there was a theme, they went all out. This party was no different.

"Where on earth did they find those dresses?" Cassidy asked.

"I have it on good authority that the three kings' capes and all of the angels' wings that were retired after last year's Christmas pageant mysteriously went missing this afternoon," Amanda said with a laugh.

"Along with some red felt," Lillian teased, eyeing Amanda's makeshift red carpet.

Cassidy gave a half-hearted wave as one of her recent customers, Mrs. Trimble, dressed in what looked like a hastily altered eighties prom dress complete with flounces and ruffles, grinned and gave an approving thumbs-up.

She gave the top of the dress another tug, and Amanda shot her a disapproving glare. "It's gonna slip down," Cassidy grumbled. The ridiculous thing had no straps, and she felt naked. And it was tight. And itchy. And weird.

"You look like a movie star," Lillian said. "That dress is much more flattering on you than it ever was on me."

Cassidy brushed her fingers across her forehead before she remembered her bangs had been plastered back with a zillion ounces of hairspray and then slathered with some other product that made it look as shiny as Barbie doll hair. "Thanks for the loan, Lillian." It had taken one of the *Living Sharpe* costume tailors hours to alter it to fit her much shorter, flatter figure. She eyed her friend's long, curvy body and snorted at the preposterous notion that she'd look better in anything than Lillian.

She resisted the urge to yank up the top of the dress again, glancing around at the Blink residents happily chattering in clusters on the deck. In addition to the usual string lights surrounding the area, Amanda had decorated with cardboard stars covered in tin foil and glitter, strung overhead on fishing line. A hand-painted sign that read, "Hello, Hollywood!" was displayed over the food table that was already half full of goodies brought by neighbors.

Today's party felt different than others. There was an electric buzz filling the place—excitement, maybe. No doubt Amanda and Niles had tipped people off that Jack Winston was in town.

As she scanned the deck and the harbor boardwalk beyond, Cassidy hadn't noticed any paparazzi lurking nearby. They were most likely still stationed outside Dolores waiting on Jack to emerge. She'd seen only a couple of them in the parking lot on the other side of the building when Lillian had driven them here from the *Living Sharpe* studio. The studio was just outside the town square where the new doctor's office had been built.

Momentarily, she wondered if Tristan had been there.

But no. She had bigger problems to worry about.

At first, getting dolled-up for this party had been fun, but after hours of being poked, plucked, prodded, perfumed, made up, and stuffed like a cannoli into this dress, the novelty of feminine pampering had worn thin enough to see through. Cassidy shifted in the tight, pointy shoes, longing for her sneakers or work boots.

"Caleb just texted. They're pulling into the parking lot right now," Lillian said. "They've got a sheriff escort because of the increased number of paparazzi. They're going to keep them off the boardwalk because of some fire code."

"Well, that's good," Amanda said. "We're already out of room on the deck."

Lillian put an arm around Cassidy's shoulders and gave a squeeze. "You and Jack are causing quite a stir."

Cassidy's muscles tightened at the mere mention of his name. She couldn't believe she was going to pretend to be in a relationship with this man. She closed her eyes and took in a deep breath of the sea air blowing off the harbor. A couple of videos together. A little bit of fake dating. Then all of this would end. It was a good deal.

"You've been really quiet since he arrived. You've avoided even the easiest of questions," Amanda said. "Something you want to tell us?"

She was bound by that NDA, so she couldn't mention her deal with Jack. Instead of trying to fabricate an excuse, she lifted her shoulder in a shrug, nearly freeing a breast in the process.

"Stop yanking on the top of the gown," Amanda scolded, slapping her hand away. She took in a gasp of breath. "Oh, look, here he comes."

Not even attempting nonchalance, Cassidy twisted to see Jack and Caleb pulling up next to Wright Boat Works in Caleb's pickup truck. Flex, dressed all in black like a TV bad guy, hopped out of the backseat and opened the door for Jack, who stepped out of the vehicle in a black tux, looking like he was ready to walk the red carpet for real and not the uneven runner of faded red felt from last year's Christmas pageant stapled to the boardwalk and up the steps to the patio. Why would he have brought a tux with him to Blink, Maine? The most formal place here was Sally's Starfish Diner.

Caleb opened the driver's side back door, and Dee stepped out in a shimmery silver dress that made her look amazing. Maybe celebrities like Jack and his team took fancy clothes with them everywhere they went in case people threw parties with themes in honor of them. She shot a glare at Amanda. No wonder the guy had an uber ego.

Not everyone had arrived for the party yet, but

those present let out squeals of delight at a real-life movie star in Blink, Maine.

As Jack waved and strolled up the steps to the deck, shaking hands with her neighbors, Flex hovered at his left side and Dee stood quietly several feet away. Cassidy wondered what it must feel like to be globally recognized and revered like that.

It must feel awesome, she decided as he confidently greeted the small mob of Blink residents who had gathered around him. Some were old-timers; others were newer to Blink, arriving to work at the mill or for Lillian's Living Sharpe enterprise.

As he signed autographs and shook hands, more people mounted the deck, bringing food to share and coolers of drinks. He never seemed disinterested or hurried as he chatted, something that must take real focus.

Cassidy noticed that Caleb had remained in the parking lot with several patrol cars and half a dozen uniformed officers who were speaking to the paparazzi that had followed the truck around to this side. No doubt other photographers had staked out the tops of buildings or sought cover like special ops snipers, waiting to take that perfect shot.

"I wonder if Tristan is going to come," Lillian said, pulling Cassidy by the elbow toward a large red-and-white cooler with the lid propped open. "Wine or beer?"

The borrowed gold and rhinestone bracelets on her wrist jangled as she waved her hand. "Nothing for me, thanks."

As Lillian fished out a bottle of beer from the ice, Cassidy scanned the crowd. What would Tristan think of her in this dress? While she preferred her work clothes, he'd probably consider the uncomfortable dress something a "knockout" would wear. Seemed she'd never know because Blink's runaway doctor had yet to make an appearance.

She glanced over at Jack and his adoring circle of admirers, and as if he felt her eyes on him, he looked up and their gazes met. He smiled as if delighted to see her, then his look heated as he took her in from head to toe.

Whoa. For a moment, Cassidy couldn't breathe. The only sounds were the blood pounding in her ears and the jangle of her bracelets. It was an act. That whole simmering look-her-up-and-down business was nothing but a fine actor playing his part in their fake relationship.

"Hmmm. That's quite a look Jack's giving you."

Cassidy jumped as Lillian's voice jerked her back into the moment. She didn't reply, uncertain if sound would even come out. No doubt, as discombobulated as she was, nothing intelligible would result anyway. *It's an act*, she reminded herself again. They didn't know each other. Heck, they didn't even *like* each other.

Lillian chuckled. "I hope Caleb is taking notes because that look scores an eleven out of ten on the panty-melt-o-meter."

Pulling her eyes away from Jack, Cassidy shook her head to clear it. "I'm sorry, the what?"

Lillian laughed and waved a hand in front of

Cassidy's face. "Earth to Cassidy. You're pretty distracted, huh?"

Yeah. Distracted. This was a mistake. She was way out of her league with this deal they'd made. This man did this for a living. She did it…never.

Amanda joined them and whispered, "Did you see the way Jack checked you out, Cass? I was over at the food table, and everyone was talking about it. I knew a formal dress theme was a brilliant idea." She squeezed Cassidy's hand a little too hard. "He's totally into you. I knew it. I told you so, didn't I, Lillian?"

"You certainly did," Lillian replied.

Ugh. This was awful. She hated deceiving her friends. She should never have agreed to this. The churning guilt in her stomach faded when she took in the animated expression on Amanda's face. Her eyes and grin were huge, and she was bouncing up and down on her toes with excitement, causing the metallic gold 1920s-style fringe on her dress to sway and shimmer in the twinkling lights over the deck. Maybe it was better this way. Telling the truth about the fake relationship deal would be like taking away a Christmas present. Besides, her friends' enthusiasm would make it more believable, since her own ability to deceive was zero.

She glanced back over at Jack as he autographed a square of fabric for one of the members of the Blink Quilting Club. Mid-signature, he looked up at her with those deep, brown eyes and again her breath caught. Dang it. He was way too good at this. Next to her, Amanda and Lillian sighed in unison as if scripted. Cassidy found herself sighing, but for a totally different reason: at the far end of the harbor, four of the paparazzi were sneaking behind the Wright Boat Works building toward the boat slips, which would give them a clear shot of the Miller Mercantile party deck. It was far away, but some of them had camera lenses as long as her arm, so the distance probably wasn't an obstacle.

"Hi, Tristan," Amanda called, waving vigorously as Tristan climbed the steps to the deck.

Jack glanced over his shoulder at Tristan as he handed the quilt square back to its owner and the men gave each other a nod of greeting. After a few handshakes and another selfie with the crowd around him, Jack came toward her in a straight line like a boat heading into a slip.

"Hi, Amanda. And I assume you are the Lillian that Caleb can't stop talking about?" Jack held out his hand and shook Lillian's.

"Hello, Mr. Winston," she said with equal nonchalance and charm. Lillian was used to dealing with famous people because of her company. Loads of celebrities were featured on her show that was filmed, in part, right here in Blink, though sometimes they took to the road with a crew. When that happened, it reminded Cassidy of the times before Blink got back on its feet.

"And fancy meeting you here," Jack said, slipping Cassidy's hand through the crook of his arm in a slick, practiced move as he led her away from her friends. Her jaw clenched. He'd done that too easily, and for some reason, it irritated her. With his looks and charm, this guy could probably swoop in and gather up any woman he wanted.

"You look amazing," he said. "Red suits you."

Before she could give him a lecture on sincerity—or his lack of it—the heel of one of her shoes caught in the gap in the deck boards, and she stopped, grateful she had his arm to hold on to.

"Death grip not necessary," he whispered. "Put the weight on the ball of your foot and push up like going on tiptoes. That usually does the trick with a stuck heel."

The heels were so high, she was practically on tiptoes as it was. "Easy for you to say," she huffed, trying to wrench the heel loose. If she leaned down, no doubt her boobs would pop right out of this ridiculous dress. "I suppose you've helped lots of women with stuck heels?"

He shot a glance to the far end of the harbor where the reporters had their huge lenses pointed at them. "In fact, I have, but in most cases, the heel is tangled in the hem of their gowns, or sometimes stuck in the grass if the event is outside. This is my first deck disaster."

"Well, bad news. This shoe is going nowhere." She could just step out of the thing, she supposed. The thought of getting out of the torture devices held some serious appeal. Sadly, it would result in the dress dragging the ground, which would ruin it. She would have to risk falling out of the dress and lean over to free the blasted thing.

Patting her hand still resting in the crook of his arm, he moved to where his side faced the reporters, then crouched down, reaching under the hem of her dress. "They're filming and photographing from where the boats are. No. Don't look at them. Just smile, Cassidy. Preferably at me."

Holding on to his shoulders for balance, she managed what she hoped was a believable smile as he wiggled the shoe, her foot still inside, back and forth.

"Man, oh man, you really did it good, didn't you?" he said, looking up at her with a grin. "You must have been walking heel first like you do in work boots."

No doubt.

"Shoe stuck?" Lillian said from somewhere behind her.

Oh, great. It was totally obvious. A quick glance at the partygoers confirmed that the feeling that everyone was watching her was spot on. Perfect.

"It happened to me all the time when I first moved here. I've gotten pretty good at heels on decks, piers, and boardwalks by now," Lillian said. "Sometimes, I had to step out of the shoe to get it free."

She should have held firm when she declined the stiletto heels. Now, she undoubtedly looked silly—not that anyone in Blink expected her to be sophisticated, but this could potentially reach a much larger audience. She shot a glance at the photographers lined up at the end of the boat slips. There were more of them now, all holding cameras with giant lenses trained directly on them. Jack was probably used to this. A guy like him probably liked it.

"Well, this leaves me no choice," he said with a grin. "Put your hands on my shoulders and step out of the shoe, Cassidy."

She stepped out of the stuck shoe, and before she could say a word, he swept her up into his arms as if he were a knight saving a damsel from a dragon or some such nonsense.

She could practically hear the blood heating her face, and she could *definitely* hear the sound of shutter clicks snapping across the water from the end of the pier.

His body was warm and hard—rock hard, like he worked out at the gym every day. She thought of his shirtless shots that were a feature of every *Mad Planet* movie. No body double there, obviously.

A tingle of excitement filled her, and she relaxed, knowing lifting her was no big deal to him and he wouldn't drop her. She slid her gaze over the deck and noticed her neighbors smiling, especially the church ladies, feather headpieces and boas swaying as they whispered to one another. This fake romance thing may not be as hard as she'd imagined. Getting her heel stuck might turn out to be a good thing after all.

She smiled in spite of herself.

"That's the spirit," he said.

She glanced back at the church ladies, whose feathers were practically quivering now.

"Shoe rescued!" Lillian announced, slipping it onto Cassidy's bare foot poking out from under the gown. "Carry on, you two."

"Hmm," Jack purred. "She gave us permission to carry on."

Okay. That rumbly voice thing he just did

should be illegal. "What do you think you're doing?" she whispered.

"I'm making good on our deal. I'm wooing my fake girlfriend for the press," he whispered back.

"Wooing?" Cassidy laughed, hoping it would add to the scene and make for good photographs—and, well, if she were being honest with herself, because she'd never been the center of a man's attention before, and she liked it. A lot. Even if it was all smoke and mirrors.

"So, um…" He grinned and released the arm under her legs, then rotated her to face him with her feet off the floor. Her body pressed to his from breasts to knees, and she slid down his body in a slow descent that short-circuited her brain. When her feet finally touched the deck, he didn't let go but leaned down and whispered in her ear, "I'm learning important dates in history. Wanna be one of them?"

It took her a few seconds to process his words, what with his hard body against hers causing all kinds of weird sensations and his heated breath on her ear making her want to squirm. The man was taking his role very seriously.

Before she could focus enough to reply to his cheesy pickup line, he arched an eyebrow and leaned back in, saying, "Are you a bank loan? Because you have my interest."

This time she laughed, body still fully pressed to his with his arms around her waist. This time the laughter wasn't to fool her neighbors or the paparazzi. It was genuine. And fun. Yes, she was having honest-to-goodness *fun*.

"Wow, those lines are awful," she said.

He arched an eyebrow. "I have lots more where those came from."

A loud clanging came from behind them, and the partygoers quieted.

Cassidy dropped her arms from around his neck, and he released her waist.

Amanda smacked a metal pot on the food table with a large, metal serving spoon several more times until she had everyone's attention.

"I know everyone is excited about Jack Winston being here," Amanda said in her loud camp-director voice. "And I know we will all get a chance to visit with him because he's going to be in Blink for a little while. That said, let's eat and give him a chance to eat, too." She gestured to the amazing spread on the table brought by the people in attendance. "Dig in!" She reached into the cooler next to the table and held up a beer. "And drink up!"

There was a cheer, and a line began to form.

Cassidy's traitorous body was still heated from where she'd been in contact with Jack. Obviously it couldn't tell acting from attraction. Self-consciously, she ran a hand down her abdomen to smooth the silk.

"You look lovely," Jack murmured.

And for the first time since her senior prom, Cassidy felt pretty. It wasn't that she had low self-esteem—quite the opposite. She liked who she was. She knew her strong points and had worked on developing and accentuating her strengths. She was a good business owner and a talented renovator. She was punctual, funny, a good planner, decent at math, and loyal to a fault. She knew she wasn't unattractive. In fact, lots of people had told her she was cute. But lovely? That was a first.

"Thanks," she said. "But you're taking this role of fake boyfriend way too seriously."

Jack leaned close and in an unexpected move brushed his fingertips across her cheek. "Method acting."

Her skin felt like she'd been lit on fire at his touch. Mind swimming, she stared up at his face to find him looking over her head.

"Hey, Cassidy," Tristan's voice said from behind her. "Jack."

The men shook hands. "Good to see you, Tristan," Jack said. "I want a beer. Can I get you anything, Cassidy?"

"Uh...I'm good," she said, mortified that her voice came out breathy.

She pulled her eyes from Jack's retreating back to Tristan, who was wearing the same tan slacks, dress shirt with no tie, and navy blazer he'd been wearing earlier.

He gestured to her dress and said, "You look... different."

Different. Still not a knockout. She took a deep breath. *Lovely*, Jack's voice whispered in her mind. *You look lovely.*

"You look the same," she said.

He chuckled. "Does Amanda throw these parties often?"

"Almost every week. Sometimes they're food-themed, sometimes there's a costume theme, like tonight."

He smiled. "That's nice. Things are really different around here."

To Cassidy, things had remained pretty much the same. Blink's recent growth had caused some changes, of course, but at its heart, Blink was a constant. Predictable, reliable, and constant.

"You should visit more often," she said.

His eyes traveled the length of her body. "Maybe I should."

There. That was the kind of response she'd imagined all these years. Tristan seeing her as a woman and not a braces-wearing band nerd. Somehow, though, it didn't have the warm, swimmy effect it always had in her daydreams.

And not near the effect Jack's "lovely" had.

She glanced back at where Jack was visiting with Sally at the drink cooler, looking completely at ease, then back to Tristan, whose tight shoulders and rigid posture indicated he was anything but. Maybe he was always uptight or maybe he was hungry. He'd probably only had one of his protein shakes for lunch. "I think I'm going to go get some food. Wanna join me?"

He stared at her, then studied the food table as if considering a major decision and not simply whether he wanted dinner. Yesterday, her insides would have been doing flip-flops, aching for him to say yes and spend more time with her. Today, she was ambivalent.

"Hey, Cassidy. You ready to get some food?" Jack's breath fanned across her ear, and a weird tremor passed through her. She hadn't even heard him approach.

She gestured to Tristan. "We were just discussing dinner."

"Join us," Jack said.

Tristan studied him for a moment, then shook his head. "Thanks, but no. There are some records sent from my Portland practice I need to review." He gestured across the water to Dolores on the hill overlooking the harbor. "I'm going to head to the house." His brows drew together slightly. "Dad told me you two are staying at the house tonight?"

"That's the plan," Jack said. "So are my two associates. It's generous of your dad to offer to put all of us up."

"Don't kid yourself," Tristan replied. "My dad never does anything without an ulterior motive. He wants something from you or he wouldn't have offered. He's never done anything generous in his life." He turned toward the stairs to the boardwalk.

Cassidy's skin burned and her head felt as though it was about to explode. Yes, Roger liked to manipulate situations and often had an agenda, but he was also one of the most generous people she'd ever met. He and Lillian had worked together to save Blink from extinction two years ago. He'd donated land, money, and lumber to rebuild the place and had given local residents jobs. And that wasn't all…

"He paid off all of my father's medical debt and covered his funeral costs so my little brother could go to college and we didn't have to sell our house," she blurted out, crossing her arms over her ribs to hide her trembling hands. Fortunately, everyone else on the deck was into their own conversations and hadn't seemed to notice them.

Tristan stopped and turned to face her. Brow furrowed, he appeared genuinely surprised as he studied her.

Jack took a step closer, and for some reason, that calmed her. She lifted her chin. "Roger has never expected anything in return, Tristan."

On and on time seemed to stretch until finally, Tristan held both hands up in surrender. "I stand corrected." He cleared his throat. "I'm sorry—not only for my harsh words about my dad, but for your loss, Cassidy. I wasn't aware your father had passed."

She gave a quick nod.

"Okay, then. I guess I'll see you at the house." Tristan tipped his head, brow furrowed. "Again, I apologize."

As she watched Tristan leave the deck, Jack reached over as if to put his arm around her, and she stiffened.

"I'm sorry," he whispered, lowering his arm. "The cameras are on us. Just trying to play my part."

Dang. She'd momentarily forgotten about the paparazzi and their little subterfuge.

"Maybe we should lay some ground rules," he said.

Cassidy glanced over her shoulder at the photographers at the far end of the harbor, then looked at the long line of her neighbors waiting in the food line. "Okay."

"Let's go where we can't be overheard." He

gestured to an area of the deck farthest from people. "In order to pull this off, we need to look authentic," he said once they were at the edge of the deck. "Believable."

She thought about her body's reaction when he'd picked her up. Believable shouldn't be a problem. "Okay, what do you mean by ground rules?"

"Well, as a couple, we would touch each other, right?"

Cassidy's heart rate escalated. "I suppose."

"What kind of touching would be acceptable to you?" he asked. Again, he had that utterly sincere expression on his face. "I want you to be comfortable."

She couldn't even swallow her throat was so dry. "Holding hands."

He smiled. "Great. How about putting my arm around you like I almost did when Tristan left?"

She nodded. "That'd be okay."

"What else are you comfortable with?"

She racked her brain for another benign type of contact. "Hugging?" That worked. She hugged her friends all the time. No biggy.

"Good. That will get us through this party for sure." He held his hands out palms up.

She studied his hands for a moment and then placed hers in them. His hands were warm and much larger than hers.

He closed his fingers around hers and gave a squeeze. "We're playing a part. It'll get easier as we get to know each other."

He would know all about playing parts.

"Are you ready?" he asked.

Cassidy glanced over at the paparazzi. "What do they say when you're about to start filming on one of your movies?"

"Well, first someone would announce 'stand-by,'" he said, dropping one of her hands. "Then, there would be some stuff about sound and cameras." He led her toward the front of the deck that offered a clear view for the paparazzi. "Then, it's marked with a slate to designate the date, project, scene, and take." He turned her to face him and placed his hands on her waist.

Cassidy looked up into his smiling face, and her anxiety dialed back a bit. This was all for the cameras. She could do this. "I suppose we should hug now to give them something to photograph?" she suggested.

His smile was truly beautiful. "Then, after the scene is marked," he said, "the director or A.D. will call, 'Action.'"

"In that case…" she said, wrapping her arms around his waist for a photo-perfect hug. "Action."

CHAPTER SIXTEEN

Jack stared up at the clear, starry sky that wasn't obscured by lights or the smog of L.A. At least the paparazzi hadn't deployed drones. That would've really freaked Cassidy out. Although in this setting, the telephoto lenses were probably more effective.

He'd been surprised when she'd suggested a hug, and even more surprised when she'd leaned her head on his shoulder. It had been a brief embrace, but no doubt enough to give the paps material.

Holding Cassidy's hand, Jack slowly headed toward the table full of food at the back of the deck. Her small hand was smoother than it had been this morning. He had noticed the short, bright red nails that matched her dress, so she'd probably had a manicure and they did something to smooth the calluses. He was honestly a little disappointed. He'd liked her work-roughened palms. They were a tribute to her talent and ambition.

He could feel curious eyes as they made their way to the food service. The sensation of being watched was second nature to him now, but he imagined this kind of scrutiny was uncomfortable for Cassidy, even though she knew these people.

After serving up their plates, they headed toward Amanda and a blond man seated at one of the bright blue tables at the edge of the deck lit in the warm glow of strings of white-and-gold lights interspersed with silver stars.

The guy stood and held out his hand as they approached. Jack recognized him immediately. "You're Niles Sharpe. Great to meet you." He shook Niles's hand. "I watch your show all the time."

Niles's chest puffed out a little, and he eyed Amanda as he shook Jack's hand. "Your movies are awesome, man. Big fan."

"Thanks." Jack took Cassidy's plate, set it on the table, and waited while she gingerly scooted onto the bench from the end, careful not to snag her floor-length gown. Then he stepped over the bench to sit next to her.

Jack had just taken a bite of a beef slider when Niles asked, "So Amanda told me how the two of you crossed paths online, but I'm not clear on why you're hanging out in Blink."

Cassidy shifted uncomfortably next to him.

He chewed and swallowed his bite, then chased it with a swig of beer. "Well, I was hoping Cassidy and I could shoot some restoration videos together."

"That's awesome. So how long are you going to stay?" Amanda asked, leaning forward, grinning as she glanced back and forth from him to Cassidy.

Before he could answer, Dee hurried up to the end of the table. "Mr. Winston. I just heard from Ms. Hill. She checked into a hotel in Bangor after she dropped the PR and legal team off at the airport and says she's waiting for her reporters' and

team's flights to arrive so she can brief them before they get to Blink. She instructed me to let you
know that they will be here sometime tomorrow
afternoon."

"But she's not here tonight." He patted the
bench next to him. "Join us, Dee. I know you've
met Amanda. Have you met Niles Sharpe?"

She smiled and extended her hand. "Nice to
meet you. I enjoy your TV show."

"It's not mine, really. It's Lillian's and the whole
Living Sharpe team, but thank you," Niles said,
flushed, clearly enjoying the recognition.

Dee slid onto the bench.

"Have you eaten?" Jack asked her. He knew
she hadn't. He'd been keeping a loose eye on her
all evening because she'd taken this whole
Instagram mess-up so seriously. "I know Marion
keeps you busy, but you have to eat." He shoved
his heaped plate between them. "I was dreaming
big. Help me out here."

Dee picked up one of the remaining two sliders
and took a bite.

"So, back to my question," Niles said, grinning
like he'd caught someone in a lie—which wasn't
far from the truth. "Why are you—and what
sounds like maybe more of your team on the
way—hanging out in Blink, Jack?"

Jack knew any mention of dating would make
Cassidy uncomfortable, so he purposely kept it
vague. "Like I said, I'm here to film some videos
with Cassidy. And to answer your question, too,
Amanda, how long we stay depends on how long
that takes."

Amanda glanced at her phone screen. "Oh! It's time!" In a weirdly awkward move, she climbed over the bench and pulled the bottom of her dress that looked like something out of a Gatsby movie back into place right above her knees. She did something with her phone, and the quiet jazz music coming from the speakers hanging on the building wall stopped.

"Ladies and gentlemen!" After the crowd quieted, she continued, "If you're finished, can you put your stuff in the garbage and help me clear the center tables to the side? It's time for some dancing!"

The small crowd cheered and clapped, then many rose and began following her orders. Jack suspected Amanda was the type of person most comfortable when in charge. He let out a chuckle.

"What's funny?" Cassidy asked.

"I was just imagining putting Amanda and Marion in a room to see who raised the white flag of surrender first."

On his right, Dee giggled.

"Creates a pretty amusing image, doesn't it?" he said.

Dee nodded and took the last bite of her sandwich. He loved seeing her smile. She was too young to be so serious all the time. In fact, it was his firm belief that nobody should be serious all the time. Life was way too fun.

A heavy bass beat started up, and Amanda pulled some older women decked out primarily in sequins and feathers to the cleared space in the middle of the deck. Before long, a number of people were shaking and wiggling on the make-shift dance floor. The beat bounced off the steep sloped sides of the harbor, returning in syncopated rhythms and amplifying the sound.

Amanda danced over to their table and took Dee's hands. "Let's go, lady." She pulled her to her feet and led her to a group of five or so young women about Dee's age, laughing and dancing at the far end of the cleared area. The women immediately greeted Dee and pulled her into their group until she was wiggling and laughing right along with them.

Jack took a chug of beer, wiped his mouth, and climbed over the bench. "Let's dance!" he said, extending a hand to Cassidy. Flex, who had been inconspicuously lurking by the railing behind their table, materialized instantly.

"You want to dance, too, Flex?" Jack teased, waggling his eyebrows.

"Please stay on the outside of the group closest to me, boss," he said.

"But I have a beautiful, capable bodyguard. I'm totally safe."

Cassidy took his hand and hesitantly stood.

"Her, too. Stay outside and close to me." Flex was practically shouting because of the volume of the music.

"I really don't dance," she said as he led her to the floor.

He acted like he hadn't heard her over the music, remaining conscious of the narrow heels on her shoes and the perilous gaps between deck boards as they slowly made their way to the edge of the floor opposite the prying lenses of the photographers lurking across the harbor.

At the edge of the space, he stopped next to a middle-aged man doing what looked like a whirring blender imitation with his arms. With a grin, he drew Cassidy to safety a few feet away. She was hesitant to dance at first, only shifting her weight foot-to-foot and snapping her fingers, but after a few minutes, she loosened up a bit and added a little hip action.

Some color had come to her cheeks, and she was finally smiling, maybe for real this time.

When he glanced over at Dee, she was holding a beer bottle aloft, teaching some kind of dance combination to her new group of friends, who were trying not to spill their drinks as they attempted to imitate her moves.

Jack heaved out a sigh. For the first time since he'd walked through Dolores's door, he felt like coming to Blink had been a good idea. Maybe even a great idea. He did a little turn he'd learned for a choreographed dance from one of his earliest movies, an indie romantic comedy that was a box office flop. On the backside of the turn, he saw Flex was stationed just outside the dance area standing as close to them as possible without joining them.

The upbeat song ended and mellowed into an old 1940s big band ballad. After flashing him a shy smile coupled with a blush, Cassidy turned as if to go back to the table.

He took her hand, and she stopped. "You look familiar. Didn't we have a class together?" As expected, she gave him a puzzled look. He smiled and leaned in to whisper, "Because I could have sworn we had chemistry."

She rolled her eyes. "Ugh. Where do you find these awful pickup lines?"

"The internet is a wonderful thing." He glanced across the almost empty dance floor to the group of photographers still congregated on the pier at the far side of the harbor. This was the perfect opportunity to give them something else to send to their bosses. They had the image of him carrying her, the hug, and now they could back it up with something even more romantic to make the story stick. Marion would be pleased.

The tune was slow and sensuous. "Dance with me, Cassidy."

CHAPTER SEVENTEEN

Cassidy scanned the people on the dance floor. There were only three couples. The two senior couples were dancing in that old-fashioned ballroom-dancing style usually reserved for father-daughter wedding dances and black-and-white movies. The other pair was Niles and Amanda, and what they were doing couldn't be categorized as dancing. It was more of a stand and sway…and grope.

Panic. Sheer panic surged like ice water up her spine. With either style of dancing, Cassidy was way out of her element. She'd fall all over herself in these heels if she attempted what the older couples were doing—which honestly struck her as something an actor like Jack would know how to do with proficiency. And if they did what Amanda and Niles were doing… Yeah, Jack was probably proficient at that, too.

"I swear I don't bite," he said.

Obviously, her emotions were easy to read. Heart hammering, she gave a half-hearted attempt to smile. "There's rarely dancing here in Blink. I haven't had much practice."

"This takes no practice." He took her hands and placed them on his shoulders. "Feel my jacket?"

What a weird question. She ran her fingers over the shoulders of his tux, trying not to imagine shirtless Captain Blake Crusher from *Mad Planet*. "Uh, yeah?"

"Good. Because it's boyfriend material."

Hands still on his shoulders, she barked out a laugh. "Jack! Stop with the horrible pickup lines. Seriously. They're awful."

He wrapped his arms around her waist and began to sway to the music. "Made you laugh, though."

"*At* you."

His grin widened. "That's okay. *At* me, *with* me…you're laughing, and that's the goal."

"I thought the goal was to act like we could tolerate each other."

"Noooo," he said close to her ear. "The goal is to make everyone think we're mad about each other."

Gah. That rumbly voice thing was a problem. She put space between them, stiffened her spine, and swayed to the music with him, hyperaware of her neighbors' eyes on them. Being the center of attention wasn't her norm, and her skin heated as a blush crawled up to her neck and over her face.

"I was sincere when I said you were lovely."

Her face grew even hotter.

He slid his hands from either side of her waist to loop them behind the small of her back.

Cassidy took a deep breath in and let it out slowly. There was no reason for her to be self-conscious. The dance they were doing took no skill, so she wouldn't make a misstep. The roles they were playing amounted to nothing in the long run, so she couldn't get hurt. It was all an act.

She relaxed a bit and looped her arms behind his neck, which brought their bodies together.

His sway in time to the music didn't stop, but there was a slight hesitation, and he drew in a breath at the contact.

She breathed in deep through her nose and closed her eyes, enjoying the smell of starch and aftershave. After several measures of music, she relaxed enough to rest her cheek against his shoulder.

Slowly, he slid a hand up her spine and back down to her waist, and she sighed, melting against him.

"Okay?" he asked.

"Yes." For a moment, she forgot about their deal, their ground rules, and the fact they had absolutely nothing in common as his fingers left a warm, buzzy trail on her skin. Then she realized her back was to the reporters and the stroke up and down her bare skin was only for show.

"I like you in an evening gown with your hair up," he whispered in her ear. "But honestly, I like you in overalls and a ponytail better."

She stopped swaying and pulled back enough to look at his face. "That was more ridiculous than one of your terrible pickup lines."

His smile was brilliant. "Thereby proving that truth is often stranger than fiction. So, I have another one for you."

She bit her lip, unable to hide her smile.

"Knock knock," he said.

She shook her head. "Oh, no. Not going to go there."

"Knock knock," he repeated, slowly and deliberately.

She heaved an indulgent sigh and rolled her eyes. She needed to be careful, or she might start liking this guy. "Fine. Who's there?"

They began to sway again.

"When Where," he answered.

She groaned. "When Where, who?"

"Now. Here. Me. You."

She stared up into his dark eyes, glad he was holding her because as silly as that line was, it had worked, and her knees were wobbly—something she thought only happened in books and movies.

"May I kiss you?" he asked. "Nothing makes a fake relationship more believable than a kiss."

She should say no. Yeah. Absolutely. She should say no freaking way. It wasn't part of the ground rules. But rules were made to be broken, right? Or at least expanded. Swallowing hard, she glanced around. She was on the deck of her best friend's store surrounded by her neighbors and friends. She should 100 percent not kiss the hottest movie star on the planet in front of all of them. Heart hammering, she took in a deep breath through her nose. Jack made no move, waiting on her answer.

And as she stood there, a series of truths dawned on her, ticking through her head like a timer on a bomb: the most handsome man on earth wanted permission to kiss her, she hadn't been kissed since the summer after her senior year in high school, this whole thing was for show, the music had stopped, he'd turned them sideways to the photographers to give them the best shot, and darn it, despite all that, she really wanted to kiss him.

She took a deep breath, and heart hammering so hard it hurt, she whispered, "Yes."

And he did.

His lips were soft and teasing at first, but the moment she kissed him back, he made a little growly noise that made her dig her fingers into his shoulders. She forgot about everything and everyone as he tilted his head to deepen the kiss. His hands roamed up and down her back as his body pressed firm and hard against her. Little shimmery stars danced behind her eyelids and her body felt liquid. The man had talent.

A noise that seemed to start in the far distance grew closer and louder. Raindrops? No. Applause. *Applause?*

With a gasp, Cassidy pulled away, but Jack kept his arms around her. "It's okay. Your friends are just happy. I'm happy." He shot a glance across the water at the handful of creeps with their cameras still up. "The paparazzi are *really* happy, but the most important thing is, are you happy?"

She stared up at him, emotions battling between embarrassment and arousal. Arousal was winning. "Yes."

"Good. Smile, Cassidy. Preferably at me." His expression was warm and open, and she couldn't help but smile.

Loud dance beat music started, and the floor filled again with energetic dancers, but as if glued to the floor, Jack and Cassidy simply stared at each other.

"In the film world, they would call 'cut' at this point."

She laughed, glad he broke the tension with a joke.

"I think I'm going to call it a night," he said. "I was at the airport early this morning."

She nodded, still unable to move. "Jack, thanks for…" For what? For coming to fix the mess the mis-tag had made of her life? For making her feel special and "lovely?" For giving her the best kiss ever? Yeah, all of that.

But, instead, she settled for, "Thanks for the dance."

CHAPTER EIGHTEEN

Jack hadn't expected to get an arm workout first thing this morning, but his biceps were burning from holding the crown molding in place over his head in an awkward position for so long. He glanced behind him at Dee, who was working on her computer in the window seat that wasn't much of a window seat, since it was draped in drop cloths to keep prying eyes and cameras out.

"Almost done," Cassidy said before the compressor shaped like a yellow flying saucer cranked back up with a deafening roar.

Pow, pow, pow. The nail gun she used was even louder than the compressor. She climbed down her ladder and moved it next to his.

"Final stretch!" she shouted over the compressor as she climbed up next to him. "You could probably let go, but wait until I put a couple more in. This piece is heavy and old, and I don't want it to crack." She blew her bangs out of her face and pulled some slack into the air hose connected to her nail gun. He noticed she bit the end of her tongue when she nailed. Her tongue… His mind kept revisiting last night's kiss every few minutes, which made standing still like this difficult.

Pow, pow, pow.

He hadn't lied last night when he told Cassidy he preferred her in casual clothes. They suited. Her hair was pulled back in a ponytail and she was wearing a multicolored tie-dye shirt, which in combination with the paint-splattered overalls made her look like she'd gotten dressed in a spin-art machine.

"Okay, you can let go," she said—well, more like shouted.

His arms burned in protest when he lowered them. He climbed down the ladder to stand next to Amanda, who'd been filming the whole time. Both he and Amanda sighed in relief when the tank of the compressor was finally full, and the thing quit making a racket.

He should have taken Cassidy up on her offer of earplugs.

Pow, pow, pow.

"That's it!" Cassidy shouted, climbing down her ladder.

Amanda pointed at her own ears, and Cassidy grinned and pulled out her earplugs. "Sorry. I suppose I was yelling, huh?"

"Yes, you were," a voice came from the stairway. "And it also sounded like you were firing pistols while jackhammering."

Tristan looked like he hadn't slept any better than Jack had. Jack knew what had kept *him* up tossing and turning, and not just the ancient lumpy mattress in what obviously used to be Tristan's room. Cassidy James.

Every time Jack had started to drift off, his mind would turn to her and the fact she was in the next room, and he'd be wide awake again.

Cassidy smiled at Tristan. "Sorry if I woke you up. I waited as long as I could to start."

He groaned and rubbed his eyes. Tristan was evidently not a morning person.

"There's a pot of coffee in the kitchen," Cassidy said.

Tristan grunted his thanks and shuffled past them toward the dining room that opened into the kitchen.

"So, what's the plan for the rest of the day?" Amanda asked. "I was thinking I'd grab Dee and take her with me to the Living Sharpe studios, since she clicked so well with the design team last night, if that's okay. They're having a cake tasting in their outdoor lot to test out some potential upcoming recipes for their magazine."

Dee's eyes lit up, then she looked down at her computer screen, businesslike mask back in place.

"I think that's a great idea," Jack said.

Dee opened her mouth to protest, but he held up a hand and she closed it.

"Marion said she wouldn't be here until late afternoon, and this may be the last bit of downtime you get for the rest of the trip," he said. "Go hang out with your friends. We'll know when Marion gets here, count on it. There'll be signs of her arrival like in one of those movies where the seas part, or the heavens go black, or the sky fills with locusts or birds, or dragons, or some other doomsday pestilence." He was pleased to see a smile pulling at the edges of Dee's lips. "Until then, we should all take advantage of this beautiful day." He looked at Cassidy. "That includes you."

"C'mon," Amanda said, holding her hand out to Dee. "We'll go to the studio and then to the

Starfish Diner. Sally's making her homemade chicken soup today, and it's delicious, so we'll have to go light at the cake tasting."

Before they made it to the door, Amanda winked at Cassidy over her shoulder. "Have fun," she mouthed before closing the door behind them.

"Your friend has totally bought into our plan, I see," Jack said.

Cassidy heaved a sigh. "She's so excited about the prospect that you and I have a thing going, I'm kinda glad I don't have to tell her the truth."

"What truth?" Tristan asked from the archway into the foyer.

Cassidy tensed, but before Jack could create a good story for the guy, the door yanked open and Flex charged in like they were under siege.

"What's wrong?" Jack asked, honestly glad for the diversion.

"Where's Dee going?" the big man asked.

"To the Living Sharpe studios with Amanda."

"But Ms. Hill told us to remain here," he said, eyes wide. "We weren't even supposed to go to that party last night."

Jack almost laughed. Even a big, bad dude like Flex was rattled by the formidable Marion Hill. "She won't be here for hours and hours. Relax, Flex. Take it easy while you can."

The man's brow furrowed. Taking it easy was probably a nonsensical phrase to this guy. He'd never seen Flex relax even a little bit.

"Okay," Jack said, hands up in surrender, "you can stay intense while Cassidy and I take it easy."

Cassidy shook her head. "I need to finish—"

"You need to finish showing me the harbor and that gorgeous blue water beyond," Jack interrupted, taking her hand. From the corner of his eye, he noticed Tristan push away from where he was leaning against the archway. "This noisy thing is not invited." Jack took the nail gun from her hand and set it on the floor, then flipped off the red power switch on the compressor.

He leaned in and whispered in her ear, "Indulge me." He smiled at her little shiver. Her ears were sensitive.

"I should change," she said, pulling her hand away and gesturing to her work clothes.

"Not on my account. Like I told you, I'm a fan of this look on you."

Tristan snorted.

"Bless you," Jack said.

Tristan raised an eyebrow, knowing full well Jack didn't think he'd sneezed.

Cassidy raked her bangs out of her face and shrugged one shoulder. "Okay, then. A harbor tour, it is."

Flex led the way out the door, no doubt to clear whatever imaginary villains lurked in their path. Jack held the door for Cassidy, and when he looked back, Tristan was standing in the middle of the archway looking like the only kid not invited to a birthday party.

CHAPTER NINETEEN

Cassidy absently ran her fingers over her lips as she descended the steps from Dolores's huge wraparound porch. Her lips tingled every time she thought about her kiss with Jack last night, so she'd been nonstop tingly, which was irritating.

She caught Jack's sly smile as he caught up with her on the bottom step, and she lowered her hand, fighting back a blush. It's not like he could know what she was thinking about or anything. He winked, and she lost the fight with her blush. Yeah, he knew. Maybe he was thinking about it, too. Other parts of her buzzed to life at that thought.

Stop, Cassidy. This guy is trouble.

There was a trail from where Dolores sat at the top of the hill that led down to the beach just outside the mouth of the harbor. Cassidy had decided that was the place she'd take Jack first because it was her favorite, and maybe the sea air would blow that kiss out of her mind. If not, a dousing in the frigid Atlantic certainly would.

Flex followed Cassidy and Jack, keeping himself between them and the photographers who had been lurking outside Roger's house, often hanging back to keep the vultures out of hearing distance.

"It's okay," Jack said from behind her on the trail after she'd turned around to look for the dozenth time. "Flex will keep them away. They're just doing their jobs. Marion will know how to get rid of them. She's done this since dinosaurs roamed the earth."

She stepped over a football-size rock on the path. "I don't know whether to be afraid or intrigued by Marion."

"Be afraid. Be very afraid!" he said dramatically.

She was sure it was some movie quote she didn't recognize. Even with all the negative things he said about her, Cassidy could tell Jack liked and respected the woman.

"She's scheduled to arrive later this afternoon?" she asked.

"That's what she texted Dee."

"Good. Because I'd rather be wearing something different when I see her this time." She gestured to her work clothes.

"You'll have plenty of time."

They stopped when they'd made it to the head of the trail before it descended to the rocky beach below. This was her favorite view. If she turned a circle, she could see the ocean, the harbor, a part of the roof of her family's little cabin in the trees on the other side of the harbor, and even some of the buildings in the new town square in the distance. Of course, she could also see lovely lady Dolores where she stood at the start of this trail overlooking it all, as she had for over a century.

"Wow," Jack said. "What a view."

For a moment they stood side by side as the wind whipped around them, like they were in a movie of their own.

"Fantastic," he said. "And you get to see it any

time you want."

It surprised her how pleased she was by his re-action. For some reason, it was important to her that Jack like Blink, even though she didn't like Jack—or at least that's what she kept telling her-self.

Resisting the urge to touch her lips again, she gestured for him to lead the way down to the beach. With a grin, he struck out. He was agile, which made sense considering his profession. She liked having him in front of her where she could look at him without him staring back.

He was wearing a hunter green T-shirt tucked into well-worn blue jeans. She sighed and forced her eyes away from his backside to his feet. Like her, he had on hard-soled boots that held up well on the rocky path to the beach.

"Gorgeous," Jack said as they picked their way over the rocky beach toward the water. "It's so raw and primitive."

Behind them, Flex was taking his time on the trail down, keeping the paparazzi at bay. A couple of them appeared to have given up, remaining at the top, probably not willing to risk their expen-sive equipment. For all Cassidy knew, the picture taking might be better from up there.

"How do you stand it?" she asked.

Jack turned his attention from the water to her. "Stand what?"

"Those creeps following you around all the time."

He hooked his thumbs in his front belt loops. "It's part of my job. Marion has a saying: with great fame comes great inconvenience."

"And no privacy whatsoever," she added, wandering away to sit on a large, low, flat rock the diameter of a tractor wheel.

"I have plenty of privacy." He waggled his eyebrows. "You'd be surprised how creative I can be."

She didn't doubt that at all.

He sat next to her, not touching, but close enough that she could feel the heat rolling off his skin. He took in a deep breath, turning his face toward the ocean as he raked his fingers through his hair. "I make it a point to not do anything I'm embarrassed about or that I want to hide so they don't bug me that much. They're a nuisance and make it hard to get around sometimes, but it's part of the job. It's a lot harder for celebrities with kids."

Cassidy scooted forward on the rock and leaned over to scoop up a round pebble the size of a shooter marble. "I don't think I could ever get used to it."

"You'd be surprised. I have an actor friend from the South somewhere—one of those states with mosquitos year-round. He says he thinks of the paparazzi as mosquitos, always annoying, but inevitable. You just learn to deal with them."

Yeah, well, she didn't like mosquitoes, either. "When did you decide to become an actor?"

"When I fell into it by accident," he said. "My sister, Bryn, was at UCLA when our mom died from an aneurysm. I'd just graduated high school. I went out there to be with Bryn." His dark eyes were focused on one of the lobster boats in the distance. "Being right out of high school, I had no real skills, so I worked as a grocery store stocker during the day and at the front desk of a gym at night. Neither job paid well, but I got a free gym membership, which ended up being the most valuable benefit imaginable."

She could imagine it. Just like she could imagine the shirtless *Mad Planet* scenes.

"A woman came into the store one day when I was unloading cans of green beans. There were stacks of boxes of them on this big rolling dolly. I had to cut open the top of the boxes and unload them onto the shelves, only someone had misloaded the cart and there were some boxes of canned peaches on top of the green beans. I picked up two of the boxes and moved them to the other end of the cart so I could get to the green beans. Well, the woman saw me and asked me how old I was, and I told her I was eighteen. She was impressed with how easily I had moved the boxes and asked me if she could see my biceps."

"That's weird." Cassidy flipped her bangs out of her face.

Jack smiled, eyes still focused on the lobster boat as if he were seeing the grocery store scene in his mind. "Yeah, I thought it was an odd request, too, but I was eighteen and proud of my body, so I rolled up my sleeve and flexed." He flashed a grin. "And that was that. A star was born."

He picked up a rock and tossed it out into the water.

Cassidy swiveled to face him. "Wait a minute. You can't just stop mid-story like that. I mean, if you end it there, it's just a flex for some pervy woman in a grocery store. Who was the woman? What happened next?"

There were little crinkles at the corners of his eyes when he smiled.

"The woman was the casting director for a TV series that was set in a high school, who fortunately for me needed a can of tomatoes for a dinner casserole and happened to see me as the perfect fit for a bit part in an upcoming episode. No lines. No shirt." He laughed. "But it got me an agent who set me up with an acting coach. I'd done a good bit of acting in high school but hadn't considered it as a career. Terrible odds of success."

"Yet here you are."

"Yet here I am. With you."

For a moment, she held her breath. Superstar Jack Winston was here, in nowhere Blink, with nobody her, and he seemed to be genuinely happy about it. His back was to the cameras, so unlike the kiss last night, this little bit wasn't all for show—at least it didn't seem that way. Something in her chest pinched—not painful, but not comfortable, either.

"Enough about me. Tell me about you. How did you end up with your own construction company?"

She stood and faced up the coastline, soothing herself with the familiar. She loved how the rocky beach seemed to go on forever as it rounded the cliffs farther north. "It was my dad's company." She ran her fingers over the smooth stone in her pocket. "He called me Little Miss Fix-It because I would hang out with him after school and help with whatever he was building. Pretty sure I was more of a hindrance in the early years, but he never let on and always made me feel useful and talented until I really *was* useful and talented. I learned so much from him. It was only natural I'd take over the company along with my brother, Luke. As you know, he has big plans to expand with crews and whatnot when he graduates. I'm happy with whatever he feels like taking on. I'll keep doing what I do."

"Restoring that cool Victorian," Jack said.

Something in her warmed at his appreciation of the old building. "That and helping with little things for my neighbors. I prefer handyman work to big construction, though I can do both."

He brushed some hair that had escaped her ponytail behind her ear, and she fought to keep from leaning into his touch. "I imagine there is very little you cannot do, Cassidy James."

There was one thing. She couldn't kiss him, and right about now, it was the one thing she wanted to do most. She glanced over at Flex and the reporters who had their cameras up and were firing off shots. Had Jack only touched her for that reason? He'd looked so sincere…and, well, that kiss last night had *felt* way more than sincere.

She closed her eyes and let the air coming off the water blow some sense into her brain. Of course it was all for show. Everything this man did was for show, including—no, *especially* their kiss last night. They'd made an agreement, and Jack was simply keeping up his end of the bargain. She would, too.

She opened her eyes. "Let's go to the harbor and visit Wright Boat Works. Caleb is always working on something cool, and if we're lucky, we can hitch a ride to the diner for lunch."

She struck out toward the lower trail that led to the harbor. As if hit by an electric shock, the paparazzi near Flex and those at the top of the hill jumped into action, gathering up their gear and falling into step to follow.

As they hit the spot where the trail widened before meeting up with the boardwalk ringing the harbor, Cassidy glanced over her shoulder at Jack, whose eyes were focused on her butt. She stopped, cleared her throat, and faced him, hands on hips.

The maddening man didn't even blush or look down. "Like I said earlier, great view."

Here, she'd thought to do a "gotcha" on him, and instead, he'd turned it right around, making her face heat in what was undoubtedly a stellar blush.

Behind them, a couple of camera shutters clicked, no doubt Jack's objective.

She turned and resumed their trek, again wondering how he tolerated it. She was certain she'd be frazzled beyond redemption if she had to put up with people following her around all the time. Fortunately, she'd never have to find out. She and Jack lived in different worlds on opposite sides of the country, and when this bargain was over, they'd never have to deal with each other again.

CHAPTER TWENTY

The Starfish Diner, like the harbor, looked like a movie set. It was a perfect, fifties-vibe small-town diner with a black-and-white checkered floor, red vinyl booth benches, a large, Formica counter with a chrome trim, and chrome-and-vinyl stools.

Jack was seated at a table across from Roger and Caleb. Next to him, Cassidy squirmed uncomfortably in her chair, no doubt because of the pack of people who'd followed them into the diner and had set up camp at the opposite end of the place.

He reached under the table and patted her knee. "They need to eat, too. At least your friend, Sally, will make some money off them. Besides"—he gestured over his shoulder with his thumb to the big man in the chair at a table directly behind him—"Flex will take care of them if they get too close."

She nodded. Jack took in a deep breath through his nose, and even through the strong coffee and baked bread smell filling the place, he picked up the faint scent of honeysuckle that clung to Cassidy's hair.

"We had a blast at the studio," Amanda said from her chair on the other side of Cassidy. "The Italian Cream Cake and the strawberry shortcake won, but they were all winners."

Sally, whom he'd met last night at the party, hustled up to the table, shoving her notebook into her apron pocket. She pushed her glasses up on her nose and scanned the table. "I hope everyone enjoyed the soup."

"Might be the best I've ever eaten," Jack said, rubbing his belly.

Sally flushed pink, then efficiently refilled water and coffee and shuffled off, disappearing through two swinging doors with round portholes.

For a few moments, the table ate in silence. There was only one empty seat between Roger and Tristan.

From the end on Jack's side, Dee's phone rang, and she excused herself to leave the table to answer it.

"Did you go to the cake tasting, Tristan?" Jack asked.

He looked up from his phone long enough to shake his head.

"Tristan is getting the Blink Medical Clinic all staffed and organized," Roger said, lifting his coffee cup in salute to his son. Then with a big grin, he said, "He's also interviewing interior designers to give the old house a new look before it hits the market."

Next to him, Cassidy jumped. "Wait. What? What about my restoration?"

It struck Jack that Roger was way too animated about this—his eyes twinkled like he was about to deliver a punchline. "You'll still keep the repairs going, Cassy. No matter what the designer does, the damage still needs repair." He gave a theatrical sigh. "The place has sat empty for too long. A house needs to be lived in."

"You don't need a designer. The design is perfect," she said, twisting her napkin in her lap. "It shouldn't be altered. In fact, the few modernizations added over the years should be restored to the way it was originally."

Tristan snorted. "Yeah, there should definitely be no electricity and no running water."

"This house most likely always had electricity," Cassidy huffed. "Probably knob and tube originally. And that's not what I mean, Tristan. Updating for safety and comfort is one thing. I'm talking about the design—the aesthetics of the house, like the vinyl flooring in the bathrooms that was probably added in the seventies." She was gripping the edge of the table. Her nails were still painted red from last night, and they struck Jack as wrong. "The aesthetics cannot be improved from the original design."

Yeah, she was right there. Maybe that's why the bright red nails seemed wrong. Like the house, the original Cassidy was best.

He glanced at Roger, who was leaning back in his seat, clearly delighted with the outcome of his little bombshell about the designer.

Jack narrowed his eyes. The old man was up to something.

Tristan put his phone down and cleared his throat. "When Dad and I had our meeting yesterday evening, we discussed the sale of the house and what it would take to unload that dinosaur." He picked up his water glass and took a sip. "A designer might be able to make it appeal to someone who wants to live in it and not just buy it as a tear-down."

Cassidy's mouth opened and closed a few times, then she said, "Tear-down?"

Roger reached across the table and patted her hand. "Nobody's tearing it down, Cassidy."

That seemed to relax her a bit. She sat back and studied the scarred Formica tabletop, no doubt deep in thought over the fate of Dolores.

Dee returned to the table wearing the emotionless face she wore around Marion, which made Jack's chest tighten. He'd loved seeing her animated and laughing last night at the party and then again today when she returned from the Living Sharpe studios. She picked up her spoon and took a sip of her soup, which by now had to be cold. The phone call had thrown her off. It had been from Marion, no doubt.

"The first designer is coming to look at the place tomorrow morning at nine o'clock," Tristan said. "She's done some great makeovers in Portland, including a friend of mine's office. She specializes in ultramodern themes with homages to the past."

Cassidy grabbed her napkin from her lap and balled it in her fist under the table. Jack wrapped his arm across the back of her chair, hoping she perceived it as a gesture of support.

"What does that mean?" Roger asked.

"It means this," Tristan said, turning his phone toward Roger.

"That's a white room with black furniture and one place on the wall showing brick behind some kind of glass," Roger said, squinting at the phone across the empty space left between him and his son.

Tristan showed the photo to Cassidy, who gasped, then turned the screen toward himself and grinned. "Yes. That's her signature look. Super sleek and monochromatic with an occasional surprise from the past. In this home, she plastered over the old brick and overdone wood trim but left a sample of the original materials with glass over it signifying the past is something we can't touch but can observe and admire."

Cassidy pushed to her feet and dropped her napkin on the table. "Excuse me," she said before striding behind the diner counter and pushing through the stainless-steel swinging doors into the kitchen.

Roger chuckled, like this was what he'd planned and expected. He met Jack's gaze with a lift of an eyebrow, as if in challenge. Or maybe it was a dare. *What are you up to, old man?*

Tristan, on the other hand, looked genuinely surprised by Cassidy's reaction. Brows drawn together, he studied the kitchen doors that were still swinging back and forth.

"Excuse me, please." Jack stood and headed toward the kitchen, Flex only feet behind him.

CHAPTER TWENTY-ONE

Cassidy leaned back against the steel cooler door and closed her eyes, heart squeezing so hard she thought it might burst. "*Why*, Sally?" she moaned. "Dolores is perfect. She was constructed back when things were built to last for centuries. And the designer's concept is that we can't touch history? It can only be looked at behind glass and admired?" She shook her head, feeling like it was full of hornets. "I touch history every time I enter that house. The ornate moldings. The details that were designed and carved by hand, not created on a computer and stamped out by a machine." She sucked in a breath. "That old saying, 'They don't make 'em like they used to'? It's true. Dolores is one of a kind."

Hornets still buzzing in her head, she allowed Sally to pull her into a hug. Cassidy relaxed into Sally's familiar arms. This woman had been like a mother to her and Luke after their own mom had died when they were children. The smell of baked bread and starch from Sally's apron enveloped her like a warm blanket, and she instantly felt better. It didn't stop the tears from stinging behind her eyelids, though.

"How could Roger do this?" Cassidy's voice was muffled against Sally's shoulder.

"Well, honey, it's too much house for him. Has been for years." Sally's voice was like a lullaby, and

Cassidy's tense muscles began to release.

"But why let Tristan decide how she's remodeled? He doesn't even *live* here." Her voice sounded like she was six again.

Sally took Cassidy's face in her hands. "Look at me, Cassy-girl."

She raised her eyes to Sally's and blinked back her tears.

Sally brushed aside her bangs. "You and I both know that Roger McGuffy holds dear what his daddy and his granddaddy built here, including that house. He won't let it be damaged."

Cassidy sniffled, irritated she felt so much like a child. "But—"

"But nothing," Sally cut in. "Roger's scheming again. That's all. He wants Tristan to move back here. Maybe if the boy feels some ownership of the house, he'd be more likely to stay."

"He plans to destroy it. You didn't see that picture. It was awful." She buried her face in Sally's shoulder.

"I agree with Sally," Jack's deep voice said from somewhere behind her.

She turned to see Flex just inside the doors and Jack leaning casually against the prep counter a few feet from where Sally's new cook was scraping the grill with a metal spatula. How long had Jack been standing there? She should be embarrassed that he'd seen her like this, but something about his calm, steady presence was reassuring. A man like him should not be reassuring. She sniffled and flipped her bangs out of her eyes.

"I think Roger's running some long game with

his son using you and the house as chess pieces," Jack said. "I'm pretty sure I play into it somehow also. Tristan wasn't far off when he said Roger invited all of us to stay at the house for a reason."

Cassidy's throat tightened, and she pulled out of Sally's embrace. "Roger's a nice man. A good man. A kind man."

"I agree. I think the game Roger's playing is motivated by love, not malice." Jack remained perfectly still. "Nonetheless, I still think it's a game. I'd be surprised if he let anyone except you touch that house."

He sounded so certain, she felt herself believing him. "Really?"

"Absolutely. When you left the table, he looked like a cat with the cream."

She huffed. She shouldn't be surprised. Roger was always up to something.

Jack held out his hand, and she stared at it, wanting to take it so badly her fingers twitched. But she didn't.

"Let's go along with his plan and see where it leads us," Jack said. "I'm pretty good at improvisation, and you know all the players. I bet we can meet or beat Roger at his own game." He pushed away from the counter and approached her, hand still outstretched.

The NDA loomed in her mind. She had to keep up the act that she and Jack were into each other. Even in front of Sally. She took his hand, and he laced his fingers through hers, as if they'd known each other for years, not a little over twenty-four hours.

"Do we have a deal?" he asked.

Her heart felt a billion pounds lighter. "You know we do."

His answering smile was stunning. Like, literally stunned her to the point her breath caught and she was frozen in place. Time stood still for a moment until it was broken by the crash of the doors being shoved open.

"Mr. Winston, I hate to interrupt you." Dee's voice was strained. "Ms. Hill is back from Bangor."

Jack's grip remained loose, and his expression was relaxed as he answered, "Thanks, Dee. Please find out where she's staying and tell her we'll meet her in an hour."

Cassidy let out her breath in relief. That would give her time to clean up and put on something presentable before seeing the woman again.

"No, Mr. Winston, I mean she's *here*." She pointed to the doors. "Like out there. Right now."

Just when Cassidy's heart had returned to a normal rhythm and the world seemed right again, *this*. Marion Hill, the person she couldn't allow to see any weakness, had arrived, and here she was, hiding in the kitchen sporting ratty paint clothes and a tear-blotched face.

Perfect.

CHAPTER TWENTY-TWO

With Cassidy's small hand in his, Jack lifted his chin and strode into the diner, expecting to find Marion the Megalodon standing in front of her squadron of carefully selected security and media soldiers. Instead, she was seated in the chair at the table between Roger and Tristan, head back, laughing.

Jack and Cassidy halted behind the counter.

She was laughing.

Megalodons laughed.

In the two years he'd worked closely with Marion Hill, he'd never once seen her laugh.

The paparazzi were still seated at their table at the other end of the diner, cameras nowhere in sight. They were watching Jack and Cassidy closely, though. No doubt the dramatic escape to the kitchen had caught their attention.

"I told them if they took so much as a single picture, they were outta here," Sally whispered. She winked. "There are a few advantages to being the only three-meal restaurant in a small town. Obey or starve." She leaned her elbows on the counter. "Your friend seems nice. She paid for everyone's meal, including theirs." She indicated the paparazzi with her thumb.

Nice? Marion? Jack shook his head to clear it. Yep. She was still smiling and laughing. "Uh, yeah. Nice," he said. Then this alternate reality flipped back to the familiar when Marion glanced up and noticed him…and Cassidy, who gripped his hand tighter under Marion's scrutiny.

The woman not only had the world's most spectacular resting-bitch-face, she'd perfected the look-down-her-nose technique that rendered the recipient powerless.

"Imagine her wearing a clown nose," Jack whispered in Cassidy's ear. "Or a mud mask. Or pink hair rollers. Or better yet, all three at once."

Cassidy bit her lip to keep from smiling, and he relaxed.

"Good to see you, Marion," Jack called.

"I was just telling Marion, here, about the time Cassidy helped Mrs. Phipps rescue the kitty cats living in her boiler room," Roger said.

Marion giggled—honest to God giggled.

"I haven't heard that one," Jack said.

"Well, it'll have to wait." Marion stood. Roger stood as well and pulled her chair back. "Thank you, Mr. McGuffy."

He took her hand and patted it. "My pleasure, Ms. Hill."

Tristan stared at his dad as if he'd spoken some long-dead language as Marion rounded the table wearing a smart pantsuit with matching navy-blue purse and shoes.

"If you're ready to leave, Mr. Winston, I'd like to arrange a word with you." Marion looked from Jack to Cassidy, pausing briefly on the paint-spattered overalls. "Both of you, if possible."

Jack nodded and gestured for her to lead the way. Marion stopped in front of the door, and Jack pulled it open for her, bells jangling overhead. Wordlessly, she walked through and headed toward a big SUV with tinted windows. A man in a black suit stepped out and opened both the front and back passenger doors.

"Do you need a ride?" Marion asked.

What he needed was a stiff drink, to be honest. "Caleb gave us a ride here, so yes, that would be great."

"I met Caleb's father, Gus, at the harbor, where I'm staying," Marion said, sliding into the front seat.

He and Cassidy exchanged looks. There were no hotels at the harbor, or anywhere in Blink for that matter.

Marion gracefully climbed into the front seat of the vehicle. "What are you waiting for? Hurry up."

Jack turned to Cassidy, Dee, and Flex. "Are you aware that prehistoric sharks called Megalodons grew as large as fifty feet, maybe even longer, and had teeth up to seven inches long?"

· · ·

"Whoa," Cassidy said as they drove under the Hideaway Harbor sign and pulled up next to Wright Boat Works. "That's a big yacht. The biggest I've seen in Hideaway Harbor for sure."

Jack leaned forward to get a better look at it through the windshield. It was a sleek vessel with a shiny black hull, not huge, but large enough to look out of place in Blink's harbor.

After they got out, Marion pulled her phone

from her handbag and dialed. "No photos now," she said to someone on the other end. She looked over her shoulder at Cassidy. "We're not ready," Marion added, phone to ear. "Tell them we'll be on the deck at three o'clock." She stopped and studied Cassidy again. "Make that four." She disconnected the call and shoved the phone in her handbag before climbing the gangway, leaving them standing on the wooden walkway.

"Well, come on," Marion said with a frustrated huff before disappearing inside the impressive yacht's cabin.

"Seven-inch teeth?" Cassidy asked under her breath as she stepped onto the gangway.

"The ultimate predator," Jack answered, following her.

CHAPTER TWENTY-THREE

When they reached the top of the gangway, a man in a crisp, white uniform complete with gold braids greeted them at the top. "Welcome aboard," he said, gesturing to a doorway.

Once inside, Cassidy blinked, trying to make out the interior of the room, which seemed too dark. Her dad had called the time needed to adjust from bright sunshine to the darker indoors "barn blindness." It wasn't long before the plush interior with its expensive woods and heavy furniture came clearly into focus, making her feel even more uncomfortable. The way Marion had studied her had made her feel inadequate, something she rarely felt. Her dad had raised her to be strong and had instilled a strong self-image in Cassidy, which was fostered by her neighbors in Blink. She wasn't going to let this woman, Marion, undo an entire lifetime of training.

Raising her chin, Cassidy faced the table in the corner where Marion was instructing a team of four people. Every now and then one would look up at her and then quickly look away.

While Flex stood just inside the doorway and Dee took notes next to Marion, Jack led Cassidy to a comfortable seating area and lowered himself next to her on a sofa.

"She's really not as bad as you think," he whispered.

MARISSA CLARKE   181

Well, that didn't say much, because Cassidy
hadn't seen anything good from the woman yet
other than her laughter at the diner about the silly
cat story. Why would Roger do that? Heck, why
Roger did anything was hard to figure out, but he
always had a motive. She suspected Marion Hill
was a schemer, too.

Dee approached and set a piece of paper on
the coffee table between Jack and Cassidy. On it
was a handwritten schedule that started with haircut and new clothes and ended with makeup and
script review. Obviously, Marion didn't like
Cassidy's usual style as much as Jack did and intended to do a complete makeover. She studied
her chipped red nails and thought about getting
ready for last night's party. Never once did she feel
like Lillian and her team were trying to change
her, but somehow, she didn't think Marion would
have that gentle a touch.

"She's here to help us," Jack said. "She makes
magic. The goal is to restore your life back to normal."

"And to make me out to be someone you're
dating, don't forget," she added with more acid
than she'd intended.

He gave a nod. "And to increase your online
visibility." There was a slight edge to his voice as
well.

She gestured to the list in front of them. "She's
going to change me into someone else."

"You could *never* be changed into someone
else. Not even by Marion the Megalodon."

Cassidy couldn't stop the little smile tugging at

the corners of her mouth.

Jack took her hand and placed it palm down on her thigh. "Like that nail polish, it's only temporary."

She flipped her bangs out of her face.

"And admit it, you could use a haircut," he added. "I trust her, Cassidy. She's only doing what we're doing. She's creating a scenario to meet specific goals."

Fair enough. "Okay," she said, picking at the polish on her thumbnail as she watched Marion giving instructions to the people around her. "But I don't like it."

Jack patted her knee. "Neither do I."

A man wearing a similar uniform to the one who greeted them when they came aboard approached. "Welcome aboard *The Illusion*. My name is Brad. May I bring you a drink?"

The Illusion?

She and Jack met gazes, and she found herself holding her breath until she couldn't anymore. The giggles started quietly, but once he joined in, they grew into a chuckle, then laughter, and eventually into full-on guffaws.

She stopped laughing when a tabloid was smacked down on the table in front of her. She'd seen this rag in the grocery store checkout line. It was one of Amanda's favorites. *The Hollywood Inquisitor*.

"They certainly move fast," Jack said, picking the paper up and placing it on his lap.

Cassidy's face grew hot and was probably as red as her dress in the pictures on the cover. The large one was of their kiss on the dance floor, and the smaller one was from when Jack had swept her into his arms when her shoe caught in the deck planks.

"You knew I was returning today, Mr. Winston. I had hoped you would afford me the courtesy of waiting." Cassidy wanted to cringe. The woman had a commanding air—like Amanda when she was feeling bossy, only more intimidating.

Jack relaxed into the cushions and draped his arm across the back of the sofa behind Cassidy. "Some things can't wait." He turned the paper so that Cassidy could see it better. "You look great," he said. "We make a lovely couple."

Lovely. The word brought back that warm feeling from when he'd said it last night. She studied the paper. Sophisticated Cassidy in the photo looked like an entirely different person from the one in her restoration videos. Different from who sat here right now.

"Kudos on this endeavor at least," Marion said. "It's a starting point I can work with rather than an obstacle to overcome." Again, she swept her eyes over Cassidy. "I already have plenty of obstacles."

Yeah, like a snotty attitude, Cassidy thought. She knew Jack admired this woman, but Cassidy wasn't feeling it. Not even a little bit.

"I assume you have reviewed the schedule?" Marion asked Cassidy.

"I have, but I need to work on the house sometime today, so—" Cassidy fell silent at Marion's icy stare.

"Working at the house is not on the schedule today, Miss James. Today, we work on *you* and launch our campaign."

Work on me?

Just as Cassidy was about to let Marion know exactly what she could do with her schedule, Jack placed the tabloid back onto the coffee table and said, "Hey, Marion. Did you know that Megalodons are estimated to have had a life span of forty to fifty years, but it's believed that some may have lived to be as old as eighty and maybe even a hundred?"

Cassidy almost busted out laughing again when Dee snorted, then covered her nose and mouth in horror.

Marion straightened and studied him down her nose. "I'm sorry, Mr. Winston. I assume that was rhetorical in that it is completely unrelated to our discussion topic."

He shrugged. "Just a fun fact I learned from one of my nephew's books." He circled his hand casually. "Carry on with your discussion topic."

Marion narrowed her eyes on him, no doubt certain he was up to something, but Jack had already accomplished what Cassidy knew was his goal: he'd defused her anger with his joke.

"Let's get started then, shall we?" Marion said, gesturing the people from the table over. "We'll start with hair and makeup while Johnathan gets measurements and makes alterations to the wardrobe we brought."

Why would they bring a wardrobe? She had plenty of outfits. "I'm not going to wear my own clothes?"

"Absolutely not."

The woman had said those two simple words with so much disdain, the hair at the base of Cassidy's neck prickled.

"Oh, here's another fun fact," Jack said. "Megalodons' jaws were strong enough to crush a car, though, of course, there were no cars back then, so."

Marion's face reddened only slightly. Other than that, she showed no change of expression. "The Riviera, Mr. Winston. You plucked me off a beach in front of one of the finest resorts on the French Riviera to take this position. That's a fun fact, too, I believe."

"A very fun fact, and I'm grateful," Jack said. "But this guns-blazing approach you've adopted is off-putting and, honestly, flat-out rude. Cassidy is mixed up in this because of a mistake on our end. She's doing *us* a favor, not the reverse. She's a great sport and part of our team, and I'd like it if we all acted like a team."

Everyone in the room remained silent as Marion said nothing. There was no movement at all except the rise and fall of Marion's chest as she took deep breaths and studied Jack's face.

"You're right," she said finally. "I've been rude. I apologize, Miss James. I tend to become hyper-focused on an end goal and unfortunately lose sight of…well, things like manners and other people's feelings."

Cassidy was pretty sure she looked like a cartoon character with her mouth gaping open in shock. She closed her mouth and nodded, then said, "I appreciate that you came all this way to help clear up the problem." She stood. "I'm all yours. Let's get started."

And just like that, Cassidy was hustled from the room surrounded by a team of people hired to trim, groom, gloss, decorate, and dress her until she became...who knew what.

CHAPTER TWENTY-FOUR

Jack tried to relax on one of the lounge chairs on the deck of *The Illusion* while the team of stylists worked on Cassidy. Every now and then, he studied the revised *Mad Planet 4* screenplay Marion had brought him, but the words jumbled together, kind of like his emotions.

Coming to Blink had been a terrible idea.

The top page of the tabloid on the table next to him fluttered in the breeze coming off the harbor, and he stared at the photo of him and Cassidy kissing.

Or maybe coming to Blink had been a wonderful idea.

Since he was surrounded by an army of security guards Marion had brought along with her, Flex had felt comfortable leaving long enough to go with Dee to get his and Cassidy's things from Roger's house. Marion had insisted they stay on the ship for the sake of security and believability, and Jack was good with that plan. He was pretty sure a yacht this swanky would be much more comfortable than Tristan's childhood room with its lumpy mattress.

The yacht had been a great idea on Marion's part, especially considering Blink's lack of accommodations. She'd driven from Bangor to where she'd chartered the ship and crew out of some nearby port, bringing half a dozen or so bodyguards and a handful of reporters with her, as well as the team of four makeover artists currently working on Cassidy. He'd resisted the urge to text Cassidy at least a dozen times over the last two hours.

He picked his phone up and considered texting to let her know it was okay to say no to something she didn't like—and to tell her to not let them make any drastic changes. He liked the way she looked as she was but ultimately decided it was none of his business. He set the phone back down with a sigh.

Closing his eyes, he pictured her on the dance floor last night as she looked up at him right before their lips met. He groaned in frustration. Imagining that was a worse idea than texting her. He opened his eyes and watched a seagull riding the wind currents above the ship, rising and falling effortlessly, only occasionally flapping its wings.

He had to stop thinking about Cassidy in a romantic sense. No more fixating on that kiss. She was only going through with this ridiculous scheme in order to get rid of the paparazzi. He needed to harden his feelings toward her. The whole thing was a dead end. And then, he remembered how upset she'd been by the prospect of someone destroying Dolores and his conviction to harden his heart collapsed.

"Hey, Dee?" he called, knowing she was sitting at a table a few yards behind him.

"Yes," she said, appearing at the side of his lounger.

"Could you please put a nine a.m. appointment

on tomorrow's shared calendar?"

"Sure. What label?"

"Label it 'Dolores designer meeting.'"

She nodded, fingers flying over her phone as she strolled back toward her table.

"Hey, Dee?"

"Yes, sir?"

"It's Saturday night. Surely your pack of girlfriends at Living Sharpe have plans of some kind?"

There was a long silence, but he didn't turn around to watch her. Finally, she answered, "I think some of the production team are taking the Living Sharpe bus and going to dinner and then a club in one of the bigger towns south of here."

"We've got things nailed down here tonight. Marion has meticulously planned a staged romantic dinner for two plus the press and whatnot. Why don't you take the night off?"

Another pause. "I would need to run that by Ms. Hill."

He'd let this go on for too long. Marion was a genius, but he couldn't let Dee become collateral damage. "Ms. Hill works for *me*, Dee. *I* am giving you the night off." He twisted in his lounge chair and was delighted to see her face lit with a bright smile. "I'll see you at Dolores tomorrow morning at nine. Deal?"

"Deal!" she said.

"When does the bus leave?" he asked.

She bit her lip. "It leaves from the Living Sharpe parking lot at five."

"Well, you'd better go get ready. Tell Flex to get

you there in my rental car."

He didn't have to tell her twice. When he turned back around, he saw her fist pumping the air as she trotted around the corner and into the cabin of the yacht.

With a sigh, he picked up the script but ended up staring over the top of it at the white Victorian house on the hill overlooking the harbor.

"Working hard, I see," Marion said as she sat on an uncomfortable-looking stool next to his lounger.

He thumped the script with the back of his fingers. "More of the same. They should have stopped after the third movie."

She nodded at his script. "It's upside down, you know."

He snorted. So it was. He didn't bother to turn it right side up.

"What errand was Miss LaPorte running off to tackle in such a rush?" Marion asked.

"I tasked her with a crucial mission," he said, dropping the screenplay on the deck next to his lounger. "Very important."

"Hmm," she said, studying her phone. "Who is Dolores and why is she on your calendar at nine tomorrow morning?"

"Dolores is the name of the house Cassidy and I are working on. We're meeting a designer there tomorrow morning." For some reason, it felt good to say he and Cassidy were working on the house, but in truth, he'd only helped with a piece of trim so far. For a moment, he allowed himself to imagine working side by side with Cassidy to restore

Dolores, then quickly shut it down.

She nodded. "As you know, I have you and Miss James scheduled for dinner here tonight, with select press. There will be no press at breakfast, or the meeting with, or rather *at* Dolores unless you want them there."

He shook his head.

She made a note in her phone. "I have you, Miss James, and some reporters scheduled for a Q&A after lunch tomorrow at one, so we need to make sure she studies the script I gave her. Maybe Miss James knows of a quaint place to have the Q&A? It would be nice to have some local atmosphere. Perhaps you could ask her since you have a better rapport." She glanced at the tabloid. "Much better rapport." She craned her neck and scanned the deck. "Where did you send Miss LaPorte? I need her to make a couple of phone calls."

"I sent her on a very important mission, like I told you."

Marion arched an eyebrow.

"I sent her out with some of her friends with strict orders to have fun and not report in until tomorrow at nine."

She glanced at her watch. "It's only three twenty in the afternoon. She ordinarily works until six."

"I didn't think we needed her on a Saturday when we're surrounded by people ready to help out in any way they can." When Marion's sour expression didn't change, he added, "Come on. She's probably only twenty-two or -three years old. She needs to have some fun."

"You would know all about that," she grumbled, studying her phone again.

And at that moment, something dawned on Jack. He knew nothing about Marion Hill's youth. The Vietnam War had been going on when she was Dee's age. Maybe she'd never had fun. Perhaps it was a luxury that had passed her by.

"Thank you," he said.

She glanced at him over her glasses. "For what?"

"For caring about me and my future."

He thought for a moment she was going to deny or protest, but instead, she blinked a few times rapidly and returned her attention to her phone. "You're welcome."

"Taa daa!" a man's voice sang from the doorway behind them. "Behold Miss Cassidy James!"

Jack pushed to his feet to face Cassidy and her team of makeover artists, feeling way more nervous than he'd expected. Marion remained seated on the stool, eyebrows lifted, as if daring them to impress her.

Jack let out a relieved breath when Cassidy walked into view, looking very much herself but with a shorter, shaped fringe of bangs and some highlights in her hair. She was wearing a loose, flowing, sleeveless dress with a scoop neckline and a ruffle at the bottom. It was lavender with a hint of gray, like her eyes. Thank goodness they hadn't done anything weird to her.

Cassidy crossed her arms over her ribs and tapped long nails against her elbows. Okay, so they did one weird thing, but the nails were painted lavender and they looked feminine and stylish, so.

"I thought we discussed a shorter, trendier hair style," Marion said.

"Well, Ms. Hill—" the short guy began to answer.

"I said no," Cassidy said, cutting him off. "I wanted to be able to pull my hair back when I worked, so we compromised. I agreed to a trim and highlights."

Jack's body grew warm all over. Not only had she stood up for herself with the team working on her, she'd stood up to Marion.

"The color is good on her. I'd like more jewelry, Johnathan," Marion said. "And higher heels."

Again, Cassidy replied before the guy could answer. "Thank you. I like the color, too, but no to the jewelry and heels. I'm not used to wearing things like that, and it would only make an awkward situation more awkward for me, and being comfortable is important considering the goal, don't you agree?"

Jack's adrenaline spiked. Cassidy was fantastic, and from the slight lift on one side of Marion's mouth, she thought so, too. "When you are ready, I'd like to go over some things with the two of you before dinner tonight."

"I'd like some time to touch base with Amanda first, if that's possible," Cassidy said. "She's been blowing up my phone for hours, and since my nails are finally dry and nobody's messing with my clothes or hair, I'd like to put her mind at ease."

"I need to change clothes," Jack said. He'd planned to remain in his jeans and T-shirt, but after seeing Cassidy's dress, he wanted to up his game a little.

Marion gave him an approving nod. "Meet me back here at four and we'll let the reporters get some photos in before drinks and dinner."

Cassidy met Jack's eyes, and his breath caught. She was a beautiful woman. Inside, outside, wearing overalls or an evening gown. Lovely.

As Jack strode to his cabin, he knew the burning in his stomach wasn't hunger. It was a deep, growing resentment for this entire, impossible situation. He wanted this woman in his world, but his world was harsh and hard with people who only showed interest in you when it served them. Cassidy didn't belong in his world. Hell, he wasn't so sure he did.

CHAPTER TWENTY-FIVE

Cassidy gave a happy sigh. She'd cleared the first hurdle with room to spare. The session with Marion's selected reporters had gone well. They were kept at a reasonable distance and were only allowed to take pictures and notes on what Marion told them. Jack and Cassidy had been instructed to say nothing, but to smile in agreement and at each other. Smiling at handsome Jack Winston had become easy. Too easy.

From across the dinner table set for two, the flickering flames from the trio of taper candles reflected in Jack's dark eyes, which had a hypnotic effect. That, combined with the wine she'd consumed on an empty stomach during the "cocktail hour" following Marion's performance for the reporters, had her feeling warm and buzzy. The reporters hadn't been invited to cocktail hour, and since she'd decided she wasn't going to let Marion get under her skin anymore, Cassidy perhaps enjoyed one more glass than she should have.

She wasn't drunk by anyone's standards, but she was certainly relaxed. Maybe that was a good thing. It had been a rough few days.

"I like the new haircut," Jack said. The candlelight was still doing that hypnosis thing in his eyes. It was almost like a movie special effect.

"Thanks. Me, too."

They were outside at the rear of the boat, and

though they appeared to be alone, she knew the reporters were taking pictures through the windows from inside the cabin where she could hear the gentle strains of a string quartet. The security guys were also lurking around somewhere in the shadows, except for Flex. He'd decided to go on the bus with Dee and the Living Sharpe crew to make sure they stayed safe.

For the billionth time, she clanked her fake nails against her wineglass when she reached for it, nearly knocking it over. "I'll never get used to these things. I said no to long nails originally, but I'd said no to almost everything else, and I felt like I had to agree to something." She wiggled her fingers. "These seemed like the lesser of all the makeover evils."

Jack chuckled. "I had to wear prosthetic fingertips when I played a troll-like creature in a bad horror movie early in my career. It gave me a great appreciation for anyone who can function with long nails."

Cassidy couldn't imagine gorgeous Jack Winston being cast as a troll. In fact, he was so attractive, she was finding it difficult to tear her eyes away from his face so that she could cut into her steak. Or maybe that was the wine making it difficult.

Nah. He was truly that good-looking.

"This seems really excessive," Cassidy said before popping the bite in her mouth.

"Dinner?" Jack took a sip of his wine.

She cut off another bite of delicious steak. It was cooked perfectly and made her want to make yummy noises. "The dinner, the candles, the string quartet…the freaking *yacht*."

He chuckled. "I have an image to maintain, you know," he said. "Besides, the yacht is chartered." He looked around. "Though I could get used to this."

Sadly, so could she. And that horrified her. She'd always kept her feet on the ground. Born in Blink, she planned to grow old and die in Blink. This man—this moment—made her wonder if maybe she'd kept her field of vision too narrow.

"So, it's time," Jack announced, putting down his fork and sitting back in his chair.

"For?"

"For the story that made Marion the Megalodon break out in laughter. That was a first and possibly only occurrence of its kind."

She speared the last bite of her steak. "The story's not as good as all that. We really need Mrs. Phipps to tell it for the max effect."

"We don't have Mrs. Phipps. We have Miss James, whom I find charming." He slid the candles to the side of the small table and leaned forward. "Tell the story, Miss James."

A pair of waiters came and cleared their plates. Once they'd moved off, she leaned in so that they were almost nose to nose. "I'll make a deal with you. I'll tell my story, if you tell me one in return."

"I like your deals," he said, bumping his nose to hers.

From inside the cabin, cameras clicked, and she wondered if he'd done it to give them photo fodder. Probably. *Keep your guard up, Cass*. Hard to do with flicker eyes and a boozy buzz, though.

"Okay," she said, sitting back and smoothing the napkin in her lap. "But first, you need some backstory. Mrs. Phipps used to be a beauty queen, like the real deal. Rumor has it, she was runner-up for Miss Maine."

"I intensely dislike those kinds of contests," Jack muttered.

"Same, but that's neither here nor there." She shook her head. "God, I sound like my dad." She took another sip of wine.

Jack tilted his head. "You loved him very much."

"Yeah. I did."

Two waiters returned and placed crème brûlée in front of them along with coffee and a maple syrup–colored cordial in a tiny, stemmed glass.

"Back to Mrs. Phipps," Cassidy said, raising her spoon. "It's important you know she had been a real beauty and it's still a large part of her identity even in her mid-sixties in order for this story to work."

Jack grinned. "Understood. Mrs. Phipps is a vain woman."

"Yeah, her appearance is her whole identity, really." She scooped a bite of the caramelized treat onto her spoon. "So, anyway, one day she calls me to check her boiler because she's worried it's too hot in her basement for all the kitties living down there."

"How many cats live in her basement?"

"Shhh. Don't jump ahead. It's my story." Okay, so maybe she was more than just relaxed, she might be bordering on tipsy. She took her first bite of dessert and closed her eyes.

"Okay. I won't interrupt again. Go ahead," Jack said.

She held up a finger, eyes still closed, and swallowed. "Hang on. You'll have to wait. I need a private moment with this food." She took another bite, savoring the creamy texture and glorious flavor, and sighed.

Across the table, Jack chuckled. He picked up his tiny cordial glass and held it up. "A toast to good food, good stories, and excellent company."

She clinked her glass to his and tasted the almond liquor. It was sweet and made her throat feel warm.

"Mrs. Phipps?" he said as she took another sip.

"Mrs. Phipps," she repeated. "So, I arrived at her house to check out her basement to be sure her boiler was functioning properly. As always, I took a work light and a headlamp, which was good, because there was only a tiny forty-watt bulb for the entire space. When I arrived at her home, she was all decked out in a dress and jewelry with her hair and makeup perfect, as usual. Before I headed down the stairs to the basement, she asked if I'd save her a trip that day and take some food to pour in the kitties' bowls. She also asked me to refill their water from the sink down in the basement." Cassidy shrugged. "No problem. I figured maybe like lots of utility spaces, the basement might be dirty or something and she just didn't want to get her nice clothes dirty if she didn't have to. She also asked me to talk to the cats. She said they'd never let her pet them, but she knew they liked it when she sweet-talked them, and she felt bad that they might be lonely down there. She said she'd tried but had never been able to get any of them to follow her up the stairs into the house."

Cassidy took another bite of dessert and finished off the cordial. Jack had sat back in his chair and was studying her with an amused look on his face. A sexy amused look, but then he *was* Jack Winston and…wine and whatever this delicious drink was.

"You went down into the basement?" he prompted.

"I did, and it was not too warm, well, not warmer than any basement with a boiler in the winter. I didn't see any cats, though, so I checked the boiler. Everything was fine."

She eyed her wine and decided she'd had enough. If she felt any more relaxed, she'd melt. Also, she needed to keep her guard up. Right. Because… She looked up at Jack. Because he looked as delicious as her dessert in this candlelight.

"The boiler checked out?" he prompted.

"It did. Perfect working order, so I set myself to the task of feeding her cats. I could hear them moving around down there, but they weren't coming out for attention or anything. I mean, that's not out of the norm, I suppose, especially if they were feral or old and fussy like Lolo."

Willpower caved, and she drank the last few sips of her wine. "So I started calling them in a sweet voice, like Mrs. Phipps suggested. 'Here, kitty-kitty. Come on out for food, kitty-kitty.' Nothing."

Jack had placed his elbows on the table with his chin resting in his palms. "What happened then?"

She smiled. She would love to have heard Roger tell this story to Marion. No doubt he would do a better job of it. "Then I finally saw the cats. I don't know if they came out because they got used to me and knew I wasn't a threat or if the sound of the cat food hitting the bowls was too much to resist, but all of Mrs. Phipps's kitty-kitties came out."

"How many were there?"

She grinned. "Dozens. Maybe over a hundred. All healthy and well-fed." She paused for dramatic effect. "So I tiptoed through the kitties, careful not to upset or disturb them, and found Mrs. Phipps in her living room. 'When was the last time you fed your cats?' I asked her. 'Yesterday. I feed them every day,' she answered. 'How long have they been down there?' I asked. She told me it had been several years. And then I noticed the eyeglasses sitting on her kitchen table next to her car keys, and it all made sense."

Jack was watching her closely, so Cassidy continued. "'Are those your glasses?' I asked her, and she said, 'I don't like how I look in glasses. I only wear them when I need to see something clearly like when I'm driving, but I almost always drive during the daytime. I wear prescription sunglasses so nobody sees me in those ugly things or knows I have to wear them.'"

Cassidy poured some cream in her coffee and stirred it. "I asked her to put on her glasses so that she could meet her kitties. She resisted, not wanting anyone, including me, to see her in glasses. She eventually gave in and put them on after I told her it was crucial for the well-being of her and her cats."

Jack shifted in his seat, but he didn't say anything, completely engrossed. Cassidy couldn't remember a time when someone had been so interested in what she was saying. She took a sip of coffee and then continued her story.

"I took the work light with me and intentionally stopped on the stairs so she could get a good look at all of them without disturbing them. And then," Cassidy grinned, "when she was three steps from the bottom, I turned my work light on."

Jack had moved to the edge of his seat.

"It was a bright halogen spot, and for the first time, Mrs. Phipps saw her kitties clearly. All of them. A basement full of them, seen in all their glory…including their beady little eyes and long, hairless tails."

"No!" Jack said, sitting back in his chair, eyes wide.

"Oh, yes. Rats. Everywhere. Huge ones. Cat food evidently grows them big and healthy."

He busted out laughing. "What did Mrs. Phipps do?"

"She screamed bloody murder, of course, and let me tell you, the woman has some lung power. Then she shot up the stairs like a rocket."

Jack slapped his knee. "That's fantastic. That poor woman." He shook his head. "Those poor rats."

"Oh, the rats were fine. After she calmed down, she found a company that live trapped them and took them to a safe place way out in the country—though I'm sure they'll miss the daily room service."

Still laughing, he sat back in his chair.

"And that," Cassidy said, "is why to this very day, you will never see Mrs. Phipps without her glasses."

Jack applauded. Cassidy stood and gave a curtsey, dropping instantly into her seat when she heard camera shutters.

"Oh, come on, Cassidy," Jack said with a wink. "You navigated a basement teeming with giant rats. What's a few reporters?"

He had a good point. She stared across the table at his handsome face, and a weird buzzy sensation filled her that had nothing to do with wine. Jack had a lot of good points, including a really kissable mouth. And from experience, she was well aware that he knew how to use it.

Nope. She needed to think of the end game, not his mouth or what he could do with it. Time for a change of topic.

"Okay. I told you a story, Jack. It's your turn to tell me one."

CHAPTER TWENTY-SIX

Jack sat back in his chair and took a sip of his coffee. Probably a mistake, since he'd had a nearly sleepless night in Tristan's old bedroom, tossing and turning on the lumpy mattress knowing Cassidy was in the room next door.

She'd be next door tonight, too.

He set the coffee cup down and met Cassidy's expectant eyes across the table. Behind her, the stars looked like pinholes in black paper, perfect and bright. They never looked like this in L.A.

From the cabin behind him, Vivaldi floated out mellow and sweet. Marion had gone to great lengths to set the mood, and like everything she did, it was spot on.

"Your turn," Cassidy said, placing her napkin on the table. "Entertain me, Jack Winston."

Oh, he'd like to do that for sure. There were a million ways he'd like to entertain her, but telling a story was not one of them.

He stood and moved behind her chair. "Let's walk."

Not only would a stroll give Marion's photographers more material, it would get his mind off creative ways to entertain Cassidy James.

He pulled her chair back as she rose. She'd had several glasses of wine and then the amaretto, but it had been over several hours and her speech was clear, so a stroll to the bow should be fine.

"It's beautiful here," he said as they walked hand in hand up the side of the vessel toward the bow.

"It is. I can't imagine living anywhere else."

When he glanced over at her, her skin seemed to glow from inside in the bright moonlight. He couldn't imagine her living anywhere else, either. She fit here in this stunning, rugged place, and it made something deep inside his chest ache.

"I always thought I'd live in Kansas my entire life," he said.

She stopped and looked up at him. "I can't imagine you in Kansas."

"It's beautiful, too, in a different way." He shrugged. "So's L.A."

Only L.A. did nothing for him, not emotionally, anyway. He loved the California beaches and parks, though he rarely visited them anymore. Marion had clipped his wings, which wasn't a bad thing, considering he'd worn those wings out by the time she came on board, but honestly, he was feeling the urge to fly again. Especially now. Since arriving in Blink, something had changed.

"Storytime. We had a deal, Winston," Cassidy said, striking out toward the bow and tugging him along with her.

He'd racked his brain, and other than silly stories from movie shoots that were not terribly relatable to someone outside the industry, he didn't have a tale that could come close to rivaling Mrs. Phipps and her kitties.

At the top of the rise straight off the point of the bow, Roger McGuffy's house towered in the moonlight.

"Why did you name the house after a cat?" he asked.

She dropped his hand and strode to the very apex of the railing at the front, staring up at the building. "It suits. Lolo is old and a bit run down, but even with arthritis and two remaining teeth, she's proud, like Dolores. And Lolo is loyal. She never left Mabel McGuffy's side in her last days." She turned to face him, and the wind pushed her hair across her face. "And like Dolores the cat was loyal to Mabel, I'm going to be loyal to Dolores the house." She raked her hair out of her face. "I can't let Tristan allow someone to ruin her."

Jack pulled her into his arms. "That won't happen."

For a while, they stared at Dolores. "The big house on the street where I grew up had a turret also," Jack said.

"That's a tower, not a turret," she explained. "Towers go all the way to the ground while turrets pop out of an upper level. There is a round room on all three above-ground floors of Dolores. It's one of my favorite features."

He ran his hands up and down the smooth skin of her arms. "It's a beautiful house."

She sighed and relaxed against him. "I hope you and Sally are right about Roger doing some long con on Tristan to get him to come home or something."

Burying his nose in her hair, Jack breathed in deep. Her hair didn't smell like honeysuckle this time, probably because it had been styled by Marion's people. He rested his cheek against her temple. "I'm certain that's what's going on." Though how letting Tristan destroy his childhood home would inspire him to leave his medical practice in Portland to move to Blink was beyond Jack.

"Ahem."

Crap. Jack released Cassidy and faced Marion, who was emerging from the door leading onto the deck.

She cleared her throat again. "Sorry to interrupt, but I've sent the reporters to their cabins, so you two can drop the act for tonight. Breakfast is at seven thirty to accommodate your nine a.m. appointment with, or rather *at* Dolores."

As if on cue, Cassidy yawned. "You lucked out, Winston. You'll have more time to figure out what story you're going to tell me." She winked at him, then strode off toward the door.

"Good night, Marion," she said, then disappeared through the door.

Jack turned to face Dolores. His feelings were scattered all over the place, like Mason's LEGO pieces on the floor of his room. The more he got to know Cassidy, the more he knew she could never fit into his world. But the more he thought about it, the more he realized that he might fit into hers. And maybe, he could find a way to make those worlds touch just enough to—

"I know what you're thinking," Marion said. "Stop thinking it."

Jack gritted his teeth but didn't face her. She probably *did* know what he was thinking, the old battle-ax.

"Another week or so and then both of your

lives will return to normal. Everything will be set right again," she said.

Normal. His life was anything but normal, and as for being set right, maybe that would apply to Cassidy's life, but his hadn't been right in the first place. It's why he'd been so restless lately. Something was missing. And every now and then since he'd arrived in Blink, he felt like he was getting close to discovering what it was.

As if his silence were dissent, Marion pressed on. "You can't have her. It's impossible, and you know it." She moved to stand next to him, forcing him to hear her. "You've fought hard to get where you are. Don't let that girl ruin everything you've worked for." She placed her hands on the railing, her large rings sparkling in the moonlight. "I've been around a long time. I've seen this over and over again. It never ends well. You belong in Hollywood. She belongs in Blink. You would destroy each other."

For a moment, he didn't move, her words bouncing around his head. Then he took a deep breath, unable to come up with a suitable response. She had decades of experience on him. In her lengthy career, she'd amassed wisdom he could only imagine.

"I'll see you at breakfast, Mr. Winston."

He nodded, not turning around. "See you tomorrow, Marion."

Her footsteps faded, and he loosened his grip on the smooth stainless railing and walked toward the back of the ship, getting a view of the gangway just as Dee and Flex walked, or more like stumbled their way up, laughing.

Flex was in his usual all-black ensemble, and Dee was in a low-cut bright pink top and tight black pants. She looked great. And happy.

Jack avoided what could have been an awkward encounter by returning to the front of the boat. Nothing like running into your boss to kill your buzz.

After he was certain Dee and Flex had made it aboard safely and had heard a crewman offer to escort them to their cabins, Jack pushed away from the railing to head to his own room. The one next door to Cassidy's. The one connected to hers by an interior door.

"You can't have her," Marion's voice said in his head. *"It's impossible and you know it."*

But the thing was, he didn't know it. He'd always believed nothing was impossible. That belief is what propelled him from poor kid from Kansas to Hollywood movie star. But this thing with Cassidy wasn't about accepting a challenge. It was about doing the right thing.

"You would destroy each other."

With a heavy sigh, he glanced over his shoulder at the grand house on the hill. "Good night, Dolores. See you tomorrow."

CHAPTER TWENTY-SEVEN

Cassidy was pretty sure her head was going to explode. Not from a hangover; she woke up feeling fine, but because of the very tall, very opinionated, and very pushy Brie Barona—a leggy blonde with a fake Italian accent. At least it sounded fake to Cassidy, most likely because she'd heard the woman on the phone with someone speaking in a clear, Midwest dialect like a newscaster.

Cassidy would have liked to write off her overwhelming dislike of the beautiful Brie as jealousy, but that wasn't it at all. It was simply overwhelming dislike. The woman wanted to destroy Dolores.

Tristan was following her and taking notes on his phone.

"All this oppressive, outdated, dark paneling should be painted an eggshell white, I think." Brie held her hands up like she was channeling spirits or something. "No, no, sage with gilded highlights as an homage to the past. The visitor will be reminded of how this house looked in its glory days."

"*Or*," Cassidy said, "we could just continue with the period-appropriate restoration so visitors wouldn't need to be reminded. They could see exactly how this house looked in its glory days."

Brie met her gaze directly, rolled her eyes, and continued as if Cassidy hadn't said a word. "As I was saying, green hues will allude to nature and have a calming effect. You had expressed that you

liked the windows to the past I created for your
friend's office, Dr. McGuffy, yes?"

"Yes."

"I could do that with this project," Brie said. "It
would be interesting to put a modern steel cable
stair rail that ends in a six-foot section of the original staircase under a box of plexiglass. It will
demonstrate how far we have come with building
materials since this house was built."

Tristan's eyes were bright with interest. "I like
that idea."

"Wait a minute," Cassidy said. "You propose
removing this glorious hand-carved stair rail, banister, newel post, and who knows what else and
replacing it with the braided steel cable railing like
I've put on beach house decks?"

"And the kind that go inside upper-end living
and office spaces."

"That's it." Cassidy strode over to where Roger
was reading a paper at the dining table. "What are
you thinking? How can you allow this?"

Roger looked up from his newspaper, appearing confused as if he hadn't heard the hot pile of
poop this woman was shoveling. "I'm sorry. Allow
what, Cassidy?"

Oh, yeah. It was all an act. There had never
been a time she'd known Roger McGuffy to be out
of it or miss what was going on in a room. Cassidy
glanced at Jack, who was squatting down in front of
Lolo's hidey-hole under the staircase. He
seemed unconcerned as well.

Satisfied that Cassidy was a nonentity that
wouldn't present a problem, Brie strode into the

formal parlor with Tristan on her heels. Suddenly, Cassidy wished Marion were here—something she *never* thought she'd wish after meeting the woman. Marion the Megalodon would chew this woman up and spit her out like the cheese she was named for.

Cassidy ran her hand over the smooth, lustrous wood of the handrail, and it calmed her pounding heart. The craftsmanship was extraordinary. Replacing it with tension cable would be a crime. She'd chain herself to the banister to prevent something like that from happening. Better yet, she'd chain Brie to it.

Jack stood and turned with Lolo in his arms. Cassidy's jaw dropped.

"She hates everyone," Cassidy said. "I'm the only one she's let touch her for three years."

"Another thing we have in common, then," Jack said with a grin. Even from this distance, Cassidy could hear Lolo's rasping purr broken up by wheezes. Stray hairs from the old cat floated through the shaft of light beaming in through the stained-glass transom over the front door. Lolo wasn't great at grooming anymore, and Cassidy hadn't brushed her yesterday.

Brie's loud voice made the hairs on the back of Cassidy's neck stand on end as she discussed replacing the leaded glass of the tower with some of her windows to the past over arrow slits. *Arrow slits?*

"It would be a window to a time even further back than the house itself. From the outside, it would look like an ordinary window. But from the inside, it would be a medieval anachronistic conversation piece. I wouldn't overdo it. I'd only install it on this floor, so it could be enjoyed by all guests. This turret is perfect for this."

Jack spoke for the first time since Brie had arrived. "It's a tower, not a turret."

Cassidy wanted to run over and hug him.

Brie turned and saw his face for the first time. He'd been talking to Roger or digging around under the stair for Lolo since the meeting had started. Cassidy spotted the second Brie recognized him. Her lips parted slightly and her breathing became rapid as she studied Jack calmly stroking Lolo in his arms.

"Oh, my. You're…" Her accent had fallen away, but she put it back in place when she said, "Jack Winston. I…I'm so honored to meet you. You know about architecture?" she asked in a breathy Italian accent.

"Not really. But even I know the difference between a tower and a turret."

The woman flushed red. "Yes, well. Would you like to join us as we discuss the project?"

"No, thanks. I've heard enough." He placed Lolo gently into her hiding place under the stairs and looked down at the sweater's worth of gray-and-white cat hair clinging to his dark blue T-shirt.

"Let me show you the upstairs," Tristan said, giving Cassidy and Jack only a passing glance as he took the stairs two at a time with Brie practically having to run to keep up with him.

"I'm feeling the need to take a sledgehammer to something right now," Cassidy said through gritted teeth. "I think this would be a good time to begin the demolition on the old shed behind the kitchen."

"Want some help?" Jack offered.

"I'd love an accomplice."

As they strode through the dining room, she glared at Roger, who was hiding his face behind his newspaper. How could he just sit there all calm and unconcerned while his son and cheese woman discussed the destruction of Dolores? Roger had lived in this house his whole life, for goodness' sake, as had his father and his father before him.

None of this made sense. Jack followed her into the kitchen and opened the door leading out the back of the house, gesturing for her to lead the way. With a huff, she did, and right before Jack pulled the door shut behind them, she glanced back through the kitchen to the dining room to see Roger lower his paper, wearing a huge grin.

CHAPTER TWENTY-EIGHT

Jack took another swallow of lemonade, watching Marion usher the reporters from Amanda's deck. On the picnic bench next to him, Cassidy relaxed and stirred her lemonade with a straw.

"That went well," he said, pushing his Ray-Bans up on his nose. "You did great, Cassidy."

Amanda ran to the table from where she and two dozen or so people had been watching the Q&A from the side. "That was awesome. Look, your romantic moonlit dinner made the front page of *The Inquisitor.*" She slapped a tabloid down on the table in front of Cassidy. "Gotta go talk to Gus. Be right back."

Cassidy turned the paper toward them. Yep, there they were in a half-page story, nose to nose at the candlelit table in a photo bearing the headline "Jack's New Flame." These people were certainly on their game; it hadn't even been eighteen hours yet. There were also pictures from the walk on the beach.

Marion had been right. This was much better than fake stories from women he didn't know. A swirl of unease churned in his gut as he watched a drip of condensation trailing down his glass. Was it better, though? This was a fake story about a woman he *did* know.

Marion's purposeful footfalls approached, and Jack looked up to find Dee trotting along in her wake. He imagined his assistant was feeling the effects of her night out, but she looked relaxed and happy. He would talk to Marion about giving Dee Friday and Saturday afternoons off unless they had an event or special circumstances. As it stood, she worked every day but Sunday, which was overkill.

"Thank you for arranging the location of today's Q&A, Miss James," Marion said. "And please pass my thanks along to Miss Miller for making her deck available. I think it was the perfect backdrop." She reached across the table to turn the tabloid toward her. "Nice. Things are going better than expected. I think the press is buying the story completely. It's almost time to announce a breakup so we can end this charade and get back to our real lives."

Amanda gasped from behind Marion, and Cassidy covered her face with her hands, her lilac nails catching the sunlight. Jack's stomach dropped. He hadn't even seen Amanda return.

"Buying the story?" Amanda's eyes were wide and her dangly butterfly earrings trembled against her neck.

Brow furrowed, Cassidy gave a startled glance to the edge of the deck at her friends and neighbors who had come to watch the interview, then put her finger to her lips. "Shhhh."

Amanda's voice came out in a raspy whisper. "You mean this whole thing is fake? You two aren't really…" Amanda clapped her hand over her mouth, then lowered it and narrowed her eyes on Cassidy. "Why didn't you tell me?"

This was the first time Jack had ever seen regret on Marion's face. She closed her eyes for a moment, obviously realizing the mess she'd just created.

Marion opened her eyes and lifted her chin. "Because she is legally obligated not to tell anyone, even you."

"We need to take this conversation somewhere more private," Cassidy said, stepping over the bench and taking Amanda by the elbow. She led her into the store off the deck and closed the door.

Marion lowered herself onto the picnic bench next to Jack, her back to the table. He assumed straddling a bench to sit in it the right way was not in Marion's repertoire.

"How bad will the fallout be from this?" she asked, pulling out a pair of sunglasses from her purse and putting them on.

"Hard to say," Jack said, picking up his lemonade. "They're close. I'm confident Amanda will understand once Cassidy explains it."

Jack couldn't see Marion's eyes behind her large sunglasses. "I had no idea she was behind me," she said.

"What are the legal ramifications?" he asked.

"None," she said. "It was a unilateral NDA. Cassidy is the only one bound. She is not in breach, and I'm not a party. We should probably get her friend to sign one now."

For a long time, Marion said nothing, but even with those sunglasses hiding her eyes, Jack could tell she was troubled. "I'm sorry this happened," she said.

"It was an accident," Jack said.

"There's too much opportunity for accidents with this situation, Jack. It's time to end it."

Jack's pulse skyrocketed. "I thought we were here for two weeks."

"You've been front page for two days now, which is all we needed. Readers will tire of this fairytale movie-star/small-town-girl storyline soon. It's not sustainable like an industry romance would be. With someone from my list, we can carry it on for months or even years. Both of you would run in the same circles, and 'dates' would be convenient and not involve traveling to insignificant little towns wasting time and resources."

Convenient. Sustainable. Resources. It sounded like she was talking about a consumer product marketing campaign.

"I think I know a graceful way to bring this to a close," Marion said.

Jack shifted on the bench, waiting for the hammer to drop. Graceful was not a word he would apply to anything Marion concocted.

"There are rumors she has a high school sweetheart. Tristan McGuffy."

Jack remained silent. He hadn't noticed anything between the two of them, but he had been distracted by Cassidy while, possibly, she'd been thinking about Tristan. An ache bloomed in his chest. A handsome doctor would be a good match for Cassidy, he supposed. He kept his expression neutral so Marion wouldn't know this was news.

"She has evidently had a tendre for him since she was little."

Tendre? Who used words like that anymore? The woman truly *was* a dinosaur.

"Where did you hear that?" he asked. It's not like the woman was out wandering among the residents hearing idle gossip.

She waved her hand like she was shooing away a gnat. "It's evidently common knowledge, which makes it perfect."

Why hadn't Cassidy told him? If this attraction to Tristan were real, surely she would have mentioned it. Jack swallowed hard. Maybe not. By agreement, his relationship with Cassidy was decidedly *not* real. She owed him no explanations.

All the indistinct chatter from people still hanging out around them didn't cover up the humming that had started up in his head. Marion was plotting the final scene.

"Yes," she said, staring straight ahead as if she were seeing it play out—or maybe she was imagining the tabloid headlines. "Cassidy James uniting with her childhood crush will give us the out we need." She took off her sunglasses, placed them in their case, and put them in her purse. "Even sooner than I'd hoped."

The small crowd of people who had gathered to the side of the deck to watch the Q&A had begun to disperse. Roger, who'd grinned throughout the entire interview like it had been a standup comedy routine, headed toward them.

Jack had no idea what was going on with the rumors about Tristan and Cassidy, but he was pretty sure Roger did.

"Ms. Hill. Lovely to see you again," Roger said

in what Jack would swear was a flirtatious tone.

Marion blushed. Holy crap. The Megalodon blushed. "Thank you, Roger. Likewise."

Roger gestured to the tabloid on their table. "Noticed you have *The Inquisitor*. The mercantile is sold out. Mind if I borrow yours?"

Marion handed him the paper. "Not at all. Please help yourself."

"Thank you, Ms. Hill." He grinned at Jack as he rolled up the tabloid and stuffed it into the inside jacket pocket of his tweed sportscoat. "Tristan will be interested in this," he said with a wink before shuffling away.

Yep. Just like he'd told Cassidy, this man was up to something, and Jack planned to find out what it was.

"Excuse me, please, Marion," he said, rising and stepping over the bench.

"Where are you going? We need to discuss our next steps and our exit strategy," she said.

"It'll have to wait."

He caught up with Roger right as he stepped down onto the boardwalk.

"Hello, Jack," the old man said without turning around. Clearly, he'd expected Jack to follow him.

Jack fell into step beside Roger as he picked his way down the wooden boardwalk toward Wright Boat Works, his cane tapping against the wood every other step.

"Good interview. Interesting to see a behind-the-scenes look at fame." Roger slid him a sly glance. "Not much acting involved, was there?"

The guy was sharp as one of Cassidy's finishing

nails. "None at all. Like I told the reporters, I really like Cassidy and enjoy spending time with her."

Roger stopped, putting his cane in front of him and placing both hands over it. "I take it you want something from me, Jack."

"I was going to say the same thing," Jack replied.

Three women Jack recognized as the quilting ladies he'd met at Amanda's party that first night walked by staring and giggling. Once they had passed, he turned his attention back to the older man. "What is it you want from me, Mr. McGuffy?"

"Please call me Roger," he said.

Jack nodded. "What do you want, Roger?"

"I want some help with Cassidy. She's had an interest in Tristan since she was in high school." His wrinkled lips widened into a smile. "But you know that already."

"I might have just heard that somewhere."

Roger's eyebrows rose. "You don't say."

"I sure do." At least Jack knew Marion's source. In fact, he'd seen them talking right before today's Q&A.

The old man took a few more steps, then said, "Since I was part of that legal meeting and all, I know that this thing between you and Cassidy is totally for show. You've no feelings for her, right?"

"How can I help Cassidy?" Jack asked.

"There's a potluck fundraiser at the church this afternoon," Roger said. "Tristan agreed to drive me to it, since I'm so feeble and all, you know."

The only thing feeble about Roger was the

misconception that anyone would believe him to be feeble.

"It would be nice if both my son and Cassidy ended up at the fundraiser together," Roger said. "Tristan is showing interest in her for the first time—probably because your public admiration of Cassidy brought her into focus for him. He sort of walks around with blinders on, always has. Anyway, he's started asking me questions about her, but I'm concerned because Tristan has never had a knack for making things happen, if you know what I mean."

Jack smiled. "Not a chip off the old block, huh?"

"Not even a little bit." He struck out toward the Boat Works building again, cane thudding on the wood. "But you, Jack Winston, strike me as someone who can make things turn his way."

"What are you about?" Jack asked, losing patience.

"Cassidy's happiness. The girl deserves some. She covered for her daddy when his memory started to go, first by handing him tools he needed but couldn't keep straight, then eventually doing the work herself and telling the customers it was a condition of her apprenticeship and he was only allowed to supervise. That stubborn fool Hank didn't want anyone to know his memory was failing, so everything fell on that girl's shoulders. And she kept his secret up until the end. Poor kid. Held herself together by placing her hopes on my son, who didn't pay her a second's notice until you were in the picture."

"I'm still not clear on how I fit into this," Jack said.

"I'm trying to help you out here, son. None of you know how you fit in. Not you, not Tristan, and not Cassidy."

That made no sense. But at this point, the whole conversation felt like a trip down the rabbit hole. "I suppose you do?"

"I have a pretty good idea."

They walked in silence for a few paces before Roger spoke again. "You'll leave Blink when this arrangement is over. You'll go back to your life in California with your movies and managers, and Cassidy will remain here with what?"

"You can't seriously think she'd be happy moving to Portland with Tristan."

Roger moved his cane to his other hand. "What I think doesn't matter. What you think doesn't matter. After waiting for him all this time, don't you think it fair she's at least given the opportunity to make that call for herself?"

Jack stared out over the water, chest aching. "I'll go along with this, but I need a promise from you. I want you to promise me you will not let that designer get her hands on that house. I also want your word after I leave here, if Cassidy needs anything at all, you'll contact me."

For a moment, Roger looked surprised, then he laughed. It was a strong, organic laugh. No mocking, teasing, or scheming.

"What is it?" Jack didn't see any humor in this situation whatsoever.

"Let's just say I didn't expect that." He patted

Jack on the shoulder. "No designer. I'll notify you if she needs anything. I promise."

Strolling beside Roger, Jack stared out over the harbor, watching gulls dive behind a lobster boat pulling in. "What time does the event at the church begin?"

"Silent auction and bake sale start at three, but I plan to get there closer to supper. So five if you can manage it."

They'd reached the door of Wright Boat Works and Roger pulled it open. "Gonna go see my buddy, Gus. His son, Caleb, said he'd give me a ride home when I was ready."

"I'll see you at the fundraiser at five," Jack said.

"Will you be bringing Ms. Hill?"

He couldn't imagine Marion the Megalodon at a small-town church fundraiser. "I'll let her know about it and invite her to join me."

Roger smiled. "Tell her the invitation is from me, will ya?"

As Jack walked back toward the deck, his emotions were scrambled. Roger McGuffy was pulling a lot of strings behind the scenes, but it was hard to determine his game. One thing was sure, though. He wanted Cassidy to be happy and so did Jack.

He sighed and watched the lobsterman tie off his boat in the slip closest to Amanda's deck. Behind it, at the farthest pier, *The Illusion* loomed like an ostentatious piece of jewelry. It was completely out of place here. Like him.

Maybe Marion was right, and it was time to pull the plug on this whole affair.

Jack straightened his shoulders and headed back to the deck to convince Cassidy and Marion that he was dying to go to a fundraiser and potluck dinner at the local church where he would finagle a way to pair Cassidy up with Tristan.

And here he'd thought Hollywood was fake.

CHAPTER TWENTY-NINE

Cassidy stood under the church breezeway and studied the crowd of people checking out booths under portable canopies scattered around the church grounds. Jack had insisted they come to the fundraiser, but he had disappeared almost immediately after they'd arrived.

She could see Flex's head above everyone else's because of his height, and she was certain wherever he was, she'd find Jack.

"Hey," Tristan called, striding across the grass looking well-groomed in his khaki slacks and dress shirt—a blue one this time. He looked around. "Dad told me I'd find you over here. Where's your man?"

Her man. Cassidy's face heated. "Jack is his own man. I have no idea where he is." She was more irritated by this than she should be, she realized as she relaxed her curled fingers. All they had was a business arrangement that could end at any time. In fact, in the car on the way here, Marion had hinted that they'd be wrapping things up soon. She should be relieved.

Tristan flashed her the charming smile she remembered and had dreamed of for years. "My good fortune. I haven't been able to talk to you alone since I arrived."

Well, that wasn't exactly true. When he'd arrived, he hadn't even recognized her.

"Want to go check out the auction items?" Tristan asked.

"Sure." She gave one last glance to where she'd last seen Flex to find he'd moved on.

"I couldn't believe it was you when I first arrived," Tristan said.

"You didn't know it was me when you first arrived," she corrected. Dang. She really needed to lose the prickles. Tristan was trying to be nice, and here she was acting grumpy because her fake boyfriend had bounced.

"Sorry about that. I was so distracted, I didn't even look at you, to be honest," he said, stopping outside a portable awning shading a table with several baskets of goodies up for auction.

She walked past him to check out the gift baskets on display.

"But I'm looking at you now, Cassidy," he said.

He certainly was. When she turned around, he was less than a foot away, staring at her with his bright blue eyes she'd fantasized about forever. Her breath caught. She had no idea what to say, so she returned her attention to the three auction items on the table. In front of each was a lined page with a starting minimum bid. There were quite a few bids on each page.

The first offering was a wine-and-cheese basket donated by Miller Mercantile; next was a gourmet cooking basket put together by Living Sharpe LLC with a cookbook, seasonings, and several clam and shellfish tools. The last was a basket with bubble bath, a soft, fuzzy blanket, and half a dozen romance novels donated by "anonymous."

"I can see why they chose to remain anonymous. I wouldn't put my name to that, either," Tristan said right as Cassidy was thinking about making a bid on the book basket.

The next booth featured quilts. The Blink quilting club held out their best efforts for the DownEast Region women's shelters fundraiser, but there were still some fine items up for auction today to fund the new church playground equipment. There was also a quilt at the end of the display obviously made by a beginner or maybe a child as evidenced by the uneven stitches and sloppy edges. Cassidy noticed the sign-up sheet in front of it was empty. She should make a bid so the creator's feelings weren't hurt.

Tristan didn't even slow down and passed the booth right by. "Silly," he muttered, fortunately too quietly for the women attending the booth to hear.

"Quilting has historical, societal, and social significance," Cassidy said, following without stopping at the booth. "It's an art form and takes great skill." The two quilts her mother had made with the Blink Quilting Club before she and Luke were born were some of Cassidy's most treasured possessions.

Tristan shrugged and stopped in front of a table with gift certificates displayed. "I'm sure you're right. My mom loved them, but they always struck me as fussy and frivolous."

And perhaps feminine like the romance basket? She was beginning to get a feel for Tristan McGuffy, and it didn't feel as good as she'd imagined in her daydreams.

They approached another table. "Sorry I'm being negative," he said. "I'm sure lots of people around here love this kind of stuff. It's just not my scene. Coming back here is kind of awkward, you know?"

She didn't know, but at least he'd apologized. "You haven't been here in a while."

He shoved his hands in his pockets. "Not since Mom died. Dad keeps wanting me to drive in on the weekends, but it's not the same."

"I'm sure you miss her."

He nodded. "Like you miss your dad."

She did miss her dad. What would he make of this deal she'd made with Jack? What would Tristan make of it if he knew the details? Thanks to the NDA, he never would.

He pointed at the third item on the table. It was Cassidy's donation: a gift certificate for eight hours of home repairs by Miss Fix-It.

"Nice of you to help these people out," Tristan said.

He said that as if she wasn't one of "these people." Cassidy gritted her teeth, then forced herself to take a deep, calming breath. Only a few seconds ago, they'd had a moment of connection, and now this. Maybe she was just taking everything he said the wrong way because she was in a grumpy mood.

She turned her attention back to the table. There was a certificate for a chartered fishing trip and breakfast for four at Starfish Diner. Cassidy made bids on both. Too low to win, but at least she'd help raise the price.

She spotted Dee and two women from the

Living Sharpe team at the cotton candy stand and waved. Dee grinned and waved back.

"So, how long are Jack and his entourage going to be in Blink?" Tristan asked.

"I have no idea." From what Marion had said on the way here, not long.

"I'm surprised he's not glued to you like usual."

"Jack and I are just good friends," she said. Surely that wasn't in violation of the NDA. She and Jack *were* good friends—something she'd never expected.

When she scanned the church grounds, she spotted Flex towering above everyone at the quilting booth, and next to him was Jack. He had a pen in hand, which he placed on the table as their eyes met. His gaze darted to Tristan and then back to her. She couldn't read his expression before he turned his attention to someone behind him.

Tristan had noticed Jack as well. "So if you and he aren't…" He let his voice trail off. "I thought maybe we…"

Here it was. The moment she'd been waiting for since she was fourteen. She held her breath, expecting her heart to crank into overdrive like it always did when she imagined this moment, but it maintained its steady, even beat.

"Since you're not seeing him, how do you feel about maybe going out with me sometime?"

She should be ecstatic. Over the moon. Instead, she was…confused. And even though she'd spent years imagining this moment, it had taken her by surprise.

"You don't have to give me an answer right

now," he said. "I'm leaving tonight so I can make a meeting in the morning with the hospital board back home. I'll be back in two weeks to finish setting up the clinic, and we can talk about it then."

She glanced back at the quilting booth. Jack was gone. Maybe she'd feel differently when he was *really* gone. Maybe that's why this moment she'd waited for felt hollow.

"Yeah, we can talk about it when you come back," she said. "I'd like that."

"Great." He gave her a grin, and her spirits lifted.

After checking out the last of the auction booths, they got into the snow-cone line behind two little boys who looked like they'd been rolling around in the grass. They had debris in their hair and green smudges on their elbows, bottoms, and knees. She glanced over at Tristan in his pristine starched shirt and slacks with crisp pleats and his perfectly polished loafers and had a hard time imagining him rolling down a hill as a little boy.

The grape snow cone was delicious and hit the spot. She was surprised when Tristan ordered one as well, since it was nothing but sugar water. Maybe he was only opposed to cheeseburgers. Her stomach growled. She could go for one about now.

"You'd love Portland," he said as they wandered toward a pen where kids were petting bunnies and baby goats.

"I doubt it," Cassidy said, leaning on the railing of the pen.

"You don't really plan to live your whole life here." It wasn't a question.

She leaned over the railing and rubbed the head of a black goat with a white splotch on its forehead. "Yeah, I do. I love Blink."

"What a waste." He backed up when the goat stuck its head through the planks to get a bite of his shoe.

"What do you mean?"

Eyeing the goat, he said, "I mean a woman like you is wasted in a place like this. You should be somewhere you're appreciated. Somewhere you can grow and can make a difference."

She closed her eyes and fought back a sharp retort by imagining pushing him into the pen.

"It's why I left this place," he said. "I have a large, successful medical practice where I'm appreciated in a city where I can meet new and different people that challenge me and make me grow. I would have been stifled here."

"I'm appreciated here. I'm challenged here, and I assure you, I make a difference," she said, glad the edge she felt didn't come through in her tone. "Everyone is different and has different needs. What I need is right here."

Tristan shook his head as if disappointed. "We can talk about that when I come back, too."

And like the final puzzle piece, what was wrong with this whole daydream come to life clicked into place. She and Tristan McGuffy had nothing in common. Not their past, not their present, and certainly not their future. She wasn't even sure she liked the guy, now that she'd gotten to know him better.

"Tristan, I don't think we should go out when

you get back."

He raised an eyebrow. "No?"

"No." She couldn't very well tell the guy she'd discovered they had nothing in common and he paled in comparison to...*ugh*, to someone she was in a fake relationship with? This was so awkward. "I'm truly sorry."

He didn't seem angry at all, thank goodness. A bit surprised, maybe.

"Huh. Well, I guess that's that," Tristan said. "This is goodbye, then."

Yep. Goodbye to wondering and dreaming. Cassidy fought down a sigh of relief, then gasped when Tristan took her by the shoulders and planted a quick, dry kiss on her lips. He pulled back with a grin. "So long, Sassy Cassy. I was right when I told you you'd grow up to be a knockout."

Too stunned to respond, she watched him walk away.

Cassidy slumped down onto a nearby bench. All those years she'd imagined what kissing Tristan McGuffy would be like. She'd always imagined his kiss making her feel all fizzy like champagne bubbles. She shook her head. Suffice it to say, fantasy was far richer than reality.

She looked up to see Jack by the cotton candy machine talking to Roger. Speaking of fantasy outdoing reality... Her heart squeezed at the sight of him striding her way in his well-worn jeans and a rust-colored T-shirt that showed off his California tan. His dark hair was messy like he'd run his hands through it. She could totally imagine Jack Winston rolling down a grassy hill. She could also imagine him kissing her. A warmth spread low in her body. She could also imagine him kissing her while they both rolled in the grass.

"They're starting to serve dinner. I bought meal tickets. You hungry?" Jack held out his hand to her. Good thing, because after imagining herself rolling around in the grass with him, she wasn't sure she could stand on her own.

One thing she knew for certain, now, was that Tristan was not at all who she'd imagined him to be for all these years. Jack had awakened something in her that her teenage self had not even imagined. Tristan might have made her feel champagne bubbles, but Jack set off fireworks—big, colorful, exciting ones—and she planned to make the most of the time they had before he left. However long that was.

"I'm starving," she said.

CHAPTER THIRTY

Jack was proud of his self-control—or maybe it was his acting skills he was proud of. Either way, he hadn't moved a muscle when Tristan had grabbed Cassidy and kissed her. And now that he thought about it, neither had she.

Could Roger have been wrong? Or was she just holding up her end of their bargain?

Their arms brushed as they walked across the grass toward the area where food was being served, and she reached out and took his hand. He looked around, expecting to see a camera pointed at them, but saw none. Only Flex following at a discreet distance. Jack laced his fingers through Cassidy's, feeling much lighter than he had moments ago.

As they made their way through the small crowd, Jack marveled at how respectful and accommodating the people of Blink were. In most settings, he had to wear a baseball hat and sunglasses, not talking to anyone or making eye contact as Flex monitored every move from every person around him. Here, he almost felt like a regular person. It was clear that people knew who he was because of the stares and whispers, but they left him alone except for the occasional kid or fan wanting an autograph. Maybe their ability to give him space was because they were used to having Niles Sharpe around. Niles wasn't a movie star, but he was a celebrity in his own right with an active fan base and worldwide notoriety from his TV show.

Dinner was, like the rest of Blink, reminiscent of something straight out of a movie. With the whitewashed church as a backdrop, friends and neighbors shared food and conversation at long tables covered in plastic tablecloths with popsicle stick and construction paper flower centerpieces made by the children's Sunday school classes. According to Sally, the classes had quadrupled in size since the recent reopening of the lumber mill and Living Sharpe's relocation from New York to Blink.

When Jack had first learned of the successful lifestyle company moving to this remote place, he didn't get the strategy behind it. Now, as he watched Dee laughing and teasing with her group of friends at the end of the table, he totally got it. Blink was special. So were the people who lived here, including Cassidy, who was seated next to him discussing the merits of bark mulch versus recycled tire mulch for the base under the new children's playground with the church pastor.

Jack loved watching her talk about things that mattered to her, like Dolores or, in this case, playground safety materials. She used her arms a lot, and even though her newly trimmed bangs cleared her eyes, she still habitually brushed them away. He'd been worried at how serious she'd appeared when talking with Tristan, but she seemed to be back in usual form now.

Lovely, Jack thought as he watched her.

From the far corner of the dining area, Marion waved to him. He waved back.

Nope. He'd read that wrong. It wasn't a greeting, it was a summons, he realized when she crooked her finger, then pointed at Cassidy and crooked it again.

"Her highness demands an audience," Jack whispered in Cassidy's ear, smiling when she shivered at his nearness.

"I'll send you the information on the recycled tire mulch," Cassidy said to the pastor. "The extra cost up front will be worth it in the long run."

The man smiled. "From what I've been told about the success of today's auction, the extra cost won't be a problem."

"What do you think she wants?" Cassidy asked as they strode toward Marion with Flex, as always, only a few steps behind.

"I've no idea," Jack answered, frustrated how he'd allowed Marion to get under his skin so easily. Maybe it was time for a sit-down with his manager. Being grateful shouldn't equate with being steamrolled by her impressive willpower and personality.

"Follow me," Marion said when they were within earshot. "Make sure no one follows us," she ordered one of the security guys she'd hired as they rounded the corner of the church. He nodded and took up a post at that corner.

Jack and Cassidy followed Marion through a short, chain-link gate into a run-down playground with a tall metal slide and a couple of rusty teeter-totters. She stopped next to a swing set with the old-fashioned kind of swings made of wood and braced her hand on the frame. "We need to discuss our exit strategy."

With his thumb, Jack pointed over his shoulder toward the dining area. "They were about to announce the auction winners. I placed some bids. Can we discuss this when we get back to the yacht?"

"No, we cannot. There's been a development, and we need to adjust accordingly."

Jack's stomach dropped, and a bit of nausea followed. This could not be good.

"One of the reporters got a photo of Miss James and Tristan McGuffy," Marion announced.

"Of course they did," Jack said. "So what? They're neighbors." He took Cassidy's hand, intending to go back to the table.

"They got a picture of her kissing him."

Cassidy pulled her hand from Jack's. "Tristan kissed *me*. I didn't kiss him."

Marion waved a hand like she was brushing away a gnat. "There's a photo of the two of you kissing. Its publication will yield the opposite result of what we had intended. Every eye will be on you now for cheating on Jack Winston. The paparazzi will be relentless. You think it was bad before? Just wait." Marion turned her attention to Jack. "We must put a quick end to this. You need to make a small scene and part. This fundraiser is the perfect place. Make sure there are at least three photographers near enough to catch it. Keep it low-key. Argue quietly. Then give each other a hug and go your own ways. We can leave town as soon as tomorrow."

Cassidy crossed her arms over her body but said nothing.

"Once we're gone, the press will lose interest in Cassidy as quickly as they became fascinated. I'll tell the press that you have parted as friends and Miss James has reunited with an old flame who only recently returned to town."

"That's not true," Cassidy said. "Tristan and I are not—"

"None of this is true," Marion interrupted. "Not the thing with Tristan McGuffy and not the thing with Jack Winston." In a more soothing tone, she said, "The sooner I get Mr. Winston out of town, the sooner your life goes back to as it was before. The liaison was a success in that Mr. Winston got headlines and you received a larger online base, which was the goal, I believe."

Cassidy sat on one of the swings, fingers so tight on the chains her knuckles appeared white.

Jack wanted to stomp his feet and yell that he wasn't ready to end this but instead, very quietly, said, "No."

Marion stiffened. No doubt she wasn't used to being told no.

"I'm not going to agree to this, Marion. A public disagreement? I would never do that." He glanced at Cassidy. "It's not either of our styles."

Marion huffed, but before she could reply, he continued.

"We'll go ahead as we are. I saw the kiss."

Cassidy's head jerked up, and she met his eyes.

"It was a nonevent. A photo will show that. I want this to end slowly and amicably, as planned.

Cassidy being seen with Tristan makes ending it easier but not immediate." He couldn't let this end. He wasn't ready.

When Marion opened her mouth to protest, he cut her off by lifting a finger.

"You are brilliant, Marion. I admire and appreciate you, but I can say the same of Cassidy. I'm not going to stage our breakup in such a way that paints her in any kind of light other than positive. That's the final word."

For a moment, he thought Marion might argue with him, but she simply nodded.

Cassidy stood and took a deep breath. "I need to go do some work if we're finished here. I've gotten way behind in my job."

"Want some help?" Jack offered.

"Not this time, thanks." She met his eyes and blinked rapidly, then said, "I'll be staying with Amanda tonight."

Jack didn't try to stop her as she left the playground and disappeared around the building. Even discussing the end of this was upsetting. He understood needing time alone to think. He needed some himself.

He turned to Marion. "I plan to work with Cassidy on Dolores tomorrow. Please keep your reporters at home."

Marion gave another curt nod. "It has to end, Mr. Winston. How long do you think this can continue before the press paints this situation in an unflattering light, undoing all the good we've done?"

The only good they'd done was put him in

proximity to Cassidy James, and as he'd watched Cassidy with Tristan today, he'd realized he wasn't ready to give that up.

"I have no idea, Marion, but I'm hopeful I won some auction bids, so I'm going back to the table. I'll see you at *The Illusion*."

When he returned to his place, which was conspicuously Cassidy-less, the people around him applauded, then stood and were soon joined by everyone at the event.

"They just announced the amount of money they raised at today's event," the pastor said to Jack. "Thank you for making it possible for us to give our children a safe place to play." The pastor clapped him on the shoulder. "You are Blink's favorite person right now."

He waved and smiled at the crowd. The only thing he wanted to be right now was Cassidy's favorite person, and luck willing, he'd find a way to be just that.

CHAPTER THIRTY-ONE

When Jack, Dee, and Flex arrived at Dolores the following morning, Cassidy was already hard at work fixing the hole she'd made in the floor to repair the support beam underneath. Amanda was filming on her phone wearing a lime-green pantsuit with beads around the bottom edges of the shirt and pants.

Jack hung back, not wanting to interrupt. The morning light through stained glass above the front door cast fist-size blotches of color around the entry room like a kaleidoscope.

"I think I have everything I'll need for this project," Cassidy said, picking up a plank of wood and displaying it for the video. "The floorboards are tongue-in-groove, and I numbered them on the bottom, so they should go back in the same order easily. At least I hope they will, but as we know, nothing ever goes as planned."

Wasn't that the truth.

Cassidy glanced at Jack, then quickly looked away. She slid a floorboard into place, then placed a block on the edge and tapped it gently with a rubber mallet. "The wood is super hard but can still break, so I made a tapping block with a cutout for the tongue. If any of the pieces don't fit like I want them to, I have a few extra boards in the same dimension from a house nearby that was torn down years ago. Since I'm sanding and refinishing all the floors on this level, it will appear uniform when I'm done. If you're doing something like this on your own project and run short on material, you can take original pieces from a place that isn't visible, like a closet, and then use modern material in the closet."

She placed another plank and tapped it into place, then another. Jack set down the bag he'd brought and silently wandered into the dining room to avoid distracting her. Roger was sitting at the table with a newspaper and a cup of coffee.

"Good morning," Jack said in a low voice, so as not to interrupt the filming.

"There's coffee in the kitchen," Roger said. "Little Cassidy always takes care of the details. Help yourself."

Jack returned with his coffee and sat in a chair opposite Roger. "Cassidy started early this morning," he said.

Roger didn't look up from his newspaper. "Maybe she got tired of waiting for you."

Dee hurried in from the parlor adjoining the dining room. "I'm sorry to interrupt, but Marion wants you to drop by the ship to sign a couple of documents. She also got an extension for your review of the HBO series."

Jack shook his head. "I told her to tell them no. I don't want to take on anything that ties me to one location for that long. No series."

Dee nodded and made a note on her phone. "The production company for *Mad Planet 4* has sent your travel information for the New Zealand location shoot. They have approved everything your agency requested, including a private trailer on-site. Marion has that paperwork, too."

Jack nodded and took a sip of coffee. "When do I have to be there?"

"Eight weeks."

Roger looked up from his paper, then flipped the page and continued reading—or looking like he was reading, anyway. After he'd flipped a few more pages, he placed the paper on the table and sat back. Jack had assumed he'd been reading a local newspaper, but it was a tabloid. And there, on the front page, was a picture of Tristan kissing Cassidy. The photo looked a lot more romantic than the actual kiss—if you could even call it that. The quaint white church in the background made it look official and oddly matrimonial. The headline read "The Other Man."

Marion had been right. Cassidy would be vilified. After a string of swear words in his head, Jack casually asked, "May I?"

Roger nodded and slid it across the table.

Muscles tight with dread, he skimmed the poorly written article. *Cassidy James, known paramour to Jack Winston of the Mad Planet franchise, was seen yesterday at the Blink Community Church Annual Fundraiser in the company of her high school sweetheart, Dr. Tristan McGuffy of Portland, Maine. When questioned by our reporter as he left the event alone, Dr. McGuffy denied any involvement beyond childhood friendship with Miss James. When asked how he felt about Jack Winston, Dr. McGuffy said he was a "two thumbs up."*

Jack let out a sigh and relaxed back in his chair.

It could have been so much worse.

He looked up from the page to find Roger watching him.

"Where's your son?" Jack asked.

"He had some meeting with some bigwigs in Portland. He left last night."

Jack gestured to the paper. "Is this the outcome you wanted when you cooked this whole thing up?"

Roger shrugged. "I didn't have a preferred outcome in mind, necessarily. It was about the process." He took his glasses off and wiped them on his sleeve. "It was about Cassidy finishing the story and closing the book herself, rather than never finishing it or having someone slam it shut before she reached the end." He put his glasses back on, making his eyes appear bigger through the thick lenses. "I'll tell ya something. It's those what-ifs that'll get you every time. You don't want to reach my age and sit around wondering what if."

Jack took a sip of coffee and studied the man across from him. He was sharp, that was for sure.

"And what about that interior designer you never intended to hire?" Jack asked. "What book were you trying to close there?"

Roger chuckled. "That was a hoot, huh?" He slapped a hand on the table. "That was way better than I expected." He waved his arms in the air and said in a terrible, high-pitched Italian accent, "A window to history—sage with gold highlights as an homage to the past." He snorted. "I have no idea how my son thought that woman's bizarre design concept—and I use that word loosely—was a good fit for this project, but it did the trick." He leaned forward. "You never realize how much you want something until you almost lose it. Cassidy protected this house from that woman like a mama bear. No way was she going to back down. In her heart, this house is hers."

Roger nodded as if satisfied with the world.

Dee scurried in again. "Sorry to interrupt, Mr. Winston, but Ms. Hill texted me again wondering when you'll be in to sign the documents."

As far as Jack was concerned, Marion could keep on wondering. He was still irritated from their last encounter when she tried to force him and Cassidy to stage a fake breakup at the fundraiser. He wasn't ready to let her go.

Jack's breath caught, and he sat back in his chair. There it was. He didn't want his relationship with Cassidy to be fake anymore.

He needed to talk to Cassidy as soon as possible. Away from this place. Away from Marion and the paparazzi. How?

"What do I tell her?" Dee asked.

Jack held up a finger as his plan fell into place. Then he grinned and sent Caleb a text.

"Tell her I am unavailable all day. I'll contact her with a time when I know more." He probably looked silly grinning like this. Dee didn't seem to notice. Typing on her phone, she wandered from the room.

Roger noticed, though. "Looks to me like you're about to try to close the book on a story of your own."

"I don't want to reach your age with a bunch of what-ifs."

Jack's phone dinged. He read the message from Caleb Wright, who had just become one of his favorite people, and grinned.

CHAPTER THIRTY-TWO

Cassidy watched as Amanda ran the gauntlet back to her car parked in front of Dolores, waving to the paparazzi as she went. They probably should have waited for Jack to film. He and Cassidy had worked as a couple since he'd been here, and the episodes he was in always blew up the stats, but she was still stinging from last night. After she'd parted ways with Tristan, she'd felt fantastic. Like she'd had a breakthrough of some kind. Then he and Marion had discussed ending this whole thing like they were talking about the weather.

She'd given Amanda the entire rundown last night, and her opinion was that Cassidy was over-reacting and it was obvious Jack liked her and stood up for her with Marion.

Cassidy pulled out her hair tie, smoothed her hair, and put it back in again. Amanda was probably right. Well, about the overreacting part, anyway.

Roger shuffled into the foyer archway and pointed at a bright orange paper bag with handles that was lying on its side by the front door. "What's that?"

"Ah. That's gifts," Jack answered, picking up the bag and pulling out an envelope from inside.

He turned his warm eyes on her, and Cassidy's insides melted. Okay, maybe Amanda had been right about everything.

"Good morning," he said.

"Hey," she said.

Jack handed the blue envelope he was holding to Roger. "I figured you could make use of a gift certificate for the Starfish Diner."

Roger took the envelope and shook Jack's hand. "Thank you. I bid on that and lost at the last minute right before they closed bidding."

Jack smiled. "I know. I made a last pass right as they were shutting the silent auction down. I'm giving most of the items I won to the second-highest bidder because swooping in like that with winning bids on so many items was not very sportsmanlike."

"It was good of you to support our community," Roger said. "Sally drove me home before the final winners were announced, but if you beat me on this one, you were mighty generous."

"From what I hear, you've done your fair share of generous actions for this town," Jack said.

Jack reached inside the bag again. "I have something else in here, too." He pulled a tissue paper–wrapped item out and handed the empty bag to Flex. He crinkled the paper, and Lolo stuck her nose out of the cutout under the stairs, intrigued by the sound. He tore the tissue paper and pulled it off a folded quilt with uneven edges.

Cassidy's heart squeezed. She'd been worried that whoever made this quilt wouldn't get a single offer. She smiled and hugged her arms around herself. The person who made it must be ecstatic that it had been purchased by a movie star.

Jack knelt in front of the opening. Lolo had

retreated into the shadows. "This is for you, Lolo girl."

Cassidy's heart squeezed even tighter. It had been purchased by a movie star for a grumpy, arthritic cat with bad grooming habits and two teeth.

After folding the small quilt in quarters, he slid it into the opening, picked up the tissue paper from where he'd set it on the floor next to him and scrunched it in his hand, then straightened it and balled it up again. The noise did the trick, and Lolo stepped onto the quilt bed to get a better look and sat down. Cassidy could hear her raspy purr from several yards away.

Jack gently rubbed her head, and the purr got louder. Then he set the ball of tissue paper next to her.

"A beautiful quilt for a beautiful girl," he said, pushing to his feet.

Roger snorted. "That's the ugliest cat in the state of Maine."

Lolo batted the tissue paper ball across the floor, and Jack rolled it back to her. "Well, I'm pretty sure that's the ugliest quilt in the state of Maine, so…"

Roger chuckled. "Gus and I have plans to meet at the diner in ten minutes if anyone else wants to go." Cassidy figured this was code for needing a ride. Roger would drive occasionally, but only when necessary. He was aware of his strengths and weaknesses, and his eyes were a definite weakness.

"Flex and I are happy to take you there if you want a lift, but I have different plans for the day," Jack said.

Cassidy's insides did an elevator drop. She was hoping to spend more time with Jack. She knew he and Marion were plotting his exit, but her time with Tristan had only brought how much she enjoyed being around this man into sharper focus.

Jack rolled the tissue paper ball back to Lolo, who was flicking her tail wildly—the most enthusiasm Cassidy had ever seen her display. Jack seemed to bring out the best in everyone.

"Could I interest you in an adventure, Miss James?" Jack had that prankster look on his face she'd seen on her little brother so many times.

She shoved her hands in her pockets. "It depends on what kind of adventure, Mr. Winston." In truth, it didn't matter what he had planned if she got to spend more time with him.

His voice was low, like a movie character plotting a crime. "It involves carefully planned subterfuge, mistaken identity, and a daring escape from a prehistoric shark."

She held back a laugh. "In that case, it sounds like an offer I can't refuse." She glanced down at her overalls. "Can I go like this?"

He grinned. "I insist."

CHAPTER THIRTY-THREE

Jack turned north onto the highway and checked the rearview mirror. So far so good.

"Stay down just a little bit longer," he told Cassidy, who was crouching on the floorboard of Caleb's pickup truck. "I think we did it."

She giggled and grinned up at him, which made this entire ridiculous escapade worthwhile, even if they got caught before they reached their destination.

When, after a couple of minutes, no cars were visible behind them, he gave the all-clear and Cassidy climbed into the passenger seat wearing a grin as wide as his. "Well, you certainly aren't boring," she said, buckling her seat belt. She glanced over her shoulder out the back window. "I can't believe they fell for it."

Her gray gaze traveled from his face to his feet, then back up again. "The work coverall is kinda sexy, by the way."

Jack's entire body tightened, and he took a deep, cooling breath. Yeah, they could get caught right this minute, and it would have been worth it.

The plan had gone off without a hitch so far. After they'd left Dolores, they dropped Roger off at the diner with a half dozen or so paparazzi following behind. Then they drove to the harbor and parked near Caleb's business. Jack had taken his time in the parking lot, so the reporters could get a good look at his bright red T-shirt and blue jeans. Then, just as planned, Caleb came out of the building. Jack had laughed out loud when the guy strolled up in mirrored shades, a Maine Mariners baseball cap, and a navy-blue coverall with Wright Boat Works emblazoned across the back.

"You said you wanted me to be seen in something distinctive and memorable that you'd never wear," Caleb said.

"Well, you nailed it."

Caleb's truck had been pulled inside one of the garage bays in the building, so once Jack and Caleb had swapped clothes, Jack and Cassidy got inside, and she ducked down out of view.

It had almost been too easy. The roll-up bay door rose, and Jack pulled out of the garage, hat brim pulled down. The reporters dismissed him as Caleb immediately. As he looked back in the rearview mirror, he saw Flex patrolling the parking lot as if he were protecting his celebrity boss inside the building, and then there was just a brief glimpse of a man in a bright red T-shirt and blue jeans walking past an upstairs window.

"This is the way to Machias," Cassidy said. "Is that where we're going?"

He nodded, wishing they were headed to an airport to escape to someplace where the paparazzi, Marion, and real life couldn't interfere.

"I hate to ask it," Cassidy said, "but is it possible for us to stop by the hardware store while we're there? It'll save me a trip in."

"Beautiful *and* practical," he said.

When he glanced over, her face was pink. He

wondered if there'd ever be a time when she could receive a compliment and simply accept rather than getting all tangled up.

"Are you hungry?" he asked.

"I'm *always* hungry." She placed her hands on her knees and relaxed back into the seat.

"No more lavender nails?" he said.

She stared down at her natural, short nails. "Nah. They got in the way. A little soak in some paint thinner this morning, and problem solved."

Eventually, he pulled off the highway into the parking lot of the restaurant Caleb had recommended.

"Buddy's! I love this place. Best cheeseburger in Washington County," she said.

Caleb had told him Cassidy liked cheeseburgers. So far, the getaway plan had been executed flawlessly.

Jack's stomach growled as the smells of hamburgers and french fries hit him the second they entered the small, wooden, waterfront building. It was early for lunch, but the place was already half full, which was not ideal. Jack pulled the brim of the hat lower over his forehead. At the far end was a counter with a huge, hand-painted sign that said "Buddy's Burgers & Shakes." There was a short menu scrawled on a chalkboard underneath, but it was hard to make out with sunglasses on.

"Cassy!" the man behind the counter called as they approached.

"Hey, Buddy." She gestured to Jack. "This is—"

"Hi, Buddy," Jack cut in. "Caleb Wright told me this was the place to come for a good burger." He hated cutting Cassidy off like that, but the last thing he wanted was to let anyone know who he was.

The man, who was about his age, glanced at the Wright Boat Works coverall. "You must be working with Gus and Caleb. Good people. I've known them my whole life." He nodded to Cassidy. "Cassy, too." He pulled a small notepad from next to the cash register. "I'm guessing you want your usual, Cass?"

She nodded. "Yep."

"Drink?"

"Vanilla shake."

Buddy grinned. "Ooh. Mixing it up. You usually order a Dr Pepper."

Cassidy rocked up on her toes—one of the things Jack had discovered she did when she was excited that night he'd watched all of her YouTube videos.

"Livin' on the wild side today," she said with a grin.

"It's about time." Buddy turned the page on his notebook. He glanced at Jack, squinting a little as if he were trying to place him. Clearly, he hadn't read the tabloids, or he would have known exactly who he was. Hopefully, the people in the restaurant hadn't recognized him, either.

"I'll have whatever she's having except make my shake chocolate, please."

Again, the guy squinted at Jack. "I feel like we've met somewhere."

Jack lowered his head slightly to avoid the guy's intense scrutiny. "Nope. I'm new to the area."

They escaped to a table as soon as the order

was in, choosing one in the corner where he could sit with his back to the restaurant so his face couldn't be seen. After several minutes during which no one so much as looked their way, let alone whipped out their cell phones to film him, he finally relaxed. They'd pulled it off. They'd tricked the paparazzi, left town without Marion finding out and pitching a fit, and so far hadn't been recognized. This was the most fun he'd had in ages.

"I'm surprised you could convince Flex to go along with this scheme of yours," Cassidy remarked from across the small table.

"He didn't go along willingly, I assure you. In fact, I had to fire him."

Cassidy gasped. "*No*."

Jack chuckled. "It's only temporary. I'll hire him back once we return. Marion hasn't figured out we've slipped away yet, but if she finds out Flex let me leave unprotected, she'll come unglued on him—a highly unpleasant experience—and then she'll try to fire him for real. I'd be forced to overstep her authority and rehire him, which would cause her to come unglued on me—again, a highly unpleasant experience. A bad deal all around. It's much better for everyone this way."

"He could have come with us," she said. "I wouldn't have minded."

Jack would have. This whole exercise was concocted so that he could be alone with her, even if it was only for a few hours. "The paparazzi would have caught on immediately. Why would Caleb Wright take a bodyguard with him?"

"Oh. Yeah." She shrugged. "I'm not very good

at being sneaky."

"You'd make a terrible spy," he said.

"Here ya go." Buddy placed their food on the table. "Let me know if you need anything else."

The burger was delicious. So good, neither of them spoke until most of the meal was down. He liked how Cassidy didn't have to fill every moment with conversation. Time with her seemed to float in an easy, familiar way.

When he glanced up, she was watching him. She smiled when their eyes met.

"Penny for your thoughts," he said.

"I was just thinking of how much fun I'm having and how different it would be if I were here with Tristan instead of you."

Jack placed what was left of his burger on his plate. He'd promised himself he wouldn't bring up this topic but was glad she had. Jack swiped a french fry in ketchup, willing her to keep talking.

She pulled her napkin from her lap and wiped her lips. "You know this already, but I've had a crush on Tristan McGuffy since I was fourteen years old." She put the napkin back in her lap. "My impression of him when I was fourteen was unrealistic and childish. Once I had the chance to spend time with him, I realized"—she sighed—"he just didn't live up to expectations, I guess."

Jack popped the french fry in his mouth to keep from saying something he'd regret. Something like asking Cassidy to give *him* an opportunity to live up to her expectations.

"Is there anything else you guys need?" Buddy asked, moving to the side of the table where he could see both of their faces. Jack had been so caught up in his own thoughts, he hadn't heard the guy approach.

"No, thanks. We're all good," Cassidy said.

"It was great to see you, Cassy. Tell everyone hello for me." Buddy studied Jack's face for several seconds that felt like an eternity, then snapped his fingers. "I've got it. I know why you look so familiar."

Jack swallowed, hating that his peaceful moment with Cassidy was about to come to a howling, autograph-signing end when the now-full restaurant was tipped off that he was here. He should have brought Flex.

Buddy wagged a finger at him. "Has anyone ever told you that you look a lot like that guy... What's his name?" He tapped his chin with a finger. "The guy who plays that Blake Crusher guy in the *Mad Planet* movies. Oh, I remember now." He grinned. "Jack Winston! You look like Jack Winston. I bet people tell you that all the time."

Jack let out his breath. "All the time. Yes."

"Man, you're a dead ringer. Like, you could be his brother or something."

"I get that a lot," Jack replied. "And you know what? You look a little like a young Kevin Bacon."

His eyes widened. "Really? Nobody's ever told me that. Cool."

With a grin, Buddy took off and resumed his post behind the cash register at the counter.

Cassidy leaned across the table and whispered, "He doesn't look *anything* like Kevin Bacon."

Jack leaned in, too. "I know. Let's get out of here before someone else confuses me for Jack Winston's brother."

CHAPTER THIRTY-FOUR

Cassidy grinned as she watched Jack walk around the front of Caleb's truck to open her door. He was probably the only man on earth who could make a zip-up work coverall look good. Real good.

After leaving Buddy's, they'd done a driving tour of the area, only getting out of the truck to see the Machias River Falls from the footbridge in the little town park. Fortunately, the annual blueberry festival wasn't for a couple of weeks, so there weren't many people around and he wasn't recognized.

Jack was funny and fun, sometimes even narrating a scene they passed like he was doing a voiceover for a PBS documentary.

Disappointed to have reached their last stop, she stepped out into the gravel parking lot of the hardware store. "I only need a couple of tubes of caulk. This will only take a sec."

"Take your time. I'm completely at your disposal," he said.

Man, oh, man. If only. She shot a glance over at him as they walked. Sometimes, people wore coveralls over their clothes to keep grease or dirt off them. Since Caleb had been wearing Jack's clothes when they left, she assumed he was only wearing the coveralls and underwear. She smiled as she wondered if Jack was a boxer or brief kind of guy.

"I would pay almost any price to find out what

is going through your mind to put that look on your face," Jack said as he held the door open for her.

Wow. Was she that obvious?

"Caulk," she said, passing through the door. "Paintable latex caulk for trim and doors."

He laughed.

She'd been in this hardware store thousands of times as a little girl with her dad and as a grown woman. Without hesitation, she strode straight to the correct aisle and grabbed what she needed.

"Did you get any paint on the walls?" a man by the drywall tools asked, laughing at his own joke.

She gritted her teeth. She'd heard this dozens of times. She could stand next to a painter with far more splatters on him, and invariably, some guy would ask her if she'd gotten any paint on the walls. She gave a thin smile and headed toward the checkout.

The people in Blink had seen her working with her dad her entire life and thought nothing of a woman working construction. Strangers sometimes didn't take her seriously, which irked her.

The usual checker, Marge, wasn't at the register today. Instead, it was a guy who looked to be about her age. She placed the box of twelve tubes of caulk on the counter and looked over her shoulder to see Jack, still decked out in the Mariners cap and mirrored sunglasses, checking out a barbecue grill on display.

"Is this all?" the guy asked.

"Yes."

He looked at her for a moment, then leaned

forward a little bit. "You know you need a caulk gun to apply this, right? These aren't the kind like toothpaste tubes."

"Yes, I know that."

Jack joined her at the checkout desk.

Again, the cashier studied her for a moment. "Do you *have* a caulk gun?" He used a didactic tone usually reserved for toddlers.

"I have several." She could feel the angry heat moving up her neck.

The look on the cashier's face bordered on a smirk. "Do you know how to use one?"

Ugh. She hated it when people assumed if you weren't a man, you couldn't make or build anything. She widened her eyes and adopted her most innocent expression, then blinked a few times. "I think you stroke it until something comes out, right?"

Jack barked out a laugh, then covered his mouth.

The guy behind the counter's jaw went slack, and his face turned bright red.

Someone got in line behind them, and when she glanced back, she noticed it was the guy who'd asked her if she'd gotten any paint on the walls.

"How much do I owe you?" she asked the cashier through gritted teeth.

He told her the amount, and she shoved her card into the reader.

"I didn't mean to offend you," the guy said, handing her a receipt.

Cassidy sighed. He seemed sincere, but ugh, misogyny, even accidental, made her angry. "Thank you for your apology. I *was* offended," she said. "A penis is not a prerequisite to operate a power tool, caulk gun, or"—she shot a brief look over her shoulder at the man behind her—"to get paint on the walls."

While she slipped her credit card back into her top overall pocket, Jack picked up the box of caulk. After they'd made it to the parking lot, she looked over to find him biting his lip to keep from laughing. At least that's what she assumed he was doing. The glasses made it impossible to see his eyes.

It wasn't until they got in the car that he finally laughed. He had a deep, hearty laugh that was contagious, and soon, she was fighting back giggles.

"So, I have a question for you," he said, catching his breath. "Exactly what is it a prerequisite for?"

"What?" And then she remembered her mini tirade. "Oh, that!" No more fighting the giggles anymore—in fact, she soon found herself laughing so hard, she was having trouble fastening her seat belt.

"Here, let me," he said.

His hands covered hers over the buckle, and they both froze.

When she looked up, she could see herself reflected in his glasses. She looked different, somehow. Better. "Kiss me, Jack."

His smile faded when she removed his glasses. For a moment they stared into each other's eyes, and then he slowly leaned in. Her heart raced, and her gaze dropped to his mouth. And then, when their lips were mere millimeters away, the bill of his baseball cap smacked her eyebrow.

She snorted, then busted out in laughter again as he groaned and flopped his head back against the headrest.

This man was so much fun. She liked him. No, she adored him.

Jack ripped the hat off and leaned across the truck console, taking her face in his hands. This kiss made the one on the dance floor seem like a warmup. After what could have been minutes or hours—no telling because time seemed to stop— she was out of breath and feeling like she had enough spare energy to lift a truck.

Jack pulled away and grinned. "You were great in the hardware store." He grabbed the baseball cap from where he'd dropped it near his feet. "I like it when you talk construction."

She leaned back in her seat and ran her hands through her hair.

He put on the cap and glasses. "I like it when you talk about anything. I like *you*, Cassidy. A lot."

Her heart was already hammering from their kiss but sped up even more. This was terrible. And great. And scary. And. *Ugh.* She closed her eyes, wishing they weren't limited by time and geography...and well, by polar-opposite lifestyles. "I like you, too," she whispered.

He turned on the radio, and Cassidy tried to focus on the words of the songs instead of her screaming hormones and hopeful heart. She wanted to be with this man. To get as close to him as possible, even knowing the odds of them working out was a long shot. She liked long shots. And she really liked Jack.

"Where to next?" he asked when they turned south onto the highway.

"The back seat of this truck?" she suggested, only half kidding.

He looked over briefly, but she couldn't read his expression because of the mirrored sunglasses.

"Borrowed vehicle. Bad form," he said. She was pretty sure he winked, but…sunglasses. "Besides, we need to get back. Flex has probably called the missing-persons hotline by now."

Half a dozen or so songs later, they pulled off the highway onto the spruce- and pine-lined road leading to the harbor. The sun was just starting to set, throwing striking shades of pink and orange across the sky in front of them.

"Thanks for lunch and the adventure," Cassidy said.

He slowed the truck slightly. "Cassidy, I…" He shook his head, evidently deciding not to finish what he had intended to say.

"What?" she asked.

He pulled off on the shoulder of the two-lane road and put the truck in park. In front of them, the line of pink and orange had dimmed and was almost even with the horizon. In only a few minutes, it would be dark.

He turned the truck off and unbuckled his seat belt, then popped hers loose. "I'm not ready for this to end," he said, taking off the sunglasses and cap before pulling her to him over the console.

She didn't want it to end, either. She wanted

this to be just the beginning.

His mouth was warm on hers. Good heavens, the man could kiss. Something inside her felt like it was clawing to get out. To run free. To take a reciprocating saw to the freaking console between them that was gouging into her hip and would probably leave a bruise.

And then, lightning flashed.

Jack cursed.

He gently loosened her arms from around his neck and pulled away. "I'm sorry," he whispered. "So sorry."

She blinked, then realized the bright flashes were not from lightning at all. They were from cameras.

CHAPTER THIRTY-FIVE

Marion's voice made Jack wince like the camera flashes had. "Where have you been?" she asked, stationed regally in the ship galley behind a massive desk. "You said you were going for lunch, and it's well after dark." She scanned him up and down. "And why on earth are you wearing a mechanic's uniform?"

Jack didn't answer but placed the cellophane-wrapped wine-and-cheese basket on the shiny mahogany desk in front of Marion.

"What is this for?" she asked.

"For the hell of it," he said, moving toward the door. "I've had a great day, Marion. I don't want to ruin it. We can argue tomorrow morning. How about ten o'clock?"

She stood. "Tristan McGuffy returned to Portland today."

"I know."

She sighed. "This is going to make everything much harder."

"You are absolutely right about that, Marion," he said, pulling the door open with a grin.

"Don't do something foolish, Mr. Winston."

He already had. He'd fallen for Cassidy James—though it was more reckless than foolish. He smiled, thinking of Cassidy schooling the cashier at the hardware store.

"Good night, Marion." He closed the door to

find Flex waiting for him. "You're hired again."

"Thank you, boss. Did you have fun today?"

Fun didn't begin to cover it. "I did. Thanks."

He knew that Flex would stand guard outside his door until ten, when one of Marion's security guys replaced him.

All day, Jack had been mulling over things he wanted to say to Cassidy. By the time he'd gotten back to the yacht, he'd formulated what he'd hoped was an effective speech.

To be thorough, he rehearsed it under his breath as he picked up the last remaining auction item from his dresser and walked to the interior door that connected his cabin to Cassidy's. A door he had thought about a lot but had never used.

He lifted his hand to knock. Then, panic tightening his throat, he lowered it. He should text her before knocking. They had gotten pretty carried away in the car until the paparazzi interrupted. Now that she'd had time to reflect, she might have cooled off.

What if he texted asking to talk and she put him off? He couldn't risk that. He had a speech to give before he lost his nerve. He lifted his hand and rapped lightly.

The door opened almost immediately. Cassidy's eyes dropped to the gift basket in his arms, then rose to his eyes.

"Is that for me?" she asked.

"It is."

To his surprise, she grabbed him by the waist of the coveralls and pulled him into her room. Apparently, she hadn't cooled off. She took the basket and set it on a console right inside the door. "I can't believe you got this for me," she said. "You might just be the perfect man."

He just wanted to be *her* man.

"We need to talk," he said.

Immediately, the fire in her eyes dimmed and her mouth drew into a thin line.

He sat on a sofa exactly like the one in his room. She perched on the edge of a chair facing it, wearing a somber expression suitable for a funeral.

Butterflies filled his stomach, and he had to grip his knees to keep from fidgeting. It was like he was auditioning. Well, he was, he supposed. Perhaps for his role of a lifetime.

He'd auditioned hundreds of times. He could do this. He took a deep breath, and…nothing.

Butterflies turned into hornets as he searched for words, insides churning. He'd been formulating this little speech in his head most of the day, and now that the time was right to give it, the words wouldn't come. His palms sweated and his pulse raced as he suffered the most intense case of stage fright he'd ever experienced.

"Is something wrong?" she asked.

"No." Dammit, why couldn't he remember the speech he'd worked out? "No, Cassidy, nothing is wrong. In fact, everything is… It's fantastic—only it's not."

She scooted back in the chair, still studying his face. "I'm not sure who's more confused right now, you or me, because that makes no sense."

But it did. It made perfect sense. He stood and started pacing. He wanted to remember his speech.

He wanted his racing heart to calm. He wanted a lot of things. Things he'd not considered before. Stability. Normalcy. Constancy. Her. He wanted *her*. He wanted to spend time with her to see if they were as well suited as he thought they were. He wanted to take this fake relationship and turn it into a real one and see where it went.

He stopped in the middle of his path across the rug. "Have you seen a movie called *Love and Other Drugs*?"

She shook her head, brow furrowed in worry.

No. Of course not. Fate wanted this declaration to be as difficult as possible. "It came out a while back. The story doesn't matter. The reason I mention it is there is a line in that movie that sums up what I feel exactly." Since he couldn't remember his own words, he might as well use someone else's. He should probably do a lead-in, though.

He walked to the far end of the room and turned to pace back.

"Are you going to tell me the line, or do I need to google it?" she asked, one edge of her mouth turned up. At least she didn't look like she'd lost a loved one anymore.

He stopped pacing in the middle of the room. This was ridiculous. Okay. Clearly, he wasn't going to remember his lines, so he'd need to improvise. "You know that my life is unconventional. I travel a lot. I fly all over the place for shoots and events. Every time I leave my house, I'm followed, and photographed, and hounded." He ran a hand through his hair. If he was trying to present an appealing prospect, he was failing miserably. She needed to know the facts, though. "I rarely go out in L.A. because of the hassle." He looked over at her. "I never date except socially—like for an event such as a premiere or awards ceremony. To be honest, I haven't wanted to see anyone romantically for a long time. No one has caught my eye."

"So is that the line from the movie?" she asked.

With a defeated laugh, he slumped down on the sofa. "No."

He closed his eyes and took a deep breath through his nose. Why was telling her how he felt so difficult? Probably because he'd never felt this way before. "So here's the line." He took another breath and met her eyes. "'You meet thousands of people and none of them really touch you. And then you meet one person and your life is changed forever.'"

She blinked several times, lips parted.

"My life has been changed since I met you, Cassidy. I know it sounds ridiculous after such a short amount of time. I've been an actor for eighteen years—half of my life. I've met so many people. I've been so many places. But you and Blink...you're different."

He thought, for several long moments, that maybe she hadn't understood, or maybe she thought he was still quoting from a movie.

Finally, she broke the silence. "Are you saying you want to date for real? Because if that's the case, I'm totally in. I like you, too, Jack. You're funny, and you like Dolores, and you're nice to a grumpy old cat, and it also helps that you are smokin' hot."

He grinned, all the stress from forgetting his

lines melting away. "I'm hot, huh?"

She stood and strode over to the gift basket he'd given her and untied the bow. He noticed her hands were shaking a bit. She reached inside and pulled out a bottle of something pink. Turning toward him, she clutched the bottle to her chest. "I never knew that there could be a bathtub on a boat until a couple of days ago. It really hadn't crossed my mind, to be honest."

Lots of things were crossing his mind at that moment, and he hoped it wouldn't cause his brain to short circuit — or his body, for that matter.

"Does your cabin have a bathtub?" she asked. Her rate of speech was super rapid, something he noticed she did when she was nervous.

"No. Only a shower." He stood very still, not wanting to do or say anything to mess this moment up. She looked adorable in her splattered overalls clutching a huge bottle of pink bubble bath like a life preserver.

"Mine does," she said. "Mine has a huge tub that's way too big for one person."

Holy crap. For a moment, he thought he might have to sit down when his knees almost buckled.

"Do you like baths, Jack?"

"God, yes."

Without another word, she pivoted and marched into her bathroom.

Feeling a little buzzed from the ridiculous amount of adrenaline raging through his system, Jack followed.

It wasn't until hours later he remembered the speech he had memorized and rehearsed.

CHAPTER THIRTY-SIX

"Ooooo, girl! Look at that photo. You guys were steaming up the windows!" Amanda said as she shoved the tabloid under Cassidy's nose.

Lillian reached across the picnic table and took a jelly roll from the box in front of Cassidy. Tuesday morning "donuts on the deck" was a standing date for the women. Lillian studied the photo. "Wait a minute. Isn't that Caleb's truck?"

Cassidy sighed and pulled out a chocolate filled. She was too happy to even feel embarrassed.

"Look at her," Amanda stage-whispered, pointing at Cassidy. "She's got it bad."

Lillian took a bite of her donut and nodded, then said, "Or maybe she got it good."

Both women laughed. Ordinarily, Cassidy would have been horrified, but nothing about this situation was ordinary. It was decidedly extraordinary.

"So I take it this means your fake romance is the real deal now?" Amanda asked.

Lillian sat up straighter. "Hold on. What fake romance?"

Cassidy was surprised that Amanda hadn't spilled the whole story to Lillian. This might be a first. Marion was going to need to print up another nondisclosure agreement.

Amanda waved her hand like she was shooing a fly. "She and Jack were putting on a show to get some good press for Jack and to drum up some business for Cassidy. And then, because Jack was interested in her, Tristan noticed her awesomeness and asked her out. But then, because Cass is smart, she realized she wasn't really that into Tristan after all. Obviously, Jack is smart, too, because when she rejected Tristan, Jack jumped right in and…" She giggled. "Jumped right in."

Cassidy finished off her donut and chased it with some coffee, pretending she was so interested in Caleb's dogs barking at a seagull perched on top of a piling in front of Amanda's deck that she hadn't heard.

"So is it serious?" Lillian asked.

"He's only been here a short while," Cassidy answered, pleased at how vague that was.

"Do you know how long he plans to stay in Blink?" Amanda asked, selecting an apple fritter from the box.

"We didn't discuss it." In fact, there hadn't been much discussion of anything after she poured the bubble bath.

"Do you think he'll want you to go to L.A. with him?" Lillian asked.

"He knows I love Blink and plan to stay here." She knew a few other things, too. She knew, for instance, what he'd been wearing under the coverall. She turned her face toward the water to hide her grin and froze when the camera shutters began to snap. She turned back around.

Nothing could kill a happy buzz faster than paparazzi.

"I thought Marion was going to do something

about those guys," Amanda said.

Cassidy set her coffee down. "I kind of killed her plan. Jack and I were supposed to stage a breakup when I started dating my childhood flame. The reporters would follow Jack and his pretend broken heart back to L.A. and forget all about me."

Behind her, a reporter shouted a question. She ignored it and continued. "Instead, I rejected Tristan, and now I'm with Jack."

She smiled. Who would have thought?

"I think this is wonderful," Lillian said. "He seems like a great guy."

He *was* a great guy.

"He's certainly generous," Amanda said. "He pretty much singlehandedly funded the entire church playground. He was the highest bidder on almost every single item at the fundraiser. And he's such a cool guy. He gifted many of the items to the second-highest bidder — well, except for a few things." She picked up her coffee and took a sip. "And you know what he paid the most for?"

"Probably the Starfish Diner vouchers, because I saw Roger had pledged an obscene amount for that, and Jack's bid won," Lillian said.

"No. The diner was the third-highest bid. Second highest was that godawful quilt that Mrs. Phipps made."

"Wait. Mrs. Phipps made that ugly quilt?" Cassidy didn't know Mrs. Phipps even quilted, but then, considering the quality of the piece, she really didn't. Maybe she'd made it before she'd started wearing her glasses.

Amanda nodded and took another bite of apple fritter. "Mmm hmm. Jack made the only bid on that quilt, and it was higher than the diner gift certificate."

And now, an ancient, arthritic cat was shedding hair all over it. Cassidy couldn't hold back her grin.

"But you wanna know what item earned the highest bid in the history of the church's annual fundraiser?" Amanda arched an eyebrow and paused for dramatic effect. "It was a gift certificate for eight hours of home repairs from little Miss Fix-It here."

"Hmmm. I wonder what Jack intends to do with those eight hours," Lillian teased.

"I bet he has something he wants her to nail," Amanda said, throwing her head back to laugh.

This time, Cassidy did blush. She rose, stepped over the bench, and threw her napkin and paper coffee cup in the garbage can at the edge of the deck, knowing cameras were probably clicking. At this point, she didn't care if they took pictures of her with a trash can.

A different group of reporters began shouting from near the piers, and Cassidy turned to see Jack waving for the cameras as he strolled casually down the yacht gangplank at the end of the harbor. His hair was wet, and he was back in his customary well-worn blue jeans and T-shirt. He'd traded the mirrored glasses Caleb had loaned him yesterday for his Ray-Bans, and he looked every bit the movie star.

Cassidy's breath caught as she watched him.

That thing where people pinched themselves to see if they're dreaming? Yeah, that was a real thing. A quick, painful pinch on her thigh convinced her that this moment was, indeed, real—that last night had been real.

"Beautiful morning," he called as he climbed the steps from the boardwalk to the deck, a gaggle of photographers in his wake. Evidently remembering Caleb's instructions, they didn't follow him up the stairs and remained on the boardwalk, cameras raised, no doubt for his reunion with Cassidy.

And from the purposeful stride and sexy smile as he approached, Cassidy was pretty sure he was going to give them something to photograph.

"Good morning, Amanda and Lillian," he said, crossing the deck, eyes still on her.

"Good morning," her friends replied in unison from the picnic table.

She held her breath as he stopped right in front of her. She could see his eyes through these glasses, unlike the reflective ones from yesterday, and they were focused directly on her, which made her body heat up like an overloaded electrical panel.

He placed his hands on either side of her waist and winked. "Good morning again, Cassidy." His voice was barely above a whisper but might as well have been shouted through a megaphone the way her insides had jolted to attention.

"We're being photographed," he said.

Breathe, she told herself. She thought that maybe since they'd gotten to know each other better last night, he wouldn't have as strong an effect on her. But this was just the opposite. She was so aware of him, it felt like she might melt.

"Smile," he said. "Preferably at me."

"Where does that phrase come from?" she asked, forcing a smile. "It's odd."

"I'll tell you after we get rid of these fine folks with the cameras. You up for giving a performance?"

"It depends on what my part is."

"First, we kiss."

Her heart lurched. "That's a part I can play."

He lowered his lips to hers and gifted her with a soft, brief kiss. She could hear the camera shutters snapping like someone walking on Bubble Wrap.

He dropped his hands from her waist. "Now, we talk to them and ask them to leave."

She let out a huff of disbelief. "Wait. After all this time of being tracked like a fox running from hounds, you tell me all we have to do is ask them to leave and they'll do it?"

He took her hand and led her to the stairs to the boardwalk. "Probably not, but it's worth a try."

The largest cluster of reporters had gathered in a bunch near the base of the stairs. Others were scattered about the harbor.

"Good morning," Jack said, still holding Cassidy's hand.

Various greetings were issued from the reporters.

"Cassidy and I would like to make an announcement."

Behind her, Amanda gasped. When Cassidy

glared at her over her shoulder, Amanda and Lillian abandoned the table and stood near the edge to get out of the background of any photos.

When she turned back around, the cameras snapped. *Smile, preferably at me*, ran through her head in Jack's deep voice, so she did. More camera shutters clicked, and some of the reporters shouted questions.

"We aren't going to answer any questions right now, but I have some information to give you. We'll also pose for photos."

Excited chatter rose from the reporters.

"But there's a catch. I'd like it a lot if you would give us a reprieve for a couple of days. I'm not asking you to leave. Feel free to hang out in Blink and spend your money, or preferably, your companies' or bosses' money, to support this little town."

Some of the reporters laughed.

Barking drew Cassidy's attention. Flex, dressed in his usual black, was sprinting toward them from the yacht with Caleb's dogs leaping and bounding by his side.

"Flex and the dogs have the zoomies," Jack said, igniting another round of laughter through the reporters.

Cassidy snorted, then covered her nose and mouth with her hand.

"It's all good, Flex!" Jack shouted. "Be cool."

Flex slowed to a jog, then a walk while the excited dogs ran in circles around him. Once it looked like the bodyguard wasn't going to pitch two dozen people and a million dollars' worth of camera and audio equipment into the harbor, Jack continued.

"I'm sure everyone knows Cassidy James. She owns a construction company here in Blink and is a skilled craftsman with a special talent for historic home restoration." He held up his hand when someone shouted a question. "I'll hit the highlights, so no need for that."

When the group fell silent, he squeezed Cassidy's hand and said, "I'll answer your top question first, then I'll give you three facts about us."

Reporters from around the harbor had joined this main group, making it much larger. "Cassidy and I met online. I became a fan of her renovation videos, as I have an interest in historic home restoration myself."

Cassidy focused on the warmth of his hand surrounding hers and not the microphones on poles that were covered in something that looked like shag carpet. It was weird to face these people rather than run from them. But in truth, she was tired of running, and obviously, so was Jack.

"Is your relationship serious?" someone yelled.

"Please wait, and I'll answer most of the questions you would ordinarily ask." He smiled, and the cameras clicked. "Well, most of your questions, anyway. Some things are none of your business." He winked at Cassidy, sparking laughter and more camera clicks.

Cassidy was impressed with Jack's composure and the way he could tell the paparazzi to bug off in a friendly way.

"I'm going to tell you three things about us as a couple, and in return, I would ask you to fade back and give our relationship a chance to develop naturally. With you guys around, we either have to hide out, run away, or be fake. It's stressful for us and you. And right now, I have a whole lot of things I'd rather do with Miss James than be stressed out."

There was a swell of laughter.

"Fact number one," Jack said, holding up a finger. "As I said, we met online because I became a fan of Cassidy's home restoration videos. I decided I had to meet this amazing woman in person, so I hopped on a plane and barged right into her life." He squeezed her hand. "So far, she hasn't given me the boot, but I'm sure it crosses her mind every time she's forced to change her plans because there are cameras pointed at her or reporters chasing her. She did not invite me or you here, and I commend her for being such a good sport about something she did not bring on herself."

The reporters were quiet. Cassidy noticed Flex had climbed over the railing and was at the edge of the deck halfway between Jack and the group, clearly ready to throw himself between his boss and whatever danger he thought needed checking.

"Fact number two," Jack continued. "I am absolutely infatuated with this woman."

Cassidy's face flushed hot. This felt like something out of a mushy movie.

"As most of you know, I'm a private person, and I don't appear in public often. I like to keep my private life private. In this case, I'll share with you that my relationship with Miss James is one of the most enjoyable, exciting, and enriching experiences I've ever had."

At this point, Cassidy was pretty sure her heart was so full it would explode. Jack released her hand and wrapped his arm around her waist. She glanced down at her paint-covered overalls, and for once, she didn't wish she'd changed into something nicer. This was who she was—what she did—and the man she adored accepted that.

"And for the third fact. I believe I can speak for both of us when I answer the question asked previously. Yes, our relationship is serious, which strikes me as an unusual way to phrase it. I mean, it seems an oxymoron to call something so full of joy and happiness serious."

Amanda made a sound that was a cross between a whine and a sigh. Next to her, Lillian was fanning herself. Even Flex was affected, but he disguised it as an itchy nose.

"So that's it," Jack said. "We're going to walk to the yacht now, and on the way, we'll stop a few times for photos so your bosses will be happy." He released Cassidy and clasped his hands in front of his chest. "In return, I beg of you—please allow us some time together so we can get to know each other." He took her hand again. "Give us space so that Cassidy can get to know me as a man, not just a celebrity."

And it was then that Cassidy knew she'd fallen head over heels for Jack Winston, the man, someone she couldn't wait to know better.

"Ready?" he asked her.

"Yeah." She was ready for anything, as long as it was with him.

With the cluster of press scrambling to gather their gear, Jack, Cassidy, and their inevitable shadow, Flex, made their way toward the yacht, stopping multiple times for photos in spots the photographers thought would make good backdrops. Cassidy was uneasy at first. She had no training for this kind of thing and had never considered herself photogenic, but Jack was so natural and genuine, she loosened up and ended up enjoying herself.

When she'd first thought of herself with Jack, it had been hard to imagine. A movie star and a construction worker. It seemed impossible. But now they were Jack and Cassidy and it felt right.

He gestured for her to lead the way up the gangway to the deck. As they began the slight climb, Cassidy looked up to find Marion standing at the top, arms folded over her ribs, a pinched look on her face as sour as lemons.

CHAPTER THIRTY-SEVEN

Even Megalodon Marion wasn't going to make a dent in Jack's good mood. He doubted anything could. Cassidy had been great during the impromptu photo shoots. No primping or rehearsed posing. She followed his lead and even came up with some fun poses herself, like balancing on short side-by-side pilings and taking a photo with one of the lobsters a fisherman was unloading as they passed.

"Good morning, Marion!" he said in the most enthusiastic voice he could muster.

"Mind telling me what's going on, Mr. Winston?" she said, following Jack and Cassidy across the deck and into the main galley, her heels tapping out a rapid rhythm on the boards.

"Well, we just did an unplanned photo session with our good friends down there in exchange for them becoming scarce for a while," he replied.

Marion, dressed to perfection as usual, glared at him...as usual. "You think a few photos will make them back off?"

Beside him, Cassidy shifted her weight foot-to-foot. She hadn't spent enough time around his manager to know this was normal behavior.

Marion strode to the corner where Dee was working away on a computer, trying to look invisible, and snatched a paper from the table beside her.

She brandished the tabloid like a weapon, displaying an impressively hot photo of him kissing Cassidy in Caleb's truck.

"If you think they are going away after this, you are delusional, Mr. Winston." She took a deep breath through her nose and lowered the paper. "You are making my job unnecessarily difficult."

"That wasn't my intention," he said, gesturing for Cassidy to lead the way down the hallway to their cabins. A lecture from Marion was not on his schedule, but another bubble bath very well might be.

"May I speak with you for a few minutes alone?"

He stopped but didn't turn around. Cassidy continued to her cabin door. "I need to wash the lobster off my hands," she said, opening her door and disappearing inside.

"Come on, Flex. I need you to help me move something heavy," Dee said, attempting to pull the big man from the room by the elbow.

"What do you need moved?" he asked.

"I don't know yet," Dee said, finally getting Flex to leave with her.

Of all the times on this trip when Jack could have used a bodyguard, it was probably right now. Marion's stiff posture had not relaxed one bit. He hadn't handled the lobster, but he considered using that as an excuse to leave. It would only postpone the inevitable. This wasn't going away. With a resigned sigh, he plopped down on the sofa and waited for the lecture.

"Mr. Winston, I've been in this business longer

than you've been alive," Marion said.

He considered a smart comeback regarding the lifespans of Megalodons but decided to not antagonize her. She didn't seem to be in a teasing mood—not that Marion Hill was ever in a teasing mood.

He shifted on the sofa, trying to get comfortable. Sitting down had been a bad idea because it allowed her to loom over him. He looked up at her stern face. Marion was good at looming.

"We had a plan," she began.

"No, *you* had a plan," he corrected.

She closed her eyes and inhaled deep, as if summoning patience. "I am here to ensure that a controlled narrative is published and the press is utilized to our advantage." She ruffled the tabloid with the picture of the truck cab make-out session on the front page. "This is not to our advantage."

He held his hands up in surrender. "Well, speak for yourself, Marion, because it felt pretty darned advantageous to me."

Her eyes narrowed. Right. Not in a kidding mood. He schooled his face into a serious expression.

"It was also my understanding," she said, "that the end goal was to create a situation that would make Miss James less appealing to the tabloids and return her life to the way it was before you drew your fans' attention to her."

Jack figured the best way to put an end to this conversation and get back to Cassidy was to let Marion get all of this off her chest uninterrupted, so he remained silent.

"Why didn't she follow through with publicly dropping you for the doctor as we'd planned?" she asked. "It would have been the perfect way out for you."

So much for remaining silent. "What if I don't want out?" He stood. "What if I told you I really like Cassidy and want to spend more time with her?"

Her mouth opened and closed a few times, and then she lowered herself into a club chair. "You can't be serious." She shook her head. "This is impossible. She's—"

Jack held up a hand to cut her off. "Be very careful what you say next, Marion."

She never looked away, chin high. "She's inconvenient. What you need is someone in L.A. who will be seen with you at the right places."

"And what *I* need is someone who sees me as more than an asset or a way out or up." An angry bloom of heat moved up his neck. He walked to the far end of the cabin and stared out a window at the mouth of the harbor, where a boat was leaving, deck piled high with wire traps. "What I need is someone who likes me for who I am and not just *what* I am."

Her voice was strained. "And you don't think this small-town girl from an obscure little town doesn't see you as a way out or up? Don't kid yourself, Jack."

He turned to face her. This was the first time she'd ever addressed him by his first name. "Okay," he said, placing his hand on the back of a chair. "Let's look at it from a pure business point of view. I know you are in constant contact with my publicity team. What do they say? How is it playing on social media? How are the fans receiving Cassidy James?"

She waved a hand dismissively. "They love her, of course."

"So do I." The words were out before he'd really thought them through. Once said, though, they acted like a soothing balm, causing him to calm and relax.

Marion stared at him with a look he suspected was pity. "You need to end this fling and get back to L.A. Your career will suffer from this kind of neglect right now."

Jack knew she was right in part. Not about ending his relationship with Cassidy, of course, but about neglecting his career. "I'm due on location for *Mad Planet 4* in two months. I know you need to return to L.A. to conduct business effectively, but I can work on preparing for my role from here."

She stood. "You can't be serious."

"I absolutely can."

Marion stared at him, face unreadable for what felt like an eternity. He felt pretty sure that Marion would be resigning on the spot.

With a slow, sad shake of her head, Marion sat back down in the chair. "I've only chartered *The Illusion* through the end of the day tomorrow. I'll leave Dee and Flex with you. I would recommend you retain at least three of the security personnel I brought with me, but I know from past experience you will turn them down."

When Marion had accepted this job two years ago, she had made it very clear it was only until his career was back on track. In all fairness, she'd stayed on much longer than that. She'd stayed until his career was thriving again, largely because of her efforts.

He'd not expected to be emotional when Marion decided it was time to leave. He knew he'd feel something, but this was akin to when his sister went off to college—a deep, hollow ache inside his chest. He'd grown to respect and like Marion, even love her like he would a great-aunt if he'd had one. He took a deep breath and steeled himself. This was the right move. Cassidy was not negotiable.

"I appreciate all you have done for me, Marion. Everyone was right when they said you're the best in the business."

She opened the tabloid and turned several pages, stopping at a story about a nasty Hollywood divorce. "Save it for my eulogy, Mr. Winston. We'll see if you feel the same way when you return after filming. I can just as easily be the best in the business by email, text, and Zoom. I'll send a proposed meeting schedule so we don't lose the momentum we've created."

Relief blew through him like a cool breeze. She wasn't resigning. Even better, she was leaving tomorrow along with her security contingent and press corps. Relief turned into a dizzy kind of energy that bordered on giddiness.

"Is there anything on the schedule for the rest of the day?" he asked, using all his acting skills to appear cool and collected.

She glanced up from her article. "No."

"Since it's your last night here, should we have a team dinner?" He wasn't sure of proper protocol, but it seemed like the right move.

"Thank you for the suggestion," she said, "but no. I have plans."

Plans?

All the way to his room, Jack pondered her words. What kind of plans could Marion Hill possibly have in Blink? Whatever they were, they didn't hold a candle to his plans.

With a grin, Jack knocked on the door connecting his cabin with Cassidy's.

CHAPTER THIRTY-EIGHT

Cassidy leaned her head on Jack's shoulder. He turned a page of his script, setting the porch swing back in motion with his foot. In the week since they'd watched *The Illusion* sail out of Hideaway Harbor, they'd spent almost every minute together, and their days had settled into a comfortable rhythm.

In the mornings, Jack worked with her on Dolores unless he had a Zoom call or online meeting. Then after lunch, she took on smaller repair projects for neighbors or hung out with Jack while he memorized lines.

Surprisingly, the paparazzi had left them alone for the most part. In fact, when she and Jack had driven into Machias the day before yesterday, they hadn't needed to disguise themselves or pull any shenanigans like they had before in order to get out of town. Only one photographer had followed them.

Jack gave the swing another push, and the chains creaked with each sway.

He looked up from his script. "Have you made a decision yet?"

"Not yet."

"You'd love New Zealand. It's beautiful and rugged, like here."

Beautiful and rugged like Jack Winston. She knew she'd need to give him an answer soon, but going with him to shoot on location was a huge decision. Too big to jump into lightly. The farthest she'd ever been away from home was a high school field trip to New York City when she was seventeen, and this wasn't a field trip. This was... What was this?

She took a sip of lemonade, breathing in time to the slow rocking of the porch swing.

"If you decide not to go, I'll understand," Jack said, smoothing the screenplay on his lap. "Location shoots are intense, and travel trailers are not luxury accommodations." He stretched his arm over the back of the swing. His fingers brushed across her shoulder, leaving little flickers of electricity like fireflies under her skin. "When filming is done, I'll rush right back to you."

They hadn't talked about this part, though she'd been pretty sure the invitation wasn't some kind of do-or-die. What they had together seemed solid with the potential to last, but it still felt good to hear the words.

From here on Dolores's porch, there was a clear view of the harbor. Amanda was on her deck with a group of people, no doubt decorating for tonight's party—luau-themed this time. Caleb's dogs were running back and forth on the walkway in front of Wright Boat Works.

This was Cassidy's idea of perfect. This place. *This man.* She sighed. He was the best thing that had happened in her adult life.

She lifted her head from his shoulder and glanced up at his handsome face while he studied the script, her heart squeezing.

She needed to stop stalling on committing fully to this man. She wanted to be with him, but something was holding her back. She wasn't sure what it was, and until she figured it out, jumping into a life that was entirely different from the one she had made her uneasy.

"You never told me where that phrase came from," she said.

He looked up from his script. "What phrase is that?"

"'Smile, Cassidy. Preferably at me.'"

He laughed. "It came from an early director of mine. When I first started acting, I tended to draw attention to the wrong thing—usually myself. An important skill for an actor is to focus the audience's attention on the most important thing going on. I was so bad at it, the director during rehearsal would yell, 'Focus, Winston. Preferably on the person speaking.' He did this all the time—so often, in fact, it became a running gag with the cast. Everyone started doing it to everyone else. If a person named Laura cracked a joke, someone would yell, 'Laugh, everyone. Preferably at Laura.' Another favorite was, 'Clap, everyone. Preferably for me.'" Jack pressed his lips to her temple, and her body warmed. "When the paparazzi made you uneasy," he said against her hair, "I used that terrible running joke to focus your attention away from what troubled you and had you focus on me instead."

At the moment, she was finding it hard to focus on anything *but* him.

"Only a little longer and I think I'll have this

scene down," he said, returning his attention to his script.

She stood and stretched. Sanding and staining Dolores's ground-level floors the last few days had left her stiff. Jack had been the one to use the heavy drum sander, he was most likely even stiffer than she was. "Too bad we don't have that huge bathtub from *The Illusion*. I could use a long, hot bubble bath."

"Me, too," he said with a grin. "And no need to speak in code. We can have a *bubble bath* any time you want." He waggled his eyebrows.

She rolled her eyes. "I was not speaking in code. I was being literal. Dolores only has two bathrooms, and neither tub holds water. Hopefully, Roger will give me the go-ahead to start the second floor soon so I can fix the plumbing."

"Are we supposed to dress up for tonight's party?" Jack asked, flipping some pages in his script.

He always did this, Cassidy noted. He changed the topic every time Roger's plans for Dolores came up. Maybe Jack knew something and he was holding back so she didn't worry.

"Costumes are optional tonight," she said. "Has Roger told you anything about when he plans to list the house for sale?"

"He has not told me when he will list it."

Good. At least he gave her a straight answer this time. She wasn't too late.

His phone rang. He checked the screen and sighed, then set the script on the little table next to the swing. "Sorry, I have to take this. It's the director."

A few minutes into the phone call, Cassidy decided to go inside and organize the tool table and give Jack some privacy. To most people, listening to an A-list actor discuss a script with his big-budget film director would be fascinating. To Cassidy, it illustrated how far apart their worlds were. His life and career were huge. Global. Her life was as tiny as her little town.

Realization prickled up her spine. That was it. It was the disparity in their lives that was holding her back.

"But you love him," she whispered under her breath as she placed a wrench she'd used to tighten the sander belt in its place in the toolbox. Surely love would overcome the differences between their lifestyles.

A ball of tissue paper rolled over the top of her boot, and she grinned. This was a man who was kind to an ancient, grumpy cat. They could definitely make it work. He'd already said he wanted to have Blink be his base, and he'd even talked to Lillian about logistics. Life here with Jack could be perfect.

He said he only had to shoot for several months of the year and could be here the rest of the time, and as he'd pointed out, she could go on location with him…like to New Zealand for his current project.

And right there, in Dolores's grand parlor, Cassidy's future expanded like a camera's focus widening from a close-up into a panoramic view.

Yes. She would go with Jack to New Zealand and anywhere else he wanted to go. She didn't have to give up Blink.

Her phone rang, but she ignored it. She wanted to enjoy the high of this moment a bit longer. Lolo padded out of her hiding place and did a figure-eight around Cassidy's ankles, purring like an old carburetor motor that needed a tune-up. "I love him," she whispered to the cat as she knelt to rub her ragged fur. "I'm going to New Zealand with him."

She startled when her phone rang again. Since the paparazzi had laid off, her phone had remained relatively silent. It was a California number. Dee, maybe?

She raised the phone to her ear. "Hello?"

She immediately recognized the harsh voice on the other end. "Good afternoon, Miss James," Marion said. "May I have a moment of your time?"

She was inclined to say no. She'd never gotten a great feeling off this woman. Why on earth would Marion Hill call her? Stomach churning, Cassidy gave in to curiosity. "How can I help you?"

There was a long pause before the woman answered. "I don't need your help. Jack does. He's in trouble, and you are the only one who can help him."

Cassidy's mind was racing a million miles a minute. She'd just seen him, and he was fine. What kind of trouble could he possibly be in?

"His career is on the line," Marion said. "He is likely to lose everything. I know you care for him, and that's why I'm reaching out."

Cassidy slid down the wall and sat on the floor,

knowing this call would change everything.

"Are you still there?" Marion asked.

"Yes." Barely. Everything in Cassidy's body felt like it was folding in on itself.

"I have a request," Marion said.

Cassidy had been right. That three-minute phone call changed everything.

CHAPTER THIRTY-NINE

Jack had borrowed a ridiculous shirt from Flex that was covered in parrots, something he'd never imagined his bodyguard owning in a million years. Flex wore nothing but black, as far as Jack had seen. The silly shirt was a good move, as it turned out. Most of the partygoers were decked out in tropical wear.

With a grin, he mounted the stairs to the deck that was lit up by strings of lights in the shapes of pineapples and flamingos.

Between autographs and handshakes, he scanned the deck for Cassidy. While he was on the phone with his director earlier, she had shot him a text saying she was taking care of some things and that she'd meet him at the party.

"Have you seen Cassidy?" he asked Amanda as she walked by with a basket full of dinner rolls.

"I thought the two of you were hot glued together these days. I haven't seen her since donuts on the deck on Wednesday."

"Thanks." He spoke with a few more people on his way to the beer cooler, keeping an eye out for her. She must have gotten held up on one of her handyman jobs for a neighbor. He smiled. Maybe another wayward raccoon or an army of kitty-cat rats.

He checked his watch, and for the first time, a trickle of concern niggled at the back of his brain.

She should be here by now.

Hey! You coming for me, babe? he texted.

She usually texted back pretty quickly, so when he didn't hear back in ten minutes, that trickle of concern morphed into full-blown worry.

Flex, much more relaxed now than he'd been when they'd first arrived in Blink, was across the deck chatting with Dee and her group of friends, but, true to form, his attention was on Jack as well. Sensing something was off, he strode over, and Dee followed.

"What's wrong, Mr. Winston?"

"Do you or Dee know where Cassidy is?"

They both shook their heads. "We assumed she was with you," Dee answered.

He texted Cassidy several more times and called her twice. Both times, her phone rolled over to voicemail immediately.

After twenty more agonizing minutes with no sign of Cassidy, worry turned to panic. Sweat broke out on Jack's forehead as he approached the food table where Caleb and Lillian were serving up their plates. He didn't even try to hide the urgency in his tone. "Have either of you seen Cassidy?"

"Her work truck was at her dad's place when I passed by an hour or so ago," Caleb said.

Jack had been to the house she'd grown up in only once. It was a small, tidy cottage that had been decorated with a man's tastes clearly in mind. She'd told him her little brother would live there when he graduated from college. She had a room, but it seemed more like a guest room with very few personal items.

"Thanks," Jack said, sliding a look to Flex, who nodded.

"You want a ride over there?" Caleb offered.

"No, thanks. Stay and enjoy your dinner."

"Keep us posted," Lillian said as Jack, Flex, and Dee hurried toward Jack's rental car parked in front of Miller Mercantile.

The cottage was on the south side of the harbor, near the top of a large hill and nestled in a grove of tall pine trees. Jack let out a sigh of relief as they neared and Cassidy's truck came into view. There was a light on inside the house where he remembered her room to be.

They'd most likely located where she was, but why she was there and had not responded to phone calls or texts had him feeling nauseated.

"Let me go in first, boss. When it's clear, I'll let you know," Flex said as they climbed the stairs to the porch. Flex didn't knock. He just opened the unlocked door and crept silently inside.

As he waited, still as death on the porch, loads of terrible and impossible scenarios played through Jack's mind.

"All clear," Flex said, stepping back out on the porch. "She's inside and safe. Go on in."

An almost overwhelming wave of relief flooded over him. "What happened?" Jack asked, grateful his heart rate had dropped below the stroke-out zone.

The big man shrugged, eyes on the porch floor. "Not sure. She says she had planned to go to the party but lost track of time. Thinks she left her phone in her truck. I'll go check."

That's all? This was totally out of character. Maybe she was sick.

"Cassidy?" Jack called, walking through the living room filled with IKEA furniture. He headed down the hallway and into the room that she'd said was hers. She was sitting on the edge of the bed wearing a floral sundress—clearly her outfit for a luau party. She didn't look at him when he entered the room.

He squatted down in front of her, putting their eyes level, but she kept hers on a photo of herself and a boy in his teens with a man in a wheelchair, no doubt her father. "Hey, baby."

Her eyes met his, but they seemed dull. "Hey."

"When you didn't show up at the party, I was worried." He searched her face, but it remained expressionless.

"I came here to change. Time got away. Sorry." She stood stiffly.

Something had happened. Maybe something with her brother? College kids were forever in trouble. "Is everything okay?"

She walked past him to the living room without a reply and stopped in the middle of the room.

Gently, he took her by her shoulders and turned her to face him. "What's wrong?" he asked.

Outside the big window, Dee and Flex chatted, leaning against the rental car in the driveway. Cassidy blinked several times as she watched them. "*We* are wrong," she said.

Raw fear closed Jack's throat. The last time he'd seen Cassidy, she'd been on the porch swing making happy sighs with her head on his shoulder. They'd teased about bubble baths. Everything had been fine. He dropped his hands from her shoulders. "What do you mean when you say we're wrong?"

She glanced at him, then quickly away. "I mean we can't be together anymore."

Tristan. That jackass Tristan had contacted her. Nothing else made sense. Hell, that didn't make sense, either. "Why not?"

She inhaled deeply. "I appreciate you coming to Blink to clear up the matter with the paparazzi. I value the time we spent together, but after careful consideration, I find it in both of our best interests to go our own ways. Your lifestyle is not something I'm willing to accept."

She'd spoken so rapidly, it took a moment for Jack to process the words. Hell, those didn't even sound like her words. His arms and legs felt numb, like they wouldn't work if he tried to move.

She took a deep breath—several of them—as she stared out the window. Her eyes brimmed with tears. "I'm sorry I worried you when I didn't show up. I was trying to find the right words to tell you what I needed to say, and then I stalled, putting off the inevitable."

"I don't understand this, Cassidy. Back at Dolores, you seemed fine, and now you want to end…" He gestured between the two of them. "Something happened. What happened?"

"I realized we could never work out," she said, still staring out the window. It was like she couldn't bear to even look at him.

With effort, Jack pulled in a deep breath. "Why don't we sit down and talk this through?"

She shook her head. "You need to go back to Hollywood where you belong, Jack."

A tear rolled silently down Cassidy's cheek. The moonlight streaming through the window made her skin look like she was made of marble. Still and cold and hard. Jack closed his eyes and waited out a wash of familiar pain.

His father had left before he was born. When Jack had asked his mother why his father had left them, she told him, "Love can't be begged, or won, or forced from someone. You can't make someone love you. They must choose to love you on their own."

True words. Cassidy had made her choice. It was the wrong one, he believed, but it was her choice to make. He wouldn't argue or plead. He couldn't change Cassidy's mind. He could only respect her decision and accept it.

"I'm always a phone call or text away," Jack said, wiping the tear from her cheek with his thumb.

Numb, he forced himself to retrace his steps to the door and down the sidewalk. Dee and Flex came around the car to meet him.

"Is she okay?" Dee asked.

"Yes." But *he* wasn't. He texted Caleb while Flex went inside to take Cassidy her phone, which he'd retrieved from her truck.

"Are *you* okay, Mr. Winston?" she asked.

He pushed down the emotion trying to fight its way to the surface and nodded.

"Where to, boss?" Flex opened the passenger door for Jack, who slid in.

"To pack and then to the airport," Jack said, reading the incoming text. "But not until Caleb and Lillian are here with Cassidy. They'll be here in a couple of minutes."

From the back seat, Dee asked, "Should I let Ms. Hill know we're on our way home?"

Home. L.A. had never felt like home. "Yeah. Let her know."

CHAPTER FORTY

Cassidy dropped the worn-out piece of sandpaper and stood, stretching her aching back. She'd been working on the ornately carved parlor mantel for two days now.

"Only a little more to go," she said to the pair of green eyes staring at her from under the staircase. Lolo hadn't come out of her hidey-hole in days. She'd been very attached to Jack. Maybe she missed him, too.

If you care for him at all, you'll let him go, Marion's voice whispered in her head. *Before your little relationship destroys him.*

Cassidy adjusted her respirator and picked up a finer grit sandpaper from her worktable, carefully folding it into eighths.

She'd been working nonstop for the last week, only taking a break when Amanda dropped in under the pretense of seeing if she wanted to film, or Lillian and Caleb stopped by with food or some feeble excuse or another, or Roger shuffled through to check on her progress—something he'd never done until recently.

They were worried about her. She placed the sandpaper on the mantel and wiped her aching palms on her overalls. If she were being honest with herself, she was worried, too. She kept telling herself that with time, things would get better, and life would eventually go back to normal.

Normal. She'd lived her whole normal life in her normal town in a normal way. Then Jack had come, and it had become extraordinary.

Now it was… She didn't know what it was now.

Since Jack left, some days had been okay, some not. This day was far into the not-okay column. She'd fought back tears all morning. Reminders of Jack that she could usually ignore had come at her from everywhere: from the floors they'd refinished together, to the porch swing they'd sat in his last day, to the freaking ugly quilt that Lolo was lying on right now. Everything was tied to Jack somehow, including her heart.

She sighed and picked up a dustcloth and wiped the area of mantel she'd just completed. Movement to her right drew her attention, and she glanced over to find Roger standing in the archway, watching her.

Familiar disappointment tightened her throat. Why, when she'd sent Jack away in no uncertain terms a week ago, did some tiny part of her hope that she'd look up and see him leaning casually in the doorframe in his sexy worn jeans and tight T-shirt?

"Good morning, Roger," she said. "Coffee's ready." Her voice was tinny and muffled through her respirator.

"Thanks. That's looking good," he said, gesturing to the fireplace. "I can remember my mama sitting in a chair, right about where you're standing, knitting socks for my dad."

"Hard to believe you allowed someone to paint over a hand-carved maple mantel," she said.

"Look at the beautiful grain."

"That was all Mabel's doing. It was during her 'light and bright' decorating phase." His smile became wistful. "If my wife had wanted to paint it purple polka-dotted, I'd have given it the green light and told her it looked beautiful." Roger turned his faded blue eyes on Cassidy. "Love makes you do silly things you ordinarily wouldn't do."

She set the dustcloth on the mantel and picked up her fresh piece of folded sandpaper. "Well, painting over this mantel was certainly silly," she said, wedging the stiff edge of the folded paper into a deep groove and filing away the last remnants of paint.

"As silly as sending away someone you care for?"

She stilled for a moment, then resumed sanding. How had Roger come to that conclusion? She'd told everyone it was a mutual decision that she and Jack part ways and that he left that night because a meeting about his movie had been called the next morning in L.A. and he needed to be there.

Totally plausible. She glanced over at Roger, who clearly wasn't buying it.

"Why did you do it?" he asked.

She set the sandpaper on the mantel and pulled off her respirator, growling in frustration when the strap tangled in her hair. "I didn't do anything. Jack and I had some fun together, then he had to get back to his career, and so did I."

Roger shook his head. "That boy was putting

down roots here. The only way to force him to leave was with dynamite or an ultimatum."

Cassidy yanked the respirator free, painfully liberating some hair from her scalp at the same time. "That's ridiculous," she said, hissing when one of her sandpaper-raw fingers brushed a rough edge of the respirator filter.

"Yes, ridiculous," Roger agreed, shuffling in the direction of the kitchen. "Thanks for making coffee. Yours is always better than mine."

A knock sounded on the door.

"Would you mind getting that?" Roger called from the direction of the kitchen.

Amanda and Lillian had already dropped in today, so it probably wasn't an irritating welfare check. Her heart stuttered. No one else ever visited. She took a couple of shallow breaths. *Stop it.* Why did she play mind tricks on herself like this? He was over three thousand miles away.

Before she could answer it, the door opened, and Sally stepped inside dressed in her waitress uniform. "Oh my word." Her jaw fell open, and she turned in a circle. "Look at this place. The house is gorgeous!"

She strode over and pulled Cassidy to her in a hug. "Sweet little Cassy girl. Are you okay?"

"Yes." This are-you-okay business everyone was pulling was a bit frustrating, really. She'd played this whole thing so cool, and it was as if everyone could see right through her like a pane of glass.

After a moment, Sally released her from the bear hug. "Oh my stars. Look at your face." Her eyes widened in concern.

Out of reflex, Cassidy raised her fingers to her cheeks. "What about my face?"

Sally reached out and flicked a finger against Cassidy's temple, sending a paint chip fluttering to the ground. "You have white flakes on you, and there's a red ring around your nose and mouth."

"I've been scraping and sanding paint while wearing a respirator."

Sally *tsked.* "You've been working too hard. Why don't you come back to the diner with me and let me make you a nice, hot lunch?"

"It's not even ten o'clock yet," Cassidy said.

"Breakfast, then. Come on. You need to get out of this house and take a break."

"Really. I'm all good." Only she wasn't. And obviously everyone else knew it, too.

"Might as well hit your head on a brick wall, Sally. It's more likely to bend," Roger called from the area of the dining room. "Girl's as stubborn as her pa ever was."

"Well, hello there, old lady. I hear that you're off your food," Sally said to Lolo, who had ventured a few feet outside her hidey-hole. It was the first time she'd come out in three days. "I brought you something." She reached into her large apron pocket and pulled out an aluminum foil packet. "Here ya go, hon." She unwrapped the packet and placed it on the floor just outside the opening under the stairs. "Nice fresh chicken. I held it out of the soup just for you."

After a few sniffs, Lolo returned to her quilt under the stairs and sat down.

"She's been drinking but hasn't shown much interest in food. I'm going to take her to the vet if she doesn't eat something soon," Cassidy said.

"She didn't eat right for a long time after Mabel died," Roger said. "She'll pull out of it." He appeared from the dining room arch. "She evidently misses Jack as much as you do."

Cassidy glanced over at Lolo and sighed with relief to see her eating the chicken.

"Call him," Sally whispered.

Like a little kid reaching for a cookie, Cassidy's emotions stretched toward that idea. She could call him. He'd said as much. Over and over this last week, with his words on repeat in her head, her finger had hovered over his contact, but she'd resisted every time. She'd assured Marion that she would cut off all communication and never reach out to him or respond if he contacted her, which he hadn't.

She shook her head, looking from Sally's expectant face to Roger's amused one.

"You're in on this together," she accused.

"Yes, we are," Sally said. "Because we love you, Cassy girl. I've known you since you were a baby, and I can tell when something is wrong. Jack didn't leave here in the middle of the night without saying goodbye to any of us because of a business meeting. You didn't go from a happy, bubbly woman to a workaholic recluse because you had an amicable parting."

Cassidy pulled a paint chip out of her hair. "He did. We did."

Sally threw her arms up. "Pfft."

"Just like her pa," Roger repeated.

If only her dad were here. He'd know what to do. He always had a solution—well, before he got sick, anyway. Cassidy blinked back some tears. She hadn't cried since immediately after her phone call with Marion a week ago. She hadn't even cried when she told Jack to leave. But she was crying now, darn it.

"Aw. It's okay, hon," Sally said, pulling her to her again. "You're not alone. We're all worried about you. Roger, Amanda, Lillian, Caleb, Dee—"

Cassidy's head shot up. "Dee?"

Sally's usually ruddy face paled, and she shot a look at Roger. "Yes, she has been in touch with Amanda every now and again, ya know."

No, she didn't know. "Amanda didn't tell me that."

Why would Dee be in touch with Amanda, and why hadn't Amanda blabbed about it like she did everything else? Gossip was her middle name. Amanda Gossip Miller.

"Well, I need to get back. Are you sure you don't want to come with me to the diner?" Sally asked.

"Thanks for the offer, but no. I have a lot to do here." Like call her best friend and find out why she hadn't told her she'd been talking to Dee.

Sally stood in the doorway and stared at Cassidy for a moment.

"It's okay, Sal," Roger said. "You gave it a try."

The door closed, but neither Cassidy nor Roger moved, engaged in some kind of weird stare-off contest.

"Looks like you're about finished on this level," Roger said.

She was, and this was the perfect time to have a heart-to-heart with Roger. Cassidy had been putting this conversation off for a long time. Years, to be honest. Ever since she got her hands on Dolores, she'd thought of little else—until Jack came along, of course. Over and over recently, Roger had mentioned listing the house for sale. At first, she'd thought it was to irritate his son somehow, but he had dropped hints even after Tristan returned to Portland.

No time like the present. "I want to make a deal with you, Mr. McGuffy."

Roger's eyebrow lifted.

"I know you plan to sell this house, but I'd like you to consider an offer first. I can't buy her outright, and I doubt I could qualify for the size of loan I'd need for a house like this, but I have a good bit saved up, and I can make a pretty good down payment."

Roger had a look on his face that was more of a smirk than a smile. She'd seen this expression from him before. It was like he was waiting to blurt out the punch line of a joke.

"This house has been in your family for three generations," she continued, "and nobody will take care of her or love her like I will. My business is going well, and when Luke graduates, it will do even better."

Roger held his hand up, a look of pity replacing the smirk. "I'm sorry, Cassidy. I've already sold the house."

That hole she'd patched in the floor might as well have opened and swallowed her. Down and down, she sank, emotion as heavy as bricks. For a moment, she became so dizzy, she thought she might lose her balance, so she placed a hand on the wall. A solid, well-built wall from when people cared about craftsmanship and longevity.

Dolores had been sold. Jack was gone.

Forcing herself to breathe, she regained her balance. She deserved this, she supposed. All of it. Her dad had always told her that the most important thing in life was to be true to who she was.

She hadn't been.

He'd said that when something was right, she should hang on to it with both hands and never let go. But she'd let go of Jack without so much as a fight. She had let Marion talk her into pushing away the only right thing that had come her way in a long time.

A headache started behind her eyes. "Who's the new owner?"

Roger shoved his hands in his pockets. "Well, I'm not at liberty to say just yet, but I can tell you they are local and have lived in the area their entire life."

At least it was someone from here and not an outsider who would tear Dolores down and build a hotel or something.

"I'll just pack up my tools, then." Her voice sounded far away. "Unless you want me to finish the fireplace mantel?"

"Oh, well, you see," Roger said. "The new owner is impressed with your work and asked if

I'd arrange to have you do the rest of the restoration, including the second and third floors."

She looked around the space she'd put so much work and love into. If she said no, then whoever had bought Dolores might bring in some wackadoodle like Brie What's-Her-Name to destroy the place.

She nodded, gathering all the pieces of her heart back together and shoving them into place. "Good. When does the new owner want the work finished? It's a big project."

"I'm sure they'll want you to take as long as you need."

"I'll have to meet with them to discuss color preferences and specifics."

"I'll arrange all that," he said. "For now, just do what feels right to you." He wandered to the back of the house, and shortly, the back door opened and clicked shut.

Do what feels right? Her headache was starting to pound in earnest now. What would feel right just about now would be to throw off this calm, accepting demeanor and rant and rave about losing Dolores and Jack. She wasn't the ranting-and-raving type, though, so any relief from that would be short-lived and most likely followed by a hefty dose of remorse.

She inhaled deeply to relieve the pain in her chest and breathed in the sharp scent of coffee. Maybe another cup would help with her headache.

She headed to the kitchen and tried to come up with a plan. Since Dolores belonged to someone else now, she supposed she'd have to move out and stay at her cabin, something she dreaded. There were no reporters chasing her that would make her feel uncomfortable there, only loneliness, which was even more persistent than the paparazzi.

Roger had left papers scattered all over the dining table this morning, which was unusual. Maybe he'd decided to work in here instead of his office in the guest house behind Dolores. No doubt, he'd set up camp in here to keep an eye on her like everyone seemed to be doing these days.

She poured a cup of coffee and leaned back against the kitchen counter, staring out into the dining room and the snowstorm of papers scattered across the table.

What was Roger up to? He was always up to something. His refusal to tell her who had bought Dolores was strange. He'd said the buyer was a local. Why the secrecy? And then she realized a potential reason. Maybe Roger thought she'd say something to the buyer or have sour grapes at losing the house. He might want her to cool off first. Or...

She took another sip of coffee. Maybe it was Tristan. She'd turned him down right before he left, so Roger building in some time before they met or interacted made sense. Roger had sold the house to his son. That had to be it.

Coffee in hand, she passed the table on her way to get back to work and paused.

Maybe the house purchase documents were among this haphazard mess. Even though she knew Roger wanted to keep the buyer's identity secret, she couldn't help herself.

Eyes scanning, she slowly circled the table looking for a purchase agreement. Most of the pages were receipts for household items like the refrigerator and furnace. There were some work orders for the roof and chimney repair a decade ago as well. Everything she saw related to Dolores.

And then she froze.

Sticking out from under a letter from an attorney with a bunch of legal jargon was a paper with tiny print. It was a general warranty deed to the house with a recent date, but the name of the grantee was under the attorney letter. Roger had not sold the house; he had evidently gifted it. Which meant Tristan. She sighed. At least it would stay in the family. Odd that he wanted her to continue her restoration, though.

She should walk away. This was not her business, and she should not be snooping.

"Go ahead," Roger said from the door to the kitchen.

Cassidy jumped, hand over her mouth.

"I'm surprised you even hesitated," he said. His smile was kind. "I certainly wouldn't have."

She gingerly slipped the page out from under the attorney letter and froze.

Stunned, she read the name of the grantor and then had to sit down when she read the name of the grantee.

"Welcome to home ownership."

CHAPTER FORTY-ONE

Jack flipped the page of the script and took a sip of coffee. Out the window of his penthouse, the morning sky was tinted with L.A.'s oppressive smog haze. It suited, he decided.

He relaxed back on the sofa and glanced across the room at the desk. Dee was studying him over her open laptop. She'd been doing that a lot since they'd returned.

Marion's staccato heel clicks approached, and instead of the customary dread, he felt nothing. "Good morning, Marion," he greeted without turning to see her.

"Good morning, Mr. Winston. I just spoke with your agent, and they are sending another project for your consideration over today."

He held up the HBO script. "When you speak to them next, tell them I'm willing to do this if the terms are good. They can start negotiations."

Marion walked around the sofa and took the script from him. "I thought you weren't interested in anything but feature-length films."

"I changed my mind."

Since he'd returned, he'd tried to fill every waking minute so he didn't have time to think. It had worked for the most part. Since the shoot would begin on *Mad Planet 4* next month, he was back in the gym with his trainer to bulk up to play Blake Crusher. Then he had loads of other preproduction things to keep him busy like costume fittings and storyboard reviews. After only a week back, he'd been told he was a month ahead.

"Hey, Dee?" Jack stood. "Will you reach out to the fight director for *MP4* and see if he can line up a session with my body double?"

She frowned. "That's not set to be scheduled for two weeks."

"See if we can move it up." Maybe a jog would help with this restlessness. "And text Flex I'm going for a run, so he needs to suit up and meet me in fifteen."

"Mr. Winston," Marion said.

He turned and waited, knowing she'd say her piece whether he replied or not.

"Perhaps you should take some time off. You've been uncharacteristically intense since your return," Marion said.

No way. Marion Hill was telling him to take time off? It's like everything had turned upside down since he came back to L.A. "I'm productive, Marion. That's the goal, right?"

"Yes, but I'm worried about you burning out."

Again, something he'd never expected to hear come out of Marion's mouth.

She was wrong, though. If he didn't fill his time, he'd burn up, not out. "I appreciate your concern, but I'm going to be honest, Marion. This is what you've pushed me to do since you came on board as my manager. I'm what you wanted me to be." He gestured to himself. "Dr. Frankenstein, meet your monster."

Horror flashed across her face.

"Please let my agent know the HBO project is a go if they can reach an agreement. When I get back from my run, I'll review the new screenplay if it has arrived."

He ran a hand through his hair. "Dee, please ask the props department to send over some of the new spears while I'm out. They're longer than the ones I've dealt with before. I'll start work on those as soon as I'm done with the screenplay."

Dee appeared rattled. He glanced over at Marion, and she looked uneasy, too. They were on edge because of him. Easygoing, affable Jack Winston had become the Megalodon.

"It's only eight fifteen, Mr. Winston," Dee said. "The production office isn't open yet."

God. She was looking at him like she used to look at Marion. He glanced at his watch. She was right. He hadn't realized it was that early. He was still on Blink time. It would be eleven fifteen there. Cassidy would be wearing her cute overalls and working on some detail nobody else would notice to bring Dolores back to her glory. At least that was one thing he got right.

"I apologize, Dee. I wasn't paying attention to the time."

"I'll go email your agent about this." Marion gestured to the HBO script. Before she made it from the room, she turned. "Mr. Winston, I'm not trying to discourage you in any way, but are you certain you want to accept this? In the past, you said you were not interested in tying yourself to long-term projects."

"Well, Marion, what else am I going to do with

my time?"

For a moment, she stared at him, blinking rapidly, and he thought she was going to say something. She evidently changed her mind and strode from the room.

His phone dinged, and his heart leaped. It always did. Every text, every call, he allowed himself to hope, which was ridiculous. He reached into his jean pocket and pulled out his phone. It was Flex saying he was ready for a run when Jack was.

"I need to change. Flex is outside waiting for me."

"Mr. Winston. Wait." Dee's voice had an urgency that made him hesitate.

She had risen and was standing behind the desk chair, clutching it. "I know this is not my place. But I feel like I have to say something." She took a few breaths, as if gathering her nerve. "Since our return to Los Angeles, you haven't been yourself."

No doubt about that.

"And," she continued, "I can't help but think it is related to Cassidy."

Bingo on that, too.

"I believe that there was some kind of misunderstanding that last night."

Why on earth was his assistant concerning herself in his private business? Maybe he should have been more forthcoming with Dee and Flex. It was clear leaving Blink on such short notice had upset them.

Okay, then. He'd set the record straight.

He ran a hand through his hair, suddenly exhausted. "It's very hard to misunderstand the words, 'We could never work out. Go back to Hollywood where you belong.'"

Her brow wrinkled. "Cassidy said that?"

"It's sure as hell not something I'd make up."

She shook her head. "That doesn't make any sense."

"That's what I told her, but she stuck to it."

"Had you guys had an argument or something?"

He flopped back onto the sofa. "No. It came from nowhere. One minute, we were talking about making Blink our home base and traveling together to locations; the next, she was telling me it was impossible and to get lost."

She frowned. "There's a cognitive dissonance here I can't explain. You're both acting completely out of character. I really think there's some outside source of interference we've overlooked."

He arched an eyebrow. "Talk about acting out of character, Miss Psychobabble."

"I received a BS in Business Administration from Berkeley with a minor in psychology."

Jack felt the niggling itch of shame over his skin. Not for the first time, he realized he should know more about someone he spent so much time with. All he knew was what Marion had told him. He leaned forward. "What on earth possessed you to apply for an assistant position? You're way too qualified to be fetching me coffee and scheduling my travel and gym time."

She shrugged. "The pay is excellent, and it's a step toward my dream job."

"Which is?"

She looked down at her computer screen, then back to him. "I want to be a business manager for actors. I want to be Marion Hill."

Jack sat back and studied her. "Dee doesn't sound intimidating enough. You'll need a stage name."

"My given name is Deandra."

He smiled. "Deandra LaPorte will inspire fear and awe. It's perfect."

Flex knocked on the wall inside the living room entrance. "Sorry to interrupt, boss. You still wanna go for a run?"

"Not yet," he said. "Dee and I were discussing cognitive dissonance and"—he studied her face, trying to recall what else she'd said, then held a finger up—"and an outside source of interference."

"Very good, Mr. Winston," she said with a nod like an approving schoolteacher and a grin like a friend.

He pointed at his head. "It's why they pay me the big bucks."

"See, now you're acting true to character. You're jovial and relaxed," she said. "The thing is, Cassidy is not."

Just the mention of her name caused Jack's spine to stiffen. "How do you know?"

"Because I'm in touch with Amanda a couple of times a day."

Don't ask, don't ask, don't ask, he chanted in his head.

Flex made himself comfortable in an over-stuffed chair by the fireplace. "Tell him. He's not gonna ask."

Okay, clearly everyone knew him better than he knew them. He was going to fix that. "What is your name for real?" he asked Flex.

The big man blushed, then, after an encouraging nod from Dee, said, "Renee Michael Smith. You're deflecting."

"Do you have a degree in psychology, too, Flex?"

"Nah. Graduate of the school of hard knocks."

Dee closed her laptop and leaned against the desk. "Cassidy told a much different story than what we heard from you. She told her friends that you guys both agreed your relationship was just a fling and you parted amicably. Her story is that you had a business meeting and we had to leave in the middle of the night to make it on time."

Jack shook his head. None of this made sense.

"Amanda says Cassidy's acting strange," Dee continued. "She's working nonstop, and whenever your name comes up, she uses phrases that don't sound like something she'd say. Like she's been given lines to rehearse and perform."

A weird sinking feeling moved down his body and settled in his feet.

"Everyone in Blink is really worried about her, Mr. Winston. They think that Cassidy ran you off against her will. That she's still in love with you." She paused. "I mean, you're obviously in love with her, right? You've been acting pretty strange yourself."

"Cognitive dissonance," he said. "And yes, you're right. I only left because she told me to. I was all in. I thought she was, too." He massaged his temples. "I was so sure of our relationship, I bought Dolores from Roger McGuffy to prove to Cassidy I was serious about making Blink my home base. I've never wanted anything as much as I want Cassidy James. I'm not sure I ever will."

"Which is why you're throwing yourself into work like you're someone else." Dee crossed the room and perched on the sofa next to him. "I'm positive Cassidy feels the same way because she's doing the same thing."

Flex sat forward. "Wait. You own that big ole house?"

Jack shrugged. "Two days ago, I deeded it over to Cassidy and paid all the gift taxes. I told Roger to tell her it was from him, since his son will never live there and she's taken such good care of it."

Dee turned her cell phone over in her hands a few times. "Something isn't adding up. You both want to be together, but something is keeping you apart. What is it?"

"It's me," Marion said, stepping into the living room.

Jack flinched. Usually Marion's heels were as loud as firecrackers when she walked. How'd she make it down the hallway without any of them knowing?

She strode across the plush area rug to stand with her back to the wall of windows, putting her face in shadows. She was thinner, Jack noticed. And her hair wasn't as artfully styled as it usually was.

"I convinced Cassidy to end your relationship," Marion said.

Jack stood, but she held up a palm, and he sat back down.

"Please let me finish before you say anything, Mr. Winston."

This woman had just admitted to ending his relationship with Cassidy. Nothing, absolutely nothing, would justify what she'd just confessed. Jack gritted his teeth and waited.

She glanced at Dee and then Flex. "I would prefer we discuss this in private."

"Not a chance," Jack said.

Resigned, she took a deep breath and tugged at the bottom of her suit jacket. "I've been in this business a long time, Mr. Winston. Too long. I automatically assumed this affair between you and Cassidy was like all the other unevenly matched relationships I've witnessed fail over the decades. I knew the girl cared for you, but I also believed with certainty that she'd be detrimental to your career. That's my job, Mr. Winston: to facilitate your success and advance your career." She paused and took several breaths as if summoning courage. "I called Cassidy and told her that if she really cared for you, she would let you go. That if she didn't give you up, she would ruin your career and destroy you. I even dictated the lines she should use to convince you."

Jack's fingers curled into fists.

Marion closed her eyes for a moment, then met his gaze and continued. "I've been in this business so long, I thought I knew everything there was to know, but I was wrong. Utterly and completely wrong. What I've learned in the time since I called

Cassidy is that sometimes, a client's happiness is more central to their success than anything else. I realized that over the decades, I had lost most of what had made me the top in my field in the first place: my compassion. I'd become hardened over the years watching clients destroy themselves with addiction and poor choices. I spared myself the potential of emotional pain by forcing myself to only focus on you as a talent, and not a man, and for that, I am, and will forever be, truly sorry."

Holy crap. What was he supposed to do with that? That had to rank in the top ten heartfelt apologies of all time.

Jack's fingers relaxed, and so did his anger. A warm, humming sensation spread through his body. He recognized it immediately. It was hope. Maybe this thing with Cassidy could be remedied. After what he'd just heard, he was certain he knew exactly who could make it right.

Marion brushed her fingers under her eyes, then stiffened her shoulders and lifted her chin. "I appreciate the opportunity to have worked with you. Please consider this my resignation, effective immediately."

Jack stood. "Oh, no, you don't. Nuh uh. No way are you going to just lay that all out and leg it out of here."

Marion had a crumpled look on her face he'd never seen before, and he felt a pang of compassion—the thing she said she'd lost. He was going to help her find it.

"Deandra, I need you to make some travel arrangements, please." He couldn't hold back his smile. "You, me, Flex, and Marion are going to Blink on the first available plane."

He pulled out his phone, heart roaring to life, and sent a text.

CHAPTER FORTY-TWO

Cassidy couldn't stand still. She had so much energy, she wanted to run with Caleb's dogs up and down the dock as they chased moths buzzing around the lights.

"Best. Theme. Ever," Amanda said, handing Cassidy a bottle of beer. "Nobody even had to raid the church costume room this time. I mean, you can do anything with a theme of travel." Amanda was decked out in a khaki pantsuit with a safari pith helmet.

Above the food table, a hand-painted sign on butcher paper read "Bon Voyage." As usual, Amanda's deck was lit by strings of lights, this time interspersed with paper lanterns and cardboard 3D airplanes like you'd use at a little kid's birthday party.

Lillian abandoned Caleb at the drink cooler and joined them. She was dressed as a flight attendant, matching Caleb's pilot uniform. "Any idea when he'll be here?" she asked.

No ambiguity as to who "he" was at all. After Cassidy had received Jack's text this morning, she'd decided Marion could go jump in the ocean. She'd replied back to him and had been on cloud nine since.

"No idea. He only sent the one text. I can't imagine he'll be here before tomorrow. I mean, he would've had to jump on a plane right after he sent that message in order to be here tonight."

Amanda squealed through her nose. "Let's see it again."

Cassidy rolled her eyes. Her friends had asked to read Jack's text at least a dozen times since she'd received it earlier.

Lillian bumped her shoulder against Cassidy's. "Oh, come on, Cass. Let us live vicariously through you."

Cassidy pulled her phone from her jean pocket and pulled up the messages.

I'm coming for you, babe, he'd texted.

I'm ready for you, babe, she'd replied.

"Eeee!" Amanda danced in a circle. "That's so awesome! I knew you were full of crap."

"Says the friend who didn't tell me she'd been comparing notes with Dee." Cassidy shoved her phone back in her pocket.

"We've already been through this," Amanda said, waving at Roger, who was climbing the stairs to the deck with Sally and Ms. Phipps. "I was being the friend you needed, not the one you wanted me to be."

"What does that even mean?" Cassidy asked, taking a swig of her beer.

Amanda clinked her bottle to Cassidy's, then to Lillian's. "I have no idea, but it sounded good when Dee said it." Her attention was drawn to a group of people arriving. "Oh, there's Niles. Maybe he'll be coming for me tonight, babe." She winked and trotted off toward the Living Sharpe team streaming up the stairs.

"You nervous?" Lillian asked.

Cassidy shook her head. "No. I'm excited."

Lillian looked over her shoulder, then quickly back. "Well, I'm going to go get some food. Talk to you later."

With a sigh, Cassidy walked to the railing at the front of the deck and leaned back against it, enjoying the breeze off the harbor blowing across the back of her neck. It didn't matter how long it took Jack to get here. He would be here. With her. That's all that mattered.

"Is your name Google?" Jack's deep voice murmured from behind her. All at once, it felt like her insides had melted like ice cream. "Because you have everything I've been searching for."

Those terrible, wonderful pickup lines of his. She spun, grinning. Their noses bumped when she leaned over the railing to kiss him.

"No paparazzi this time?" she asked.

"We moved so fast *I* could barely keep up with us. I'm sure they'll turn up soon."

Behind him, Dee and Flex looked on with huge grins. Marion stood apart from them. Her expression was drawn and tired.

Marion approached the railing. Cassidy liked this. Up here on the deck, she was at least two feet above Marion.

"Miss James. I owe you an apology."

"Stop!" Cassidy ordered. "You certainly do, but a repeat is not necessary. I've already heard it."

Marion's brow furrowed. "I beg your pardon?"

"Pardon given." She reached down and wiggled her fingers, and Jack placed his hand in hers. "Dee recorded your conversation with Jack this morning and sent it as an audio file. I've heard the whole story. I get it. You care for Jack, too. We're alike in that way." Cassidy was pretty sure that was the only way they were alike. She squeezed Jack's hand. "So let's move on. I have lost time to make up for."

The old-fashioned slow song from before played—the one that had ended in their first kiss. She glanced across the deck to see Amanda giving her a thumbs-up. Man, oh, man. Her friend was in rare matchmaking form tonight. Her efforts were appreciated but unnecessary. This match was already made.

Jack vaulted over the railing and pulled her into his arms. "I believe this is our song."

With a sigh, she melted into his embrace.

When she opened her eyes, the dance floor had filled. Closest to her, Lillian and Caleb looked like Barbie and Ken airport edition, completely perfect and at ease. To their right, Amanda and Niles appeared to be one step off needing a cooldown with a garden hose.

Jack turned them, and across the floor were Roger and Marion, arms around each other, swaying in time to the music.

Jack stopped and gaped. "Megalodons dance!"

Cassidy threw her head back and laughed.

"Hold on," Jack said, staring down at her. He took a step back and took in her "costume."

"The theme of the party is travel," she explained.

She loved the look of surprise on his face.

"Lillian had one of her costumers make it for

me. Do you like it?" she asked.

"Yes," he whispered. Face completely serious. "I love it, Cassidy. I love *you*."

She stared down at her T-shirt emblazoned with "New Zealand or Bust," and her heart did a couple of somersaults. With a grin, she took his serious face in her hands.

"Smile, Jack. Preferably at me."

He did a lot better than that. He kissed her until she saw lightning flash behind her eyelids, and this time, it had nothing to do with cameras.

EPILOGUE

"How long do we have?" Cassidy asked, finger hovering over the button to accept Amanda's FaceTime call.

Jack stared out the tinted limousine window at the crowds lining the theater entrance. "We can stay in the car a little while longer." He nuzzled her neck. "A lot longer, if I had my way."

"Hair," she said with a laugh, pushing him away. "It took hours. Hey, Amanda!"

From her phone, a crowd cheered. The whole town must be on Amanda's deck from the sound of it.

"Hey, you two," Amanda shouted over the cheers around her. "We've got you streaming on one of the entertainment channels. Look!"

Cassidy squinted at her screen. It looked like they'd rigged a bedsheet and a projector hooked up to a computer—probably Dee's, since it was in her lap.

"They're covering the red-carpet stuff for the *Mad Planet 4* premiere, so we'll get to see your first real red-carpet walk."

The nerves Cassidy had felt earlier returned with a vengeance. "Great."

"Let's see the dress!" Lillian shouted from somewhere nearby.

Cassidy panned the phone down her body, and she grinned at Jack when squeals came from her friends.

"Can I tell them?" she whispered to Jack.

"They'll find out in a few minutes anyway."

She held up her left hand in front of the phone and adjusted the distance to focus on her ring finger. She had to turn the volume down this time.

"Let me talk to Marion," Jack said.

"Hang on." From the bouncing of the screen, it looked like Amanda was searching for her on a pogo stick.

"Hello, Mr. Winston," Marion said. She looked good, Cassidy thought. Maybe she'd gained some weight, or maybe it was because she was smiling.

"Thank you for the champagne," he said. "We're going to save it until we can enjoy it with you."

Roger popped his head into the field. "Well, sonny, you're going to have to wait a while for that. Ms. Hill and I are going to take a little trip. I've never been to the French Riviera, you see, and she says she knows a great resort there that I'd like."

Jack and Cassidy exchanged a startled look.

Bang, bang, bang.

Jack lowered the window a couple of inches, and Cassidy could see Flex, decked out in black with shades and an earpiece.

"I'm sorry to interrupt you, boss, but it's time. We're holding up the line." He gestured to the cars behind them.

"I've gotta go, Amanda," Cassidy said. "See you soon."

"Ready?" Jack asked as Flex opened the door.

Cassidy arranged her skirt, grateful the designer had agreed to let her wear low heels. "Like I've told you dozens of times, I'm ready for you, babe."

He grinned at her. "Say that again, and we'll be really late for this thing."

She took his hand and stepped out of the limousine. For the first of many times to come, Cassidy took Jack's arm and, with cameras flashing from all sides, strode down the red carpet knowing this was only temporary and that soon, they'd be back home, in her favorite spot in the world: Blink, Maine.

ACKNOWLEDGMENTS

Heather Howland, you are my hero. Thank you for coming to my rescue.

Shout out to Liz and the entire team at Entangled who always go the extra mile. It has been a delight to work with all of you.

Love to my family, of course, for always supporting whatever plan, project, or scheme I concoct on a whim.

But most of all, thank you to my readers who make it possible for me to do what I love the most.

Fans of RaeAnne Thyane and Brenda Novak will adore this sparkling frenemies to lovers romance...

come what maybe

KERRI CARPENTER

Social media strategist Lauren Wallace plans everything. But when she returns to the charming—if not too small for comfort—town of Seaside Cove, it's only about a second before her tough-love Grams is already on her case. So when Grams tells her *not to go to that bar*, Lauren decides it's time for a temporary rebellion. Which is exactly when the trouble starts.

Grams was right. The bar was *not* a good plan. Because suddenly super-cute bar owner Ethan McAllister has gone from being Lauren's (kind of) high school nemesis to a very unexpected one-night stand. And worse, Lauren's attempts to resume her ultra-responsible life keep getting thwarted by more unwelcome spontaneity. And a pregnancy.

Now there's a baby on the way, Lauren's the talk of the entire town, and all her planning has gone right out the window. All that's missing is childbirth to make her pain complete. But it'll be nothing compared to Grams's reaction when she finds out that Lauren broke the biggest rule of all...falling for the wrong guy.

*Find something luckier than catching
the bouquet in this delightful small-town
romance perfect for fans of* Virgin River...

The
MATCHMAKER
and the
COWBOY

ROBIN
USA TODAY BESTSELLING AUTHOR
BIELMAN

Callie Carmichael has a gift for making bridesmaid
dresses—some even call them *magical*. Somehow, every person who's worn one of her dresses has found
love. *Real* love. And as long as that happily-ever-after
is for someone else, Callie is happy. Because she's
fully over getting her heart broken...which is why her
new roommate is *definitely* going to be a problem.

After being overseas for six months, Callie's only
choice is to stay with her best friend's ridiculously hot
brother, Hunter Owens. Cowboy, troublemaker, and
right now, the town's most coveted bachelor. Only,
Hunter isn't *quite* the player she thought. And if it
weren't for her whole "no more love" thing, their set-
up could get confusing *really* fast.

Now, Hunter wants Callie to make him a best man
suit—a "lucky for love" kind of suit. But what hap-
pens if she makes the suit and he finds true love...and
it isn't her?

Return to Blossom Glen, where two opposites must put their differences aside to help the small town they both love…

the
SWEETHEART FIX

MIRANDA LIASSON

Juliet Montgomery absolutely loves her small town of Blossom Glen, Indiana, and everyone loves her. Except for the fact that she's a couples counselor who suffered a *very* public breakup that *no one* can forget. And now her boss asks her to take a step back… which is exactly when the town's good-lookin' and unusually gruff mayor offers her an unexpected job.

Jack Monroe absolutely loves being the mayor of his small town. Except when he actually has to talk to people. Can't he just fix the community problems in peace? Like right now, he's mediating the silliest dispute two neighbors could possibly have. When the town sweetheart steps up and solves everyone's problems in five minutes flat, Jack realizes what this town really needs…is a therapist.

Juliet is able to soothe anyone—other than the surly mayor, it seems. But there's a reason they say opposites attract, because all of their verbal sparring leads to some serious attraction. Only, just like with fireworks, the view might appear beautiful—but she's already had one public explosion that's nearly ruined everything…how can she risk her heart again?

A shy woman. Her outdoorsy crush. And the bet that could bring them together…or implode spectacularly.

first
Bride
to fall

NEW YORK TIMES BESTSELLING AUTHOR
GINNY BAIRD

Nell Delaney will do almost anything for her parents and her two sisters. But enter a marriage of convenience to save the family's coffee shop? *Too* far. So Nell and her sisters strike a deal: whoever hasn't found love in thirty days has to step up to take one for the team. The good news? Nell knows the perfect guy to fall in love with. The bad news? She's going to have to pretend she likes the outdoors…a lot.

Adventure guide Grant Williams knows immediately that Nell is not exactly Little Miss Outdoorsy. She's a walking natural disaster—an amazingly *adorable* disaster. And whoa, their chemistry is unbelievable. Everything between them is so perfect, he's not even a little bit shocked when he starts thinking of forever…

Right up until he catches the town gossiping about the Delaney sisters' bargain and realizes she's just using him to win a bet. Unfortunately, his family's unreliable reputation means he can't just dump one of the town's sweethearts. No, she needs to dump him. If she's going to pretend to be the perfect doting bride, well, he'll just pretend to be the worst bachelor on the market.

Let the games begin…

AMARA
an imprint of Entangled Publishing LLC.